**GROW
WARS**

**Two Manchester families
locked in a fight to the death**

KAREN WOODS

EMPIRE
PUBLICATIONS

First published in 2014

EMPIRE PUBLICATIONS
1 Newton Street, Manchester M1 1HW
© Karen Woods 2014

ISBN: 978-1-909360-31-0

Printed in Great Britain.

ACKNOWLEDGEMENTS

Thank you to all my readers for your continued support. Thanks to my publishers John Ireland and Ashley Shaw for always believing in me. Thanks to my children Ashley, Blake, Declan and Darcy for always being there. Big thanks to James, my mother Margaret and my father Alan for all your support.

My next novel is called "The Square" and should be out later this year.

Love to my son in heaven Dale, always in my thoughts.

Karen Woods
www.karenwoods.net
follow me on Twitter – @karenwoods69 – and Facebook for exclusive

CHAPTER ONE

Harry Jarvis stood at his cell door, small beads of sweat trickled down his forehead as he listened. It was his time to leave this shit hole for good. This was a day he'd imagined in his head for months, a day every prisoner longed for. Keys jingled outside the door let him know his jail sentence at Strangeways prison was finally over. This sentence had nearly broken his back and he'd pledged to himself that he would never come back here again, ever. Five years he'd been locked up behind bars, and for what, a stupid, silly mistake that could have been avoided. Prison life was hard and the torment of the years that had passed was visible all over his face. Death threats, drug usage, and men who had no shame all existed behind these prison walls. Harry had dark circles under his eyes, deep set wrinkles tunnelled around his face. This sentence had aged him.

Harry was thirty-four years old. A good looking man with a toned body most men would have been proud of, he'd injected a few steroids over the years but this was just normal inside the jail. Everybody did it if they wanted a ripped body. Like most inmates Harry had spent most of his sentence in the gym getting stronger. He needed to be fit if he was ever going to take his throne back on the Manchester crime scene. The Collins brothers should be scared. Very scared. A voice from behind him made him jump, he was edgy. "So, are you going to write to me or what?" his pad mate asked. "You better sort me some parcels out while I'm in here pal, don't leave me to rot in this gaff, you know how hard it is without fuck all," his pad mate sighed as he continued. "Now you're leaving it's going to be hard for me to survive in here you know. I'm a marked man. Dead man walking I am."

Harry turned his head slowly; he could see Jona sprawled out on his bed with his hands looped behind his head feeling sorry for himself. He nodded his head slowly. "Just chill your beans will you. Give me a fucking chance to get back on my feet. Fuck me, I'll have to start from scratch when I get out, test the water and all that, you know how it is." Harry inhaled and his chest expanded as he stretched his arms above his head. He turned to face his pad mate and spoke slowly. "Things change Jona, people change. I don't know who's running the scene anymore, but I've got a feeling it's the Collins clan. It's been a long time since I've had to graft, so, like I said, just give me time to find my feet and I'll sort you out."

Jona sat up on his bed and cracked his knuckles nervously. He was half the size of Harry and looked like a smack-head. "I'm out soon Harry, I've only got a shit and shave left to do so make sure you've got some work lined up for me. You know what I'm capable of. I'll take anyone on and I always have your back, we're a team." Jona ran his fingers through his thick crop of greasy dark hair, his heart was low. "I've got fuck all to come home to anyway. No woman, no kids, no fuck all. I may as well top myself, nobody would miss me anyway."

Harry held his head back and chuckled. Jona was such a smacked arse and he teased him. "Well, that's what you get for putting it about isn't it. I told you Mandy would find out about you and your antics, she's a wise head she is, nothing gets past her, ever. You live by the sword, and you die by it mate."

Jona blew a laboured breath. He knew Harry was right and raised his eyebrows flicking invisible dust from his legs. "Anyway, if you see that slapper tell her I'll be home soon and then we'll see whose laughing then, won't we." Jona took hold of the end of his grey blanket and twisted it with force. "I swear to you Harry, that bitch is getting her head shaved for what she's put me through. I could have been dead for all she cares, the heartless slut. One woman, she's heard rumours about me banging and she cuts me out of her life just like that, no, she's getting wasted the tart."

The cell door opened and Harry lifted his bag from the floor keeping eye contact with the screw. He wasn't taking all his belongings home with him, just the things that meant something to him; mainly the letters from his beloved wife Gill, the words that had kept him going throughout his sentence when he thought he couldn't go on. Gill had been his rock whilst he'd been banged up and without her he would have lost the plot for sure. She knew how his head worked, she knew what to say to keep him sane, he owed her his life. Gill was his childhood sweetheart, they were inseparable. Her name on his lips made him melt inside. She was the only woman he'd ever loved, the only person he let get close to his heart. Since being fifteen years old Harry had lived and breathed for her, she was his world. His family was his life. Walking to the door he turned and spoke to his pad mate for the last time. "Right, speak to you soon, just keep your head down and do your rip. You'll be home before you know it. Just keep your head down and keep out of trouble."

Jona sucked hard on his gums as he watched Harry leave. A lump appeared in his throat as he dipped his head low. "Yeah, take it easy Harry; I'll catch up with you soon. Make sure you keep in touch and don't leave me here to rot." The cell door banged shut and Jona sat on his bed moping. Punching the wall with his clenched fist he hid away under the blanket, hiding his tears, hiding his hurt.

Harry and Jona were old mates; they'd grown up together in Harpurhey and ran the area. It wasn't given to them. No, they had to fight their way to the top. It had never been easy, but they had done whatever it took to be Lords of the Manor. Tavistock Square is where they earned their reputation. In their day they were feared by all who knew them. They never let anyone get the upper hand, they were ruthless and cunning. They had to be, it was a dog eat dog world where you could trust nobody.

The screw walked slowly behind Harry and hoped he'd make a wrong move so he could nick him before he was a free man. The officers in the jail all knew Harry Jarvis well. He'd been a thorn in their sides in the time he'd spent behind bars, everyday he was up to something. They all knew he was running things in the jail, yet not once could they prove it. Harry was too clever for them, and he always made sure nothing or nobody ever pointed the finger towards him; he never got his hands dirty. The other inmates shouted across the landing to the prisoner as he strolled towards the exit, they were banging their steel cups on the banister making loud noises. Harry nodded his head slowly and smirked at them all as he licked his lips slowly. This ceremony was always performed at the end of everybody's sentence and today was no different.

Harry cupped his hands around his mouth and

shouted over to the other wing. "Do your sweat guys. I'll see you all when you get out. Look after Jona for me; you know he'll be missing me, the soft twat. He's probably bawling his eyes out now the fucking tart." The other criminals cheered as Harry walked out from the jail. He was a free man now and ready to take on anyone who crossed him. He wanted what he was owed and he would stop at nothing until he got it. People were going to get hurt for the time he'd spent in prison. Hurt badly. They knew who they were and they knew he was coming to find them. It was just a matter of time now. The clock was ticking.

CHAPTER TWO

"Will you two bleeding hurry up," Gill shrieked. "He'll be home soon and I don't want him to see you two layabouts like this. He'll go off his head if he knows what you've been up too," she looked directly at her sons and snarled. "I've covered up for long enough now and I'm glad your dad is coming home to sort you both out. I'm sick to bleeding death of it all, sick, sick, sick." Gill picked the dirty washing up from the floor and tried to make the place look half decent, it was a shit tip. Beer cans lay all over the place, ashtrays were brimful of cigarette stubs. Nobody cared about it except her.

Gill looked tired, her blonde hair was tied back from her thin face and although she'd tried to apply some make-up she still looked haggard and worn. Preston rammed his middle finger up towards his mother. He was still on a come down from the weekend and was off his rocker. Magic was the new drug on the street and he was always off his head on it.

"What's my dad going to do mother, ay? Sit me on the fucking naughty step," he held his stomach and chuckled. "Ay our kid, listen to this crazy bitch trying to lay the law down to us now. As if that's going to happen, she must be tripping."

Callum who was the eldest brother at eighteen years old turned to face his mother and waved his hands above his head. He was stoned and talking in a slow manner.

"Get a grip mam, we're not kids anymore. My dad will have to take a back seat in this house now. We're the ones who are running things around here, not him. How does he think we've been surviving while he's been banged up, on fucking fairy dust or what?"

The brothers chuckled and high-fived each other, they were taking the piss. Gill banged her clenched fist on the table and gritted her teeth tightly together. "Right you cheeky bastards, you can stop it now with this attitude. Your father is coming home today and I want us to be a family again, a proper family, do you hear me?"

Preston bolted up from the sofa and grabbed his cigarettes from the arm of the chair. "Things change mam, we've changed. My dad's not been around for years, so don't expect us to lick his arse when he comes back home. We've kept this family afloat whilst he's been in nick, and," he shot a look towards his mother, "if we're putting our cards on the table here, I didn't hear you complaining when you were getting a bung of cash did you?" Gill went white, her jaw dropped.

The Jarvis boys were well and truly out of hand and if she was being honest to herself they were the ones who'd been calling the shots in her household for as long as she could remember. Whatever happened to her two sweet boys, they were always as good as gold, angels they were. Gill just didn't have the strength to lay the law down anymore, she was exhausted. Her boys were out of control. Harry had it all to do when he got home, his sons had changed and not for the better, little bastards they were, who had respect for no one, not even their mother. Gill was forever at the police station with her lads; thieving, fighting, drugs were just a few of the crimes they'd been involved in. Callum reached for the remote for the TV and turned the volume up to the highest level. Listening to MTV he sang along with the track playing, the tunes were pumping and he was nodding his head to the beat of the music.

Gill ran at him and grabbed the remote from his hands. She was struggling to get it. "You hard faced prick. It stops now, do you hear me? Don't wind me up. Your dad doesn't need the stress of you two when he's just got out of jail. I'm up to here with it all, sick to the back teeth with it," she raised her hands above her head and shook them rapidly. "It's a wonder I've not had a bleeding nervous breakdown with you two doing my head in all the time. When's it going to stop ay, go on, when are you two going to sort yourselves out and stop being dickheads." Preston walked up to his mother's side and blew a cloud of thick grey smoke into her face. He was pushing her buttons now and he knew it. Gill waved her hands about and choked on the smoke. "I swear Preston, you carry on treating me like this and you'll see what I'm all about. Where's the respect gone in this bleeding house, ay? I'm not a stranger, I'm your mother."

Callum turned the volume down on the TV as his brother sat next to him on the sofa. Preston looked Gill straight in the eyes and spoke to her. "Respect? Do you know what that even is mother? You didn't have any respect for us when you were in bed with that Ray Clough did you?" He nudged his brother in the waist and gave a cunning grin. Gill swallowed hard, that was years ago and she'd made a mistake by bringing a man back to her family home. Her kids were supposed to have been staying out but they came home unexpectedly and caught her in the act.

Callum jumped on the bandwagon now and sat back on the sofa with his arms folded tightly across his chest. "Yes mother, did you think we've forgotten about that? How do you think it felt to be lying in bed listening to your mother getting her brains banged out by another man?"

Gill bit hard on her bottom lip. She had to play it cool, her face was beetroot. She stood tall and placed her hands on her hips. "Get a bleeding grip you two. For your information Ray wasn't banging my brains out. He'd had an argument with his wife and he just needed a bed for the night, that's all. So, you two know fuck all, wind your neck in and get your facts right before you start accusing me of being unfaithful to your father." The two brothers shot a look to each other. This was the first time they'd ever spoke about their mother's infidelity.

Preston sniggered and poked his finger into the side of his forehead. "Yeah, she thinks we're daft doesn't she bro, don't worry mam, our lips are sealed. We won't say a word, well," he opened his eyes wide and licked his teeth slowly. "That's unless you start grassing on us."

Gill was backed up against a brick wall; she knew one word of this to her husband and World War Three would break out. Her sons were evil and she knew she had to tread carefully. Checking her wristwatch she changed the subject quickly. There was no way they were ruling the roost, she needed to buy some time and think about this before she answered them. Gill pottered about the living room looking for her handbag, she changed the subject. "Right, do I look okay or what? Matty will be here in a minute to pick me up. I don't want to be late."

Callum lay down on the sofa and closed his eyes, he was still twisted from the weekend and he'd not slept for days. He knew once he'd found sleep he would be out of it for days, he was always like this after a bender. He never answered his mother. Preston kicked his shoes off and curled up in a tiny ball on the sofa. So what if his dad was coming home today, he didn't give a shit anymore. And, if his father had something to say about his life he was more than willing to take him out of the picture for good. He closed his eyes and pulled his hoodie over his eyes. Gill looked at her boys and shook her head, she mumbled under her breath as she left the room. "Little bastards, God help you when your dad see's what you've become." Gill was gone.

Harry Jarvis walked from Strangeways with a few other inmates. The sun was shining and he covered his eyes as the sunlight hit them. His breathing changed and his chest was rising with speed, his body was in shock. "Keep safe Harry," an inmate giggled as he shook his hand before he left. Harry took a few steps forward and said goodbye to his former inmates. His legs were buckling from underneath him, he was weak and panicking. A voice shouted him from the side street made him stop walking. Stretching his neck to see who it was he flung his bag over his shoulder and headed towards the car with a spring in his step.

There she was, stood waiting for him just like she promised him she would be, his woman, his heart's desire, his Gill. She ran towards him with tears trickling down her face, big bulky salty tears. This sentence had broken her in two and Harry didn't know the half of the things she'd had to cope with since he'd been banged up. It had been hard for her, so damn hard. "Come here you and give me a kiss," Harry choked.

Gill flung her arms around his neck and sank her head deep into his chest. She was safe again, protected. Her man was home at last. "Oh, I've missed you so much Harry, please promise me you'll never leave me again? Promise me." Harry bit down hard on his lips and shot his eyes behind him. There was no way he could promise her that, she was asking too much. Things needed to be sorted out and prison was something that went along with the lifestyle he led, he never replied. Matty came to the side of the car and shook his hand. "Good to have you home Harry, it's been a long time coming." Harry's nostrils flared as he inhaled the fresh morning air. This was a new day for him, a new start for his family, things were going to change. Gill would never want for anything again now he was back on the scene. He was ready to take back what belonged to him.

The engine ticked over as Harry sparked a cigarette up in the back seat. Gill opened the window slightly and wafted the fresh air onto her hot body, she was nervous and hyperventilating. Matty looked into the rear-view mirror and spoke to Harry as he pulled onto the main road. "The lads are ready to meet up whenever you're ready. Things are different now mate, you don't know the half of it. I'll fill you in later when your head stops spinning. Anyway, it's good to have you home pal."

Harry inhaled hard on his fag and his fists curled up in tiny balls at the side of his legs. He was ready for action and eager to get the ball rolling. The veins at the side of his neck was pumping with rage. "I'll see the lads tomorrow Matty. I want to know everything that's going on. And, if anyone's dealing or earning cash in Harpurhey then I want to know about it. Get me their names, addresses, the lot. We're going through their fucking doors if we have to. I'll show these dick-heads what I'm all about. It's time to take back what's owed to us."

Matty nodded his head and smiled, he'd missed his mate so much. Gill dipped her head low, she was welling up. She knew to keep her mouth shut; this was men's business and nothing that concerned her. She knew not to tackle Harry about this now, she kept her trap shut. "Where's the lads Gill, why aren't they here to pick me up?"

Gill coughed to clear her throat and her eyes opened fully. "Oh, I told them to wait at home Harry. I mean, there would have been no room in the car for them both anyway. I thought we could just have a bit of time together before we got home, if you know what I mean." she winked at him and flicked the speckles of dust from her skirt.

Harry flicked his cigarette butt from the moving car. He looked out of the window and rubbed his hands together. "Oh, I've missed you Manchester. It's good to be home I can tell you." Gill snuggled up next to her husband. He stroked the top of her head slowly as he felt her warm breath warming his body. "I'm back now love. You just watch this space. Nobody will fuck with us again. It's our time to shine."

Matty smiled at Harry through his rear-view mirror and nodded his head slowly agreeing with him. He knew more than anyone that now his partner in crime was back home things were about to change in the area. The Collins brothers should be worried. Very worried.

CHAPTER THREE

Harry Jarvis opened his eyes slowly and scanned the bedroom. It was strange to wake up in such a fresh looking room. Cream curtains and light lemon walls. His old pad was painted in grey. They were stone walls that stank of past inmates' regrets, misery and depression. The smell in this room was different – fresh, uplifting, calming. Harry was used to smelling Jona's crusty feet first thing in the morning but today he could smell flowers, sweet, refreshing aromas of roses and he could smell freedom. Rubbing his knuckles into his eyes he turned his head slightly to see his wife lay next to him. Tickling her back slowly with his fingertip he kissed her neck with soft lips. "Good morning special wife. How does it feel to have your man back in your bed again?"

Gill turned to face him and her eyes were still closed. She wasn't his special wife anymore; she was a dirty, unfaithful slut. She'd not slept a wink all night long and had only just drifted off to sleep, her head was in bits. She spoke in a low soft voice. "I love you Harry Jarvis. It feels like you've never been away," she was lying of course but hid it well, she had to if she knew what was good for her, there was no other option.

Gill held a lot of secrets, secrets that would destroy her marriage, her life. The fear inside her eyes was looming and it was only a matter of time before her world fell apart, she was living on borrowed time. The couple shared a passionate kiss and lay entwined in each other's arms. A noise outside the door startled Harry. He bolted up from the bed and his eyes were wide open, his chest was rising rapidly. Harry reached for his baseball bat from under the bed keeping his eyes on the bedroom door at all times. It had never been moved in all the years he'd been gone, he made sure Gill kept it there to protect herself if anyone broke into the house. Prison life had made him like this, he was never this nervous before his sentence. Jail does that to a man you know, it's a dog eat dog world and everybody inside the prison walls slept with one eye open, even Harry. The criminals inside the jail were ruthless and the minute your back was turned they would dig a knife in your back just to earn a few extra quid.

"Who's that?" Harry shouted, he was alert and ready to attack. His leg was hanging out of the side of the bed and he was picking his shorts up from the bedroom floor. The door creaked opened slowly. Harry gripped the bat tightly in his hand ready to strike, ready to take the bastard out.

"Alright dad, how's it going? Sorry I didn't see you last night, I was knackered." Harry looked relieved and smiled. His boys were the apple of his eye and he could never see any wrong in them. Placing the bat on the floor he started to relax and held his two arms out wide. "Come over here son and give your old man a cuddle." Harry chuckled and poked Gill in the side of her waist with his finger. "Don't tell me our son is too old for a bit of TLC from his old dad now, look how embarrassed he is. Come on then, come and feel the love."

Preston made his way to the side of the bed and hugged his dad, he didn't look comfortable. All this showing affection to his family was new to him and he made it quick, this wasn't for him. Preston sneered at his mother as his head hung over his father's shoulder causing her to sit up in the bed. "Where's Callum? Don't tell me he's still in bed," Harry asked. "Bloody hell, what's happened to you both? When I was home last you two were up at the crack of dawn, what's changed since then?"

Preston sniggered and sat on the end of the bed as Harry lay back down. "Dad, we're not babies anymore. I keep telling my mam to cut the apron strings. Me and our kid are sorted now. We look after ourselves. We don't need anyone. We're sorted." Harry examined his son further and watched him with a close eye. He knew he'd changed but just couldn't put his finger on exactly what it was. Preston shot a look at his mother and stood up from the bed. "Are you making something to eat or what ma-dukes? Just because my dad's back home now it doesn't mean you can start slacking."

Harry sniggered at the nickname his kids had given their mother, it made him smile, he liked it. Gill went to get out of the bed when Harry pulled her back down. "Oi, bleeding ma-dukes is no slave. You should be making us breakfast in bed, not the other way around. Those days are over when she runs about after you two lazy arses, like you just said; you're not babies anymore, so go and make your own scran. And," he sat up and placed a pillow behind his head, "make me and your mother a brew too. We're coming downstairs now anyway, so bang the kettle on."

Preston held his head to the side and he was about to say something when Gill stopped him dead in his tracks. There was no way she needed this so early in the morning. She wanted peace. "I'm getting up now anyway

Harry. I can make us all something to eat. There's no need for you to do it Preston, you only make a mess anyway. I'll just do it myself." Preston smirked as he left the room. Harry watched Gill getting ready and realised she was on edge, nervous. Something wasn't right in his household and the sooner he uncovered it the better. He watched Gill put her housecoat on and sat thinking.

Harry was alone in the bedroom; looking out of the window he could see the back garden. The grass was long and overgrown, nothing like he'd left it. Spare motorbike parts were scattered all over and the fence at the bottom of the garden was broken in two. He used to love sitting in the garden, he loved how relaxing it was listening to the birds. Even Gill loved it there; she'd even planted some flowers around the borders of the lawn to make it look special, but now there was nothing – it was barren, lifeless. All traces of any plant life were gone. The lawn was bald in parts and all that grew there now were weeds. Harry hung his head into his hands. Life had been hard for Gill and it was only now he was seeing just how much his imprisonment had affected his family. He had some making up to do and he knew it. Pulling his new slippers on his feet he headed downstairs. As he walked into the front room he could see Callum still asleep on the sofa. Snoring his head off he was, saliva dribbling from the side of his mouth. Harry held a single finger up to his lips and smiled at Gill and Preston.

Gill realised what he was going to do and ran to his side grabbing his arm tightly, she was panicking. "Don't be waking him up Harry, let him sleep. He'll go mental if he's not had enough kip. Just leave him alone until he wakes up on his own. He's like a bear with a sore head if he's not had enough sleep." Harry chuckled and pulled the big toe he could see hanging out from the corner of the sofa. Screams, shrieking, high pitched moans filled the room.

Callum was bouncing about the front room like a mad man. His eyes were dancing with madness. "What the fuck is going on. I'll tell you what Preston if you think you can dome me while I'm asleep then just watch."

Callum scrambled across the furniture and ran at his younger brother, he'd not even seen his father. Harry ran between them and held Callum back by the scruff of the neck. "Ay, fucking turn it in, Charlie big spuds. It was me who woke you up, not Preston. Don't you want to see your old dad or what?" Callum walked back to the sofa and pulled the duvet back over his head in a strop, he was livid. Harry looked about the room and shot his eyes to Gill and Preston. Holding his hands up he hunched his shoulders. "What the fuck was all that about?" he snapped and walked over to the sofa pulling the duvet from his son's body. Harry had lost the plot. "Who the hell do you think you're talking to? Since when do you fight with your brother like that?" Callum wriggled free and went nose to nose with his father, his eyes were menacing and he was clenching his fists into two tiny curled balls at the side of him ready to attack. Gill plonked down at the dining table and lit a cigarette. She knew this day was coming and she kept her mouth shut, it was out of her hands now and she left her husband to deal with it. Callum was flung across the living room by Harry like a ragdoll. He ran back at him but he didn't stand a chance, Harry just twisted him up and put him on his arse.

Preston was anxious and he was pacing the floor.

"Dad, just get off him. You don't know what he's like, he just needs to sleep and he'll be fine. Just leave him and let him get his head down will you?"

Harry grabbed Callum by the scruff of his neck and pinned him up against the wall. "This is my house boy, and if you're living under my roof, you live by my rules, do you hear me?"

Callum just stared deep into his father's eyes and said nothing. He looked like he was in some kind of trance. Once Harry released his grip Callum headed towards the door. He turned his head back over his shoulder and growled. "This isn't over you muppet. Just you wait and see. I'll show you what I'm all about. I'm not no nob-head you know. Don't think you can take the piss out of me because I'll bang you out old man." Harry was going to run after him but Preston closed the door and stood in front of it refusing to move.

Gill pleaded with her husband from the other side of the room, she was in tears. "Harry, just leave him. We can sort this out later. Please, for me, just come and sit down and calm down. I don't need this so early in the morning. You can sort it out later." Harry was fuming, if he had been dressed he would have followed him and given him a proper hiding. Who did he think he was talking to his dad like that? No, this was far from over, he was getting it.

Harry popped a cigarette in the corner of his mouth. Once he'd lit it he inhaled deeply trying to get his fix of nicotine as soon as he could, his hands were shaking and his temper was boiling. "He's a cheeky cunt that one is. I swear to God if I would have had my clothes on that runt would have been six foot under. Who the fuck does he think he is talking to me like that?"

Preston sniggered and looked at his mother. He spoke in a low voice with his hand covering his mouth. "As if that's really going to happen. Mam, you need to put my dad in the picture before he ends up getting hurt. You know what Callum's like when he loses his rag. You better word him up before it kicks off big time."

Gill growled at her son, he was testing the water for sure; he was a right trouble causer. "Preston, will you just fuck off out. Why do you always make things ten times worse than what they already, just zip it will you?"

Harry couldn't believe his ears, was this really happening in his own house. He stood up and walked towards his son, bending down to his eye level. "What did you say Preston, do you really think Callum can tackle me? Take your head from out of your arse, before you get hurt son. Nobody fucks with me, not even my own son!" Gill screwed her face up and darted her eyes at her son pleading with him to keep schtum. She knew this was never going to happen – Preston loved every single minute of it and voiced his opinion in a cocky tone.

"Dad, me and Callum do our own shit these days. Callum is not behind the door you know. He can get whatever he wants when he puts his mind to it. You need to back off and leave us to it. We're not kids anymore."

Harry snapped and launched his cup at the wall. Gill scrambled to her feet picking up the shattered pieces on her knees. Harry was in Preston's face. "You and your brother are playing with fire lad. I swear, let me hear one bit of news that you two are involved in any kind of shit and you'll see what I'm all about. Trust me, I'm not joking."

Preston grabbed his coat from the side of the chair and

sniggered as he left the room. "Yeah yeah dad, whatever, we'll see about that."

Gill and Harry were alone. Harry was raging and he ran upstairs to get ready. "Gill, you can sack making me anything to eat. I've got more important things to do this morning and sorting them two pricks out is first on my list. Do they really think they can take the piss out of me? They're in for a shock love, a big fucking shock."

Harry left the room and Gill sat crying at the dining table, she was mumbling under her breath. "Please God, make it all stop, please."

CHAPTER FOUR

Callum Jarvis fed the cannabis plants, he was humming a tune and nodding his head. This grow was going to get him back on his feet, put him on the map. 'Easy money' he called it with little risk of ending up in jail. The room was filled with plants, around sixty of them. Feeding them all carefully he smirked as he stroked his fingers across the watering can. "Come on my babies, not long now and you'll make me a rich man. I'll tell you what Tina; I'm like Alan fucking Titchmarsh with my green fingers. Look at these babies growing." A mobile phone ringing in his pocket made him place the feeder on the floor. A quick glance at the screen and he chuckled as he answered it. "Preston, where the fuck are you bro?" He listened carefully and paced the floor with his phone held closely to his ear. "Just hurry up and get your arse around here. And, make sure nobody is following you. These fuckers are nearly ready to be chopped down and we don't want anyone getting onto us. I swear bro this place stinks of weed now so bring some air freshener or something to try and get rid of the smell." The call ended and Callum carried on feeding the plants. The room was boiling hot and he was sweating his nuts off. Lots of small lights from above hung over the plants and the heat was overwhelming, it was like a sauna.

Tina sat playing with her hair, twisting it out of boredom. She was Callum's girlfriend and she was never far from his side especially now he was getting ready to cut these plants down. She was a money grabber and she would have done anything to line her pockets. Kicking her legs out in front of her she spoke. "So, are we going on holiday when this lot is bagged up or what?"

Callum raised his eyebrows and sighed. "Will you just relax woman. Rome wasn't built in a day. I've told you when it's sold me and you will live like royalty. We'll want for fuck all."

Tina played with her fingernails and replied in a stroppy tone. "I'm just asking that's all. There's no need to bite my head off is there. Ay, will you buy me them Ugg boots I've seen in town. Orr, I just love them and I can wear them with my skinny jeans. Joanne Marsland's got a pair you know. They look mint on her too. I'd love a pair."

Callum walked to her side and sat next to her, he was confident as he stroked her lip with his finger. Tina was pretty and she was a girl who knew what she wanted and more than anything, she knew how to get it. She was a flirt and always used her good looks whenever she could. From the first moment she found out Callum was earning money she was all over him like a rash, she'd never bothered with him until she knew he was grafting. Tina's mother was the one who put her onto him. Trish smoked weed a lot and she knew who was dealing in the area. Trish Brown was a cunning old tart and she would have had anyone over to earn a quick few quid, she was the lowest of the low. From an early age she'd showed Tina how to use her body to get what she wanted, she had no shame. She even put her on the pill in case she got pregnant, there was no way she wanted her tubbed.

Callum answered her in a animated voice. "You can have the boots if you want, and I can kit you out with some new clobber too," he sniggered. "Nothing is too much for you babes, nothing. You know you can have what you want from me don't you?"

Tina licked her teeth slowly; she knew she had him where she wanted him. He wasn't her type really, he made her cringe, but the money he was earning made it easier to call him her boyfriend. A couple of months she'd been with him now and already he was doing her head in, she would be glad to see the back of him if the truth was known. Callum leaned over and kissed Tina. His hands disappeared up her skirt and he was horny. Loud knocking at the front door made him stop dead; he panicked and jumped to his feet. Running to the window he dipped his head low and peered through the grey net curtains. He waved his hands above his head and shouted over to Tina. "Fuck me, why does he knock like that, he's a right prick sometimes. He's so on top." Callum went to answer the front door as Tina straightened her skirt. She was in no mood for sex anyway and she was glad they'd been interrupted, she was off the hook.

The front door opened slowly and Preston had to fight his way inside past Callum who was guarding the door. There was no way he was taking any chances and he always made sure he checked the area before letting anyone inside the house. Callum was paranoid and he had every right to be, he was sitting on a fortune and he knew the front door could have been boomed in at any second now. That's how this kind of graft worked, everyone was out to have you over, and nobody was safe. Preston sat next to Tina and placed his hand on her knee. He was a loveable rogue and loved flirting with the ladies. He had the gift of the gab and he was liked by most of the girls in the area. Preston smirked at Tina and rubbed her leg slowly. "Any day now and me and our kid will be wadded, fucking rolling in it. I can't wait, I'm on my arse. I owe pure dough out too."

Tina tried to act cool. She'd been waiting on the money for weeks too and knew that as soon as the plants were chopped down she would be treated like a princess. Preston walked up and down and smelt the aroma from the cannabis plants. "Has Dan been on the blower or what? He's been hounding me for weeks waiting for his cut."

Callum snarled and sparked up a cigarette. "That prick is doing my head in you know and if he carries on chatting shit I'm going to wipe him clean out. I mean, he goes on as if it's him running the shit around here, when all he does is he gets us a gaff to do the grow in. I swear down, let him carry on being a stress head and he's getting fuck all." Preston looked at his brother in more detail and knew he was already thinking about having Dan over. Callum was a snidey bastard and wouldn't lose any sleep about ripping someone off, even his own brother. Dan was a nobody, just someone wanting to earn a few extra quid and what could he do about it anyway, nothing.

The plants were fed and it was time to leave the house. The next time they would be here, the grow would be ready to cut down. Preston had a lad coming around soon anyway to guard the house; he would stay there all night and sleep there protecting their pot of gold. There was no way they were taking any chances; they had too much to lose.

★

Gill sat at the table sipping at her cup of tea with shaking hands. Every now and then she sighed as she sat back, clock watching. Harry had just left the house and he was raging about how his sons were treating him. You couldn't really blame him for being annoyed, they were out of control and didn't give a flying fuck about anyone. The letterbox rapped loudly and Gill looked edgy as she went to answer the door. She was still in her pyjamas and her hair was stuck up all over the show.

"Fuck me Sally, where have you been, you said you were on your way hours ago. I'm stressed to death here, come inside; hurry up, my head's going to pop if I don't get this sorted soon."

Sally walked into the hallway, she chuckled. "Well, you will play with fire won't you? I told you this day would come didn't I?" The women walked into the front room. Gill popped a cigarette from her packet and passed Sally one. Sally Smith was Gill's best friend. 'Partners in crime' Harry called them. Sally was plain looking but her chestnut brown hair and green eyes complemented her face.

Gill sucked hard on her cigarette. "He's going to find out isn't he; someone will blab to him I just know it. It's just a matter of time. What the hell am I going to do?"

Sally nodded her head slowly, she knew Gill was right but tried to calm her down. "Listen, if you carry on stressing like this, Harry will know something is wrong, so just calm down will you. Nobody will say a word trust me."

Gill plonked down on the sofa and brought her knees up to her chest. "The lads know about it too. Preston said the other day that he heard us in bed together. Oh Sally, it's all a mess. Why didn't I just say no? I should have known better. Harry will rip his bleeding head off when he finds out."

Sally sat down next to her and sat thinking for a few seconds. "Right, you need to go and see Ray and get a story sorted out. Fucking hell Gill, if Ray's wife gets wind of this, she'll do you in. Regina is a head the ball trust me."

Gill had never even thought about her before now and she sat sobbing as the reality of her actions hit home. "How on earth could I have let this happen?"

Sally should have kept her mouth shut but she just wasn't like that, she was always straight talking and sometimes she put her foot in it with her big gob. "Regina is the last of your worries. We need a plan, and fast. If Preston is threatening to bubble on you it's just a matter of time before he spills the beans. He's a cheeky runt that one is. He's always trying to have you over, he's blackmailing you isn't he?"

Gill hated that Sally was right and tried to stand up for her son. He was a cocky fucker yes, but surely he would never put his mother's life at risk. "I think the lads are just testing the water. I denied it anyway and I think they bought my story. My only hope is to never mention it again to them, if I show I'm arsed they will have me over. I know them both too well. Yes, I'll never mention it again and hopefully it will be forgot about."

Sally stubbed her cigarette out in the ashtray at the side of her. "So, move your arse then. Get on the phone to Ray and arrange to meet him. Harry is out all day sorting his shit out, so there is no time like the present is there?"

Gill bolted up from her chair and ran to the mirror.

"Look at the state of me Sally. You're right, I'm going to get ready and go and see him. This affair has to stop. It was a mistake, a bad mistake."

Sally watched as Gill pulled at the baggy skin around her eyes. Her heart went out to her. She'd been lonely and missed the loving touch of a man. Five years was a long time to go without any affection, surely Harry would understand that. Sally kissed her friend on the cheek. "Right, I'm off. Phone me later. Just move your arse and get to Ray as fast as you can before somebody else does. Just end it and walk away; it's your only option." Sally left and Gill was alone. Picking her mobile phone up she sent a text to Ray telling him to meet her as soon as possible. Running upstairs, she ran into the bathroom and started to get ready. She was a woman on a mission and knew time wasn't on her side. This had to be over as soon as possible, her life was in danger.

Harry Jarvis walked into the Shiredale pub in Harpurhey. The vein in the side of his neck was pumping at the side. There was silence and people whispered as he marched towards the bar. In his day he'd been a bastard and he knew he'd hurt a lot of people in the area, but in his eyes they only got what they deserved. He never took anyone out that didn't deserve it. A quick nod of his head to the punters soon put them at ease. A man around thirty years old quickly gathered his belongings and scarpered, his face was white and he looked like he'd seen a ghost. This man had had dealing with Harry in the past and knew after a few scoops he could blow at any time. There was no way he was chancing another beating, he'd lost his front teeth the last time he'd crossed Harry Jarvis. There was no way he was chancing it again! He was getting off.

Matty was by Harry's side as he shouted over to Bernard the landlord. He was Harry's wingman and now that he was back on the scene he was confident to take on anyone now that he had the backing. "Get them drinks rolling Bernard, we have a hero returning home here, where's your manners man?"

The landlord rushed to the bar and stretched his hand over to shake Harry's. He was nervous and you could see his eyes twitching rapidly. "Nice to have you back home Harry, you've been missed pal." Bernard was lying of course and he'd had his own troubles with Harry and his crew. The time this man had been locked behind bars had been heaven for everyone in the area and now that he was back on the scene he knew things were going to change and fast. Bernard brought two large brandies over and passed them to the men. "These are on the house lads, glad to have you back home Harry."

Harry didn't reply, he picked up the glass and necked the drink in one. Banging the glass on the bar he shot a look at Bernard and raised his eyebrows. "Same again mate, keep them coming." Matty swigged his drink and followed suit. Most thought he was a brown-noser who thought he was hard as nails by association.

Harry grabbed another drink from Bernard and turned his head to face the punters. From the corner of his eye he could see Mandy, Jona's ex-girlfriend sat to the left of him. He chuckled to himself and went to sit down. Matty was on his phone and he was arranging for the lads to come and meet up with them. This was going to be a long day, shit needed sorting out and Harry would want to know the ins and outs of a cat's arse-hole before the day was over.

The music played in the pub and it was night time now. Harry was team-handed and still sat in the pub in the corner of the room. Matty was pissed and his voice was getting loud. "Harry, when are we going to see the Collins brothers. They must think we're shitting our pants. They'll have got wind that you're home, that's why they are keeping their heads down."

Harry held his head back against the wall and nodded his head slowly. "It will all come back to us soon lads. They know what I want and they know I'll be coming for it. Five years I spent in the nick for them bastards, they owe me big time." Harry closed his eyes and seemed to be in some kind of trance. He was remembering the night he got arrested and how his wife lay on the floor screaming for the police not to take her husband. Harry by his own admittance knew he dropped a bollock by leaving his jacket behind at the scene of the crime. He was sloppy and paid the price for his mistake. Tony Johnson deserved everything he got that night and he was lucky that the ambulance got to him before he choked on his own blood. Tony Johnson was a no good, dirty lying scab who had double-crossed Harry and his boys. He ripped them off for over twenty grand. The Collins brothers were in on it too and Harry knew they were the ones to blame for his arrest. John Collins, the youngest brother, grassed him up. Harry was sure of it. And the money? Yes, don't forget that. Where did that go? Harry knew Tony had been working for the Collins brothers and just before he half-killed him he told them exactly who had set him up. Harry knew he should have finished him off when he had the chance and regretted every day that the man was still breathing.

Popping a cigarette into his mouth Harry stood up and headed towards the toilets, he was swaying and he was unsteady on his feet. Jona's girlfriend saw him heading her way and dipped her head low. She knew Harry couldn't keep his mouth shut and she prepared herself for some verbal abuse. Harry walked straight past her and went inside the toilets. Mandy let out a laboured breath and carried on talking to her friends, she was off the hook. Minutes passed and she thought she was safe. Suddenly there was a banging noise behind her, Mandy turned anxiously and came eye-to-eye with Harry Jarvis. "Long time no see yo-yo knickers, are you still putting it about or what? Jona is raging about you and he's coming to shave your hair off as soon as he gets out!"

Mandy swallowed hard, she knew she had to back her mouth up and stand tall. If she showed one bit of fear Harry would wipe the floor with her and humiliate her in front of everyone who was there. Taking a deep breath she answered him. "Oh Harry, Jona is off his head, you know what that rat was like, he was shagging anything with a pulse. What did you expect me to do, lie in bed all day bleeding crying over him?"

Harry liked this woman's balls; he pushed her shoulder for her to move over in her seat. "Are you getting the drinks in then or what?" Mandy asked in a cheeky voice.

Harry stuck two fingers in his mouth and whistled over to Bernard. "Oi, can I have a bottle of Brandy over here for the ladies, bring some glasses too."

Bernard was like a blue-arsed fly running around. Small droplets of sweat were visible on his forehead and he had wet patches under the arms of his blue shirt. "Yeah, I'll sort it Harry, just hang fire, give me a few minutes and I'll be with you."

Mandy smirked and looked relieved, she loved a free night out and knew if she sat in Harry's company for the rest of the night she wouldn't have to put her hand in her pocket again. Harry words were slurred as he rested his head on her shoulder. He'd known Mandy since he was a kid and she had always been in the same circle of friends as him. They'd been good friends in the past. Mandy had never had any luck with men, and she always seemed to go for the bad lads who she thought could change her life with money. It never happened though, she was always left with a broken heart and bruises on her body. Mandy was attractive with raven black hair and piercing blue eyes, yet her skin was very pale. She could look like a princess. Snow White perhaps. Men thought the small gap between her two front teeth was sexy and as Harry looked at her in more details he wondered why he'd never seen her true beauty before.

"How's Gill now that you're home Harry? I bet her world has been turned upside down now hasn't it? I mean, five years without a man in her bed that must be hard," she giggled and patted his arm. "I wouldn't have lasted five bleeding minutes." Harry looked deeper into her eyes and he seemed in a deep trance. Giving his head a quick shake he sat up straight and reached for his glass from the table.

The other women with Mandy left them both now and headed to the dance floor. "See you later Mandy, we're going to the Tavern pub after this dance if you want to follow us up."

Mandy just smiled at them and watched them leave. She knew which side her bread was buttered on, and stayed put. "So, is Jona alright or what? He's been writing to me for months but I've just binned his letters, he only chats shit in them anyway, promising me the world and all that. It's just all prison talk. I don't believe a word that comes out of his mouth anymore the spineless bastard," Mandy looked Harry in the eyes and continued. "I wish he would just leave me alone to get on with my own life. He made his choices when he was out of nick. What, did he seriously think I wouldn't find out?" she held the lower part of her stomach and giggled. "Come on Harry, I always find out stuff around here, you'd be surprised what I get to know." Mandy stared at him a bit longer than necessary and she was going to say something but stopped at the last minute.

Harry was onto her and urged her to continue. "Do you want to tell me something or what, come on, don't beat around the bush, just say it."

Mandy knew she'd said too much already and quickly changed the subject. "Ay, them Collins brothers are raking it in I hear. They've got grows in nearly every house around the estate and they have kids grafting for him, bastards they are. They're paying them peanuts too. Liberty takers if you ask me."

Harry edged closer to her and his hot breath was in her face. "Oh, is that right? I'll tell you what Mandy, you can earn yourself a right few quid if you want. I could do with someone in the know like you. What do you say, ay? You can be my eyes and ears around here? Our little secret, what do you think?"

Mandy was pissed and the brandy always made

her have loose lips, she was confident now and stroked Harry's arm slowly. "Yeah, I'm up for that. I'm on my arse and why shouldn't I rake it in too. It's about time them Collins brothers came down to earth with a bang anyway. They're too smug for their own good. I'm up for it Harry, count me in." Without thinking she kissed him. Harry responded and he seemed to forget he was a married man for a few seconds. Pulling his head away from hers he quickly looked around the pub in a panic, hoping nobody had seen him. He was safe, everybody was deep in conversation and his infidelity had gone unnoticed. Harry stood up and he was desperate to get away from Mandy now. What the hell was he thinking? He'd never looked at another woman in a long time, why now? He picked his glass up and spoke slowly to Mandy before he left.

"That was wrong, keep it to yourself, do you hear me?"

Mandy held a cunning look in her eyes and licked her lips slowly. "It was good though, wasn't it? Harry, come and see me tomorrow and we'll talk business. Perhaps we can carry on where we left off?" Harry didn't answer. He walked off to join Matty and the others who were still sat on the other side of the room.

Matty waited until Harry sat down and whispered in his ear. "Fuck me mate, don't be messing with her, she's got the biggest gob around here. I swear, Gill will cut your balls off if she gets wind of this."

Harry ragged his fingers through his hair, his head was spinning and his eyes were closing slowly, he'd had way too much to drink and his vision was blurred. "Matty, take me home mate, I'm twisted, fucking wrecked I am. I never meant to kiss her it just happened."

Harry left the pub, much to Bernard's relief. Mandy sat on her own and poured herself another glass of brandy; she lifted her glass up towards Bernard and sniggered. "Cheers love."

Harry staggered through his front door. The house was in darkness and only a small light from upstairs guided him to bed. He'd never planned to get this pissed, it just happened. Alcohol never agreed with him and he always promised himself after each hangover he would never drink again, it never happened though, he was full of shit. Gill was asleep in bed and he could see her thin body lay on her side beneath the duvet. Sitting on the corner of the bed he placed his hand on her leg and stroked it slowly. "Sorry I'm late love, I just got talking with the lads. You know how it is don't you?" Gill kept her eyes firmly closed; if her husband knew she was awake he would keep her talking for hours about nothing of real importance, she tried to control her breathing and remained still. Harry fell onto the bed and seemed out for the count in seconds.

Once he was asleep Gill sneaked downstairs. Stood in the kitchen she pulled her mobile phone out from her housecoat and started to ring a number. The voice message came on and she whispered as she left a message. "Ray, you better get in touch with me as soon as possible. I've been trying to speak to you all day. You better not be leaving me to deal with this on my own, phone me tomorrow." Gill ended the phone call and lit a cigarette. She heard a door creak behind her and nearly jumped out of her skin. Running to the kitchen door she couldn't see anyone, holding her hand to her neck she gripped her throat tightly. "Fuck, fuck, fuck, "she mumbled as she headed back to the table to finish her cigarette.

Harry plonked back on the bed after he'd been to the toilet. His head was spinning and he was wobbling all over the place. Lay staring at the ceiling a single tear rolled down his face. Closing his eyes slowly he pulled the duvet over his head and fell fast asleep. Gill sneaked back into her bed and turned the opposite way from Harry. Staring at the moonlight through the window she shook her head slowly, she needed a miracle to get her through this. Time wasn't on her side and the shit was about to hit the fan.

CHAPTER FIVE

Tony Johnson hammered on the door with both hands; he was in a panic and desperate for somebody to open up, head squeezed up against the glass pane he shouted out in a distressed voice. "Open the door will you, this is important, let me in. I need your help" The front door opened suddenly and Tony ran inside screaming at the top of his lungs. "He's out, fucking Harry Jarvis is out of the slammer. I've just drove passed him, he's on Moston Lane with Matty. What the hell am I going to do? I'm a marked man, I know I am."

Peter Collins stood tall and inhaled the morning air that seeped in from the backdoor. Everyone was waiting for him to speak, but he remained silent. He was a man of few words and only spoke when required. Tony marched about the kitchen ragging his fingers through his hair, his lips were trembling and he was holding his neck as if he was struggling to breathe. "I swear lads; you promised me you'd protect me when he got out. I've done everything for you lot and I put my neck on a line. I need to know you've got my back. "

Peter grabbed Tony by his cheeks and made his lips touch together. "Listen you spineless bastard, just relax. Harry Jarvis knows where we are, and, if he has a beef with us then let him bring it on. He's getting fuck all from us, not a carrot."

John Collins, the youngest of the four brothers, pulled Peter's arms from Tony. He was scared too and knew

41

Harry would have him down on his hit list too; he was the one who'd grassed him up after all. "Just relax Peter, for fucks just calm down. Tony's right in what he's saying, we did say we would protect him when that cunt got out of jail. Tony nearly died at the hands of that nutter, are you forgetting that or what?" John watched his brother for any reaction but there was none. Peter just stood at the back door looking out into the garden as if he was inhaling the fresh air.

The four Collins brothers didn't look alike. I think they must have had different fathers because Peter looked foreign and John was completely the opposite – fair and pale. None of them resembled each other. Susan Collins walked into the kitchen, she smiled at her boys and kissed John on the top of his head as she walked passed him. He was the apple of her eye and she had a soft spot for her youngest son, he could do no wrong in her eyes, he was an angel. "Well, cheer up you lot, you've got faces like smacked arses. Who's died?" she asked in a sarcastic manner.

John couldn't hold his tongue and blurted it out before anyone could get a word in. "Mam, its Harry Jarvis, he's out of prison."

Peter snapped and ran at his youngest brother and slapped him across the head with a swift swipe. "Shut it gob-shite, why do you feel the need to tell her everything you big wuss, grow some balls ay and keep it shut?"

Susan ran to her son's side and stroked her palm gently across his head. "Peter, don't you dare hit him like that again. I want to know everything that goes on under my roof. You did right in telling me. I mean, if the dibble come here I need to be clued up too don't I?" She pointed her finger at her sons and snarled. "Or would you prefer it if I just told them everything I know and you all land up in the bleeding chokey?" Susan knew she was talking sense and Peter calmed down. Susan Collins was not behind the door, all her children's fathers were grafters and she'd never gone without anything in her life, she was always looked after. Her looks had gone over the years but you could tell she'd been a good looking woman in her day. Her blue eyes shone brightly as she spoke. They were light blue in colour, like the sky on a hot summer's day. "If Harry Jarvis and his boys want to start any trouble then you lot need to be ready, not sat on your arses moping about all bleeding day. You need to be on your guard twenty-four- seven," she poked her son in the arm. "Peter you know what that snidey bleeder is capable of; he's a shady fucker that one is. I wouldn't trust him as far as I could throw him." Susan stood with her hands pressed firmly on her hips and folded her arms in front of her, she'd made her point.

The two other brothers Connor and Ben sat smoking at the kitchen table; they were anxious and waiting on Peter to come up with some kind of plan. They sat in silence. Tony Johnson walked to the kitchen window and lifted up the crisp white net curtain; he was nervous and knew his days were numbered. "I've not slept a bleeding wink all night lads, look at me I'm shaking like a shitting dog," he held his flat palm out and he was right he was quivering. "I'm going to stay in a hotel tonight with Marlene. She's a nervous wreck too, she's saying she's never going back home again, ever."

John tapped his fingers on the table; he lifted his head up slowly and shot a look at his mother. "Why don't we just pay him the twenty grand we took from him and shake hands, past is the past isn't it?"

Susan growled and flicked her son's ear causing him to jump. "Are you really right in the head John? Listen, Peter go and get the lads together and go and face him, man to man. You're bigger than you were five years ago, and you have the back-up now to take him on. What's up are you scared or what?" Susan could always wind her son up and she knew he'd react to her comment.

Peter went white with rage and he was just staring at the wall. His mother was right, he did know men too, bad men who would chop Harry and his men up for a few grand, but he was hesitant, something was stopping him. "Right Tony, just go and stay in the hotel and let me have a think about this."

He pulled a wad of cash from his pocket and bunged it to Tony. There must have been at least five hundred pound there. Tony licked his lips as he cast his eyes over the readies; he was pleased and knew for the next couple of days he would be safe. He was a money grabber and tried for some more cash to tide him over. "But what after this money has gone, who's going to fund my hotel bills then?"

Peter ran at Tony and dragged him out of the room by the scruff of the neck. Connor held Susan back as she tried to follow them. Peter pinned Tony up against the wall, their noses were touching and Peter's hot breath was in Tony's face. "Listen you money grabbing cunt, don't you ever come knocking on my door again. I'll sort Harry out don't worry, but stay the fuck away from my door, do you hear me?"

Tony was turning blue and his eyes were nearly

popping out from his head. He struggled to break free. Scrambling towards the front door he opened the catch with shaking hands. "Don't leave me to rot Peter, you owe me, remember, if Harry gets hold of me I'm a dead man, you owe me Collins and if you don't protect me I'll go to the police. I'll sink the ship, I swear, don't you worry about that I'll do it you know." Tony ran out of the house as fast as his legs could carry him. As Peter tried to get a grip of him he was in his car driving out of the avenue. Ben put his hand on his brother's shoulder as he came to his side. "He's a grassing cunt, him. I don't trust him one little bit, he's a double agent. He needs to go missing, taken out for good."

Peter nodded his head slowly as headed back into the house. "You're right, he has to go."

Susan was brewing up and five cups were on the side. "Right, you lot, let's have a nice cup of tea and calm down. We need to think about this. I don't want you all running in with guns blazing, this needs thinking about. Let's have a cuppa." As the brothers sat round the table, you could have cut the atmosphere with a knife. Susan passed the drinks to her sons and placed a packet of biscuits on the table. She could see they were all stunned by the news of Harry's return. "I can put a bit of pressure on his wife," Susan stressed. "I mean, come on, we all know what that tart's been up to so I could pull her strings and make sure she tells Harry to back off."

Peter shook his head. "No mam, this needs sorting properly. Harry won't just leave this alone; you know what he's like. He'll try to take back what he thinks he's owed. Mark my words lads he'll already know exactly what we're up to and who's paying what. You just watch how things change." John placed his head on his mother's shoulder and she stroked his brow slowly. He wasn't like his brothers; he was different, feminine even. He hated that he was born into a family of criminals and he would have much preferred working in an office all day long, earning his money the proper way. John never took part in any 'real stuff', as he called it. He was too squeamish for all that. Once, he was there with his brothers and they were dealing with a man who'd had them over. John fainted as soon as he saw the claret splurging all over the walls; he was a mess and vowed he would never go with them again. No. This wasn't for him; he stayed well away from any violence after that. John just collected the money when he needed to, he liked it like that. He liked a simple life with no comebacks.

Kenzo walked into the kitchen, she was still half asleep and wearing her pyjamas. She looked at her brothers sat around the kitchen table and raised her eyebrows as she reached over to grab a biscuit. "So, I take it you must know Harry Jarvis is out then. I was in the boozer last night and that's all anyone was talking about," she carried on talking with a mouthful of biscuit. "I believe he looks as hard as nails, pumped up to death. The girls said his body is hench, his muscles are ripped up to death."

Susan threw a tea towel over at her daughter's head. "Will you shut that big trap of yours? The lads know he's out so they don't need you adding your two pennies worth."

Kenzo smiled cunningly, she knew exactly what she was doing and stood with her hands on her hips still nibbling on her biscuit. "I'm just saying that's all. God, shoot me for even breathing in this house. I'm just warning you, that's all." Kenzo walked around the table and placed her hand on Susan's shoulder. "Mother, I don't want my brothers getting hurt that's all. I am part of this family too you know."

Susan snarled at her and knew she was up to no good. Kenzo was always into something hooky, she could never be trusted. Aged twenty-two she was a thorn in her mother's side. Susan could see herself in her daughter and tried her best to keep her out of harm's way. This was never going to happen though; she was a handful who listened to nobody, not even her brothers. Kenzo was sleeping with an older man. Nobody knew his name at the moment but he was always bunging her cash and buying her expensive gifts. Her brothers had told her straight, as soon as they found out who it was he'd be getting a visit from them. Nobody dated their sister without them knowing about it first. Nobody.

Kenzo reached over and slid a biscuit from the packet on the table; she had a sweet tooth and always craved sugary snacks. "I thought you were dieting again porky," John chuckled as he made pig noises. Kenzo flicked her long blonde hair over her shoulder and blew a laboured breath. Here it was, the same banter they had every single day, they fought like cat and dog and everybody was used to the heated arguments they had with each other.

Kenzo licked her lips and held her head to the side. "Listen you little fairy, take your head from up my mam's arse and grow a set of balls. When was the last time you had a bird anyway? I'm sure you're a sausage jockey. Come on, when was the last time you had a woman in your bed?"

Susan bolted up from the table and ran at Kenzo.

There was no way she was having this kind of talk in her house. "That's filthy talk, you're supposed to have respect for each other, not speak about your brother like that. Go and wash your mouth out with soap you filthy cow. You'll get a name for yourself talking like that."

Kenzo stamped her feet and crossed her arms tightly in front of her. "Yeah, how did we know goldenballs would have his mummy fighting his corner for him as per usual. Just sit back down will you and let the runt fight his own battles instead of you fighting his corner all the time."

Peter banged his clenched fist on the table and everyone was quiet, the room shook. "Kenzo, fuck off back to bed will you. You and John can sort this out another time. We have more important things on our plate at the moment than you two dickheads arguing. So just do one and let me think. I need a clear head."

Kenzo fluttered her eyelashes at Peter, he was putty in her hands and he'd always protected her from her other brothers. Well, he did when it suited him. His temper could turn like a clock and he was so unpredictable at times. Kenzo scratched the top of her head and smiled at him. "Peter, can you lend me some money to go shopping. All the girls are going out tonight and I've got nothing to wear. You don't want me to be skanky do you?" Susan let out a laboured breath and sat back down in her seat. She knew what was coming and shot a look at the others.

"Yeah, come and see me later," Peter answered, "I'll sort you out. But for now, fuck off and let me sort this shit out." Kenzo smiled and reached for another biscuit from the table, she gave a cunning smile to John and headed towards the door.

Just before she left Peter shouted her back, his face was serious. "You need to watch your back now Harry's out. He's an evil bastard and he wouldn't think twice about knocking ten tons of shit out of you just to prove a point. So, keep your phone on you at all times and make sure I can contact you."

Kenzo giggled. She didn't realise how much danger she was in. It was all just a big game to her and she never took his words seriously. "Yeah, I'll be on guard. I'm not daft you know. Harry wouldn't touch me anyway, what good am I to him? I can't give him what he wants?"

Kenzo left and Susan was champing on the bit as she watched her leave. "I swear that girl will come to earth with a bang one of these days, she's too gobby for her own good. Mark my words, she's nothing but trouble. God help us with her."

John patted his mother's hand slowly. "You're right mam. She's a loose cannon with that gob. It's just a matter of time before she gets her comeuppance. And I for one will laugh my nuts off I can tell you. That's what she gets for thinking she's untouchable isn't it?"

Peter Collins grabbed his car keys from the side of the table and nodded at his brothers. "Come on; let's go down to the pub. We'll get our house in order there without any more interruptions. It's like a fucking kindergarten in here, I can't think straight. I need peace and quiet."

Susan rolled her eyes and sucked on her gums. "Oh, I suppose that's my bleeding fault too is it? I don't know. I can't do right for doing wrong in this bloody house. Go on, piss off out and sort it. I can't stand all the doom and gloom anyway it's like a mortuary. Just go and see Harry and end all the torment, what's the worst that can happen?" The lads all kissed their mother on the cheek as they left, not Peter though, he was to cool for that. John stayed by his mother's side and helped himself to more biscuits. There was no way he was going to see Harry Jarvis, no way in this world, he valued his life too much.

Gill stood at the park gates near some bushes; she was edgy and constantly biting at her fingernails. She never used to be a nail-biter but ever since Harry had got out of jail she was constantly nibbling and picking at them. Gill kept checking her wristwatch and pacing up and down. Ray should have been here ten minutes ago. Where the hell was he? The heavens opened and the rain poured down. Big fat bulky rain. Gill pulled an umbrella from her bag and stood under it with a face like thunder, she was watching the oncoming traffic eagerly. A car approached from the other end of the street and Gill stepped out from the bushes. As soon as it pulled up near her she opened the door and jumped in.

"Where the hell have you been Ray? You're late. Fuck me, I've been ringing you for days, why haven't you returned any of my calls?"

The car pulled off from the roadside and Ray took a few seconds before he answered. He was a good looking man of similar build to Harry. "I've been busy Gill. Regina has been around me like a fly around shit. I've not had a second to spare. I'm sure she's onto us."

Gill choked up and her emotions were there for him to see. Tears streamed down her face and she was struggling to talk. She swallowed hard and took a deep breath "He's going to find out Ray, it's just a matter of time. What the hell are we going to do? The lads know about you staying at the house too. I swear, I thought we'd been careful but too many people know about us, the game's up. We're up shit-street."

Ray popped a cigarette into his mouth and dragged on it hard. He was nervous but hid it well. "Just deny it, Harry knows fuck all and until he comes to me about it I'm keeping schtum. I'm a married man Gill. Regina would leave you for dead if she ever found out about us. You know how she is about me, she's a crank."

Gill had her back up; she grabbed at his arm and ragged it about. "I'm not bleeding arsed about you having a wife. I'm arsed about Harry finding out," she stared at him and tilted her head to the side. "Oh, so is this how it is now, every man for himself? Yeah, just as long as you're alright you don't give a shit about me do you? I swear to you Ray, I'm not dealing with this on my own. I need you to help me. I'm going crazy here. I've not slept proper for days, look at me, I'm a walking wreck." Ray glanced at her and knew she was at breaking point. He continued driving for another five minutes until it came to a halt at a hotel. This was the place they regularly met and for years everyone at the hotel thought they were a married couple just sneaking off together for some private time. They'd had a few near misses, people they knew had seen them together but Ray had fed them some cock and bull story and it seemed to work. He was a right jack the lad, a joker, always up for a laugh.

Gill yanked the curtains to close them, she was shaking and her chest was rising with speed. She'd been to this room so many times before but now her husband was a free man she was on edge, she couldn't settle. Ray started to get undressed; he was humming a tune and didn't seem to be bothered that Gill's husband was out of jail. Ray could handle himself yes, but he wasn't in Harry's league, nowhere near. Harry would slaughter him in seconds. Gill growled at Ray and plonked herself onto the bed. "What the hell are you doing? I've not asked to meet you here for a quick shag. I'm here for closure, to end it, to never speak about it again."

Ray was a cocky fucker and he held his head back and chuckled as he stroked the sprinkle of dark hairs on his chest. "Come on Gill, we can't just end it. You want this just as much as me. Why end a good thing, ay? Come on, get your kit off and get into bed. We can talk about it more then." Gill kicked her shoes off, and collapsed flat onto the bed. She was fighting a losing battle, he wasn't listening, he just wanted sex. Ray climbed on top of her and looked deep into her eyes. "You still love him don't you?"

Gill inhaled deeply and closed her eyes slowly. She was so mixed up and her head was in bits. Yes, she had feelings for Ray but Harry was her husband. "I can't just stop loving him Ray. He's my husband. He was in prison. I was lonely, what did he expect? Oh, I don't know how I feel any more. My head's fucked up."

Ray snapped and grabbed at her face forcing her lips together. "So, it's him you love and not me?" Gill had to think fast, Ray was pressing her for an answer. He was raging and she knew he could switch at any second now. He was scaring her and his eyes looked menacing. "Ray, just calm down will you. I do love you, but it's just," she held her flat palm on her chest. "We'll hurt so many people. I mean, Regina would cut your dick off.

You know what she's like, she's a fucking lunatic. And, then there's Harry, he'd put you six foot under, you know he would."

Ray rolled onto his side and sighed. He knew she was right but tried to ignore it. "All I know is that I love you and I want you. We both knew this day would come so its D-Day isn't it? You have to make your choice." Ray stretched his arms over his head and sat thinking. "I know what Harry is capable of but I'm willing to face it all as long as I have you at the end of it. I'll do whatever it takes."

Gill dropped her head low and sobbed. "I can't give up on him Ray. I'm all he's got; he's loved me all his life. It would hurt him too much. He'd be devastated."

Ray let out a laboured breath and placed his arm around her shoulder. "We'll find a way. We can just fuck off from around here; we can go and live abroad. We can go to Spain or something, Harry's on licence from jail, he can't leave the country can he?"

Gill reached over and kissed him slowly. She looked deep into his eyes as her finger stroked slowly over his lips. "Do you really love me that much Ray?"

He nodded his head and started to caress her body. He held a cunning look in his eyes and he was up to something, he wasn't to be trusted. "Sssh now Gill. Let's have some fun, open your legs so I can get inside you."

Gill hadn't got the answers she wanted she was taken in by this man, she was a fool.

★

Peter Collins sat in his car outside the club debating his next move. He knew Harry was inside and he was ready for him, ready to take him out. Ben and Connor were sat in the back of the car and Ben had something stuck down the front of his jeans. Connor spoke to his brothers, he was ready to rumble. "Right let's do this now. Play it cool when we get in here and if that dick makes one wrong move I'll shoot the cunt, stop him breathing. We can't take any chances he's fucking deadly." Peter opened the car door, his nostrils flared as the night air hit his skin. The tips of his ears were blood red and he was constantly curling his fingers at the side of his legs. Peter walked into the club first with his brothers close behind. They were brothers in arms and nobody was taking them down, nobody. The club was busy and Peter was scanning the room trying to locate his enemy.

Walking towards the bar it wasn't long before Ben spotted Harry Jarvis and his men. "Eyes to the left bro, three men with him sat in the corner. Don't take your eyes off him, watch like him like a hawk. If he moves he's getting took down." Peter turned his head slowly; his heart was in his mouth, his adrenalin was pumping. There he was after all these years, sat there as bold as brass as if he owed the place, Harry Jarvis.

Connor ordered the drinks as Ben found seats for them to sit down. It was as if everyone in the club knew what was going on and lots of them started to leave in a panic. A few more of Peter's men came to join him. They were whispering to each other. "Let's just take him down now", Ben ranted. "I can get a good shot from here; he'll be on the floor before he knows it."

Connor's eyes danced about the room, he was edgy and ready to strike too." Don't make a move yet, let's see what this prick has got up his sleeve first. Look at him; I don't even think he's seen us yet. He's a sitting duck."

Ben stood up to get a better look and his jaw dropped. "I don't fucking believe it, look who's sat with them all." Peter moved to get a better view and snapped as he ragged his fingers through his hair. "What the fuck is she doing sat with them. Is she right in the bastard head? She knows what's going on the fucking Judas."

Peter bit hard onto his lips and banged his fist onto the bar. "That's it, I'm going over, Ben, Connor watch my back." Peter marched across the dance floor with a look to kill in his eyes.

Matty was sat with Kenzo whispering sweet nothings into her ear. She was all over him and off her head on sniff. Peter Collins stood tall and his chest expanded as he neared the table where they were sat. Harry was startled as he clocked his enemy nearing. This man had more balls than he first thought, he'd underestimated him. Harry moved the table from near his legs making sure he could get to Peter if needed. Reaching over the table Peter grabbed his sister by her hair, ragging it with force. Kenzo was fighting back and doing her best to break free. Matty never helped her once. He was more concerned about what was happening next. Eyes locked, it was going off big time. Peter snapped at his sister. "What the fuck do you think you're playing at you slag, get your arse home now. Since when did you sit with these wankers?"

Harry was ready now, teeth gritted together tightly. He stood to his feet and shot his eyes to Kenzo. "Sit yourself back down love. This prick is clearly asking for trouble. You're going nowhere."

Peter turned to face Harry for the first time. They were like gun-slingers at dawn. Peter's boys all stood around nervously as did Harry's men. They were waiting on the next move, ready to fight. Harry was aware this wasn't the time or place to sort his business out. It was a public place, too many witnesses, CCTV. He sat back down in his seat and reached for his bottle of beer, casually drinking from it. "I suggest you and your muppets fuck off out of here mate. We both know what needs to be sorted, and you know what you owe me." Harry's eyes were wide open as he sat forward holding the look. "We can do it the easy way or the hard way, it's up to you."

Ben was bouncing about now and his hand was down the front of his pants itching to pull the shooter out. Peter stood his ground and nodded his head slowly. "You're getting fuck all mate. If you want to bring it on, then let's do it. We're not kids anymore Harry, we're ready for whatever you have to throw at us. Trust me, there's only one loser here."

Matty was held back by the other men, his eyes were bulging with rage and he was ready to take one of them out. He rammed his finger over to Peter. "Listen wank stain, you knew this day was coming and now Harry's back on the scene it's time to pay up what you owe."

The bouncers ran over and parted the men. Around ten men dressed in black clothing pulled them apart. Harry was calm, he never flinched. He was as cool as a cucumber. He stood from his seat and nodded his head slowly at the Collins brothers. "Game on lads," he growled as he left. Matty was bouncing about with his hands waving above his head as he followed closely behind him. "Fuck me Harry, why don't we just do this cunt in? Come on we'll get him outside" The crowds around them were all watching as Peter and his boys came out of the club.

Ben pulled the gun out from the front of his pants and pointed it at Harry. "Boom, boom" he shouted as he got into the car. "You're going down."

Kenzo was by Matty's side and you could see him pushing her away. She was smitten with him and she wasn't giving up that easily. Matty lost his rag with her. "Just fuck off home will you, can't you see I've got some serious stuff going on here, just do one. Go on, jog on." Kenzo tried to put her arms around his neck but this time he made sure she knew he meant business. Digging into his pocket he pulled out a small bag containing white powder and passed it her. "Here, go and party and I'll catch up with you soon. There should be enough there to keep you going all night. Go and get twisted."

Kenzo took the bag of sniff and shoved it into the front of her bra. "Matty, ring me when you've sorted this shit out. Promise me, go on, promise you'll ring me."

Her jaw was swinging, she was off her head chatting shit. Matty blew a laboured breath and pushed her away with force. "For crying out loud, yeah I'll ring you. Just fuck off out of my face will you."

The men got together and they were discussing their next move. Harry jumped into the car and told the others to follow him to his house. Both gangs knew lives would be lost and blood would be shed soon. It was war.

★

Gill sat drinking a glass of wine with Sally. This was a Friday night ritual for them, something they had done for as long as they could remember. Preston and Callum had just come in and they were sat in the front room playing on the PS3. She could hear them shouting and screaming at each other as they played Grand Theft Auto. Sally closed the kitchen door and staggered back to her seat. "So, how did it go with Ray? Please tell me it's all done and dusted now?"

Gill took a deep breath and twiddled with her hair. "I think I love Ray, Sally. I've been with him nearly five years, how can you expect me to just walk away. I do have a heart you know. You don't pick who you fall in love with, do you?"

Sally pulled at Gill's hands and spoke directly to her. "Oh my God, are you right in the bleeding head? Where has all this love stuff come from? Gill you said he was your fuck buddy, nothing else. Since when have you been in love with him?"

Gill rolled her eyes. "Oh, shut up Sally. What does it matter if I love him or not? Harry's home now and it will have to stop won't it?"

Sally reached for her cigs and passed Gill one. "You bet your life it will have to stop. Well, if you want to keep breathing anyway. What the hell has Ray Clough got that Harry hasn't? You've loved Harry for as long as I can remember. You're a fool if you ask me. Harry's the full package." Sally blew a thick cloud of grey smoke through her mouth and continued. "Ray is a married man. He's not behind the door either with the women. I bet he's still been seeing other women even though he's been seeing you. The guys a rat, a dirty cheating low-life."

Gill raised her eyes to the ceiling and shook her head. "He's not a player at all. He treats me well and he loves me too."

Sally chuckled and played with the cuff off her blouse.

"Don't tell me you believe his bullshit. Take your head from up your arse, the guy's a player?" Studying Gill for a few seconds she sighed. "You do don't you. You actually love the guy? For fucks sake Gill. I hope you've written your will out because your days are numbered. It's just a matter of time before Harry gets wind of this. So, you've been warned, on your head be it."

The kitchen door opened and Harry was stood there with Matty and the other men were stood behind him. "Who's been warned?" Harry enquired.

Sally swallowed hard; she was on the spot and struggling to speak. Thinking on her feet she chuckled and tried to make light of the matter. "Oh, some guy I'm seeing. I swear Harry, you can't find a decent man these days. They're all fucked in the head. Gill's found a diamond when she met you. I just hope she knows how lucky she is?"

Sally shot a look at Gill and made sure she got the message. Harry walked to Gill's side and kissed the top of her head. "Can me and the lads sit in here, love. We just have a few things to sort out. You go and get in bed, you looked knackered. I'll be up soon anyway."

Gill looked tired and once she picked her belongings up from the table she headed off to bed. Sally said goodnight and left in a hurry. Harry was watching his wife like a hawk and he knew something was playing on her mind. He knew her inside out and licked his lips slowly as she pecked his cheek with a kiss and said goodnight.

★

"That cunt is a dead man walking. Who the fuck do they think they are? Did you see them walking onto our turf as if they own the fucking gaff. Harry, this is war. I'm so ready for it now, let's take them pricks out." Matty snarled.

Preston walked into the kitchen and he was necking the remainder of his beer from the bottle. "Alright dad, what's going down here then? If you need some extra hands me and our kid can hook you up with some manpower. I swear, we're hardcore when we get going. You should see our Callum when he lets rip, he's a fucking head case. He just goes sick and lets them have it."

Harry growled at his son. He was pissed and humiliating him, he needed him to leave as soon as possible. Placing his hand on his shoulder he smirked. "Listen Charlie big spuds, when we need some teenager sorting stuff out we'll give you a shout but for now, fuck off to bed and leave us alone. This is big boy's stuff," Harry paused and his face changed. "Ay, is Callum in there with you because if he is I want a word with him before he goes to bed? He's not forgotten about his attitude towards me this morning has he?"

Preston grabbed another two bottles of beer from the fridge and left the room, he was singing a tune as he left. Harry tapped his fingers on the table. This was the moment they were all waiting for, the plan, the revenge, the moment they took their throne back on the Manchester crime scene. "We start by attacking them where it hurts. Tomorrow we'll start by going through a few doors and taking the grows we know they have. We need some money to build on first, because we all know money talks around here doesn't it? Matty, I want you to shag that little slut a bit harder. We need to know exactly what her brothers are up to and Kenzo will tell us anything for a few grams of Charlie. So do your work on her." Harry paced the room, thinking. "We need guns sorting, machetes, anything we can hold of. Tomorrow is a new day and I'm ready to take back what belongs to us. We need to stay strong lads and keep this on the low. No one must know it's us who are having these grows away, nobody."

Matty stretched his arms above his head. "I'll sort it Harry. I'll get Kenzo talking later. I'm going to shag her brains out. She'll be grassing them up like fuck, the dirty coke whore."

It was agreed, they would meet again tomorrow night. The men knew what they had to do. It was time to make it happen. Time to destroy them. Harry said goodnight to the lads and let them out. He was heading upstairs when he suddenly stopped and turned back around. Opening the living room door he could see his sons sitting on the sofa playing their game. He was in no mood for any back chat and it was time to lay the law down. Harry walked straight over to the TV and turned it off. Preston jumped up and he was bouncing about. "Whoa, what's going down? Why are you turning it off you dick-head. I was winning then. I was on a top score."

Harry sucked hard on his gums, and turned to face Callum. "So big boy, come on then hard man if you want to tackle your old man. That's what you want isn't it, a shot at the title?" Callum swallowed hard, yes he could fight, but he'd never imagined he would have to battle with his own father. He looked at Preston and wondered if he would have his back if the fight wasn't going his way. No, Preston would have bailed on him. There was no way he would turn against his father like that, he had more respect for him, unlike Callum. "So, have you lost your tongue or what lad? You want to play with the big boys, so come on then. Let's see what you've got?" Harry rolled his shirt sleeves up and he was ready to rumble, a bare knuckle fist fight. Preston sat on the arm of the chair and nibbled on his fingernails. He sniggered nervously; he was watching them with eager eyes. He knew his brother could talk the talk but now it was time to walk the walk, he wasn't sure if he could handle it.

Callum held his hand out towards his father. "Listen dad, I was just on one, women problems and all that, you know what it's like. Let's shake hands and forget about it."

Preston screwed his face up, his brother was a pussy and he'd never listen to a word he said again about standing up to his father, he was such a bull-shitter. Harry knew he'd won, he would have fought with his son too, just to prove a point. Bite his ear off if he needed to. This was his domain and no smacked- arse kid was ever going to challenge him for his title. He demanded respect in his household and there was no way he was taking any backchat. Harry was the king of his castle again, both his sons knew that now, the pecking order was back in line. Harry shook his son's hand and said goodnight to them both.

When he left there was silence. Preston and Callum was alone again. Preston walked back to the TV and flicked the power button back on. He smirked as he turned to face his brother. "Got domed then didn't you our kid? What happened to you taking him out and all that? I knew you were full of shit, it was proper funny though watching your arse twitching. You were going to get twisted up."

Callum's pride was hurt and he bit down hard on his

lips. He'd lost face in front of his brother and knew he had to regain the respect back from him. "Listen, nobody domed me at all. It's just I couldn't be arsed fighting the old fart at this time of the night. You know me bro, the next time he gives it the big-un I'll put him on his arse. You know me I'll leave him for dead."

Preston started the game up again and looked at his brother from the corner of his eye. "Yeah, whatever bro, seeing is believing isn't it?" They both played on the game and not another word was spoken about what had just happened. Callum was boiling inside. If his old man thought he could speak to him like that he had another think coming. He was going to show him who ruled the roost from now on. He wasn't a kid anymore. He was a man.

A big man who feared nothing.

CHAPTER SIX

Kenzo opened her eyes slowly; she was licking her dry cracked lips and gagging for a cold drink. Glancing to the side of her she could see the back of Matty's head. She loved this man with all her heart and would do anything for him, she was obsessed. Kenzo could have had her pick of any of boys her own age, but she wanted something different, a challenge. A bad boy who could give her everything she wanted. Checking Matty was still asleep she dropped her arm from the bed and searched for his jeans. She knew there would be some cocaine in them somewhere and she was doing her best to locate it. Kenzo had a habit, a bad one at that, and each day it was getting worse. The drug had taken her prisoner and now she was a slave to it. If she was being true to herself she couldn't function without it, she couldn't concentrate. Matty started to stir, he was mumbling. Kenzo clutched the bag of sniff and headed to the toilet. She twisted her head back over her shoulder to make sure he'd not clocked her. Matty knew she liked to get wired and he just thought she only had it when she was out partying. He was right at first, she did only take it when she was on a night out but over the last few months she needed a hit every morning just to keep her going, just a bump, nothing much, just something to give her some energy.

Stood looking at herself in the mirror, she drew her face closer, she was a mess. Dark circles had formed around her eyes, her skin was spotty and sore and the glow she used to have was gone, her skin was dull, tired and exhausted. Kenzo dropped to her knees. She needed a hit and fast. Making a neat white line on the toilet seat, she snorted hard. Head held back she felt the rush from the drug hitting her body. She loved the feeling it gave her, an instant high. She craved it every day, she couldn't live without it. Standing to her feet her naked body felt cold, she had goose pimples all over her. Tiptoeing back to bed she was ready to wake Matty up now she felt normal again. Normal, what was that? It had been ages since she'd felt anything but normal, she was twisted most days. She never ate, she never did half the things she used to do, she'd lost all her old friends and Matty was her life. He was all she had and she was holding on to him for dear life. Stroking her finger slowly across his back she watched him move. Her hot lips nibbled at his ears. She was horny and seeking his affection.

Matty turned over and looked at her. Such a waste of life, she was gorgeous when he first started seeing her, but now she looked like a woman twice her age, haggard. Matty grabbed hold of his penis and flopped it about. "Get your laughing gear around that, come on, you know how I like to be woken up in the morning. Get them gums around my plums." Kenzo disappeared under the duvet and Matty lay with his hands looped over his head enjoying the blow job. Kenzo was good in bed and even from the first time he'd had sex with her he knew she was no virgin, she had too much experience. She was only sixteen when he started sleeping with her. She was hot on his trail from the minute she set eyes on him. Matty knew she was jail-bait, but still he couldn't resist her sexy slim body. Kenzo straddled on top of him and grinded hard against him. He knew she'd had drugs he could see white powder resting on the edge of her nose. Sexual groaning, hot sweaty bodies, Kenzo held her body back and a wave of pleasure filled her body as she reached orgasm. Matty was sweating, his heart was beating ten to a dozen, this girl could fuck, she was riding him hard and he knew he was going to come at any moment.

Once the sex was over, Kenzo snuggled deep into Matty's chest. "Can't we just stay in bed together today? It would be great, just me and you all day?"

Matty stroked her hair and he would have loved to have spent the day in bed with her but business came first. Shit was going down and he was needed. "Sorry love, no can do. I've got loads on today I'm too busy. Come on anyway, move your arse and get ready. I swear to you if all this was over with your brothers we could spend all week together, not just a few hours. I mean, we could fuck off to the sunshine for a couple of weeks, just me and you, chilling."

Kenzo's eyes were wide open, she was listening now, excited. Two weeks in the sun with her lover would have been pure heaven; she could have had him all to herself. Matty watched her with cunning eyes and sat back waiting for her to answer. He knew she was thinking about what he'd just said. "How could it all stop then, I mean, what needs to happen?"

There it was, the moment he'd been waiting for. He could see by her face this was going to be like taking candy from a baby. He looked directly into her eyes. "Your brothers owe Harry cash. If we could get the money back it would all be over. If I knew where all their grows were we could just take it back that way. I mean, they would never know it was us, and Harry would be happy, and it would all stop."

Kenzo was thinking. Matty reached down to his jeans and pulled out some more sniff, he needed her talking and the white powder was a sure-fire way to unlock that information. After a quick line each Kenzo was ready to betray her own flesh and blood. She teased her finger along his cheek slowly. "I could find that out for you. They meet at my mam's all the time, they trust me. I can get you all the information you need," she chuckled and gripped his hand in hers. "We can piss off from around here and have some fun in the sunshine if I found out can't we?" Kenzo was such a self-centred bitch and didn't care who she hurt, as long as she got what she wanted. She rubbed her hands together with excitement. "I've seen some lovely bikinis too. You're going to love me in them. Should I start getting my case packed then or what?"

Matty had to rein her in she was going way over the top. "Just chill will you. Fuck me, we don't even know where any grows are yet and you're planning a holiday. Just get me some news and then we'll start planning our getaway." Matty reached over and kissed her on the cheek. He was late; he should have been with Harry over half an hour ago. Kenzo sprawled out on the bed. She was all skin and bones these days, nothing like she was when Matty first met her. She was curvaceous back then, something to grab hold off, not now though, she was wasting away.

★

Harry sat watching a house from his car. Mandy had put him onto this graft. She'd said young kids were in charge of a grow at this address. Harry and a few of his men were ready to boom the door in, hammers at the ready, but they were just waiting for Matty who said he was on his way. Harry looked edgy and kept checking his watch. He was constantly licking his lips and cracking his knuckles. This was his first piece of work since he'd left prison and his arse was twitching, his bottle was going. Matty opened the passenger door and jumped inside. He was flustered; he'd been running and gagging for breath. "Sorry I'm late mate, fuck me, it's been rush, rush, rush this morning non-stop."

Harry never spoke, his eyes were on the house, he was concentrating. One young lad was in the house and they were ready to take him out if needed. He must have been on the night shift because no one had come out of the house and no one had gone inside. Harry inhaled deeply. "Right, let's have it then. Let's get in and out as soon as possible. Tie the fucker up if needed and let's take the fucking lot." The van pulled away from the cul-de-sac and headed straight towards the house. All the men jumped out and the door was off its hinges in minutes, boom. Matty was leading this heist and he was running in each room screaming at the top of his voice. He saw a man lay on the floor. "Move you little scrote and I'll blow your fucking brains out." A young lad aged around seventeen years-old covered his head with his hands on the floor. He'd been sleeping and looked off his head. His words were slurred and he was trying to talk as Matty yanked him up from the floor.

"Mate, just take it all. I'm just watching it for someone I know. Go on, take the fucking lot, just don't hurt me." Matty knew this kid would give him no trouble but he had to be sure. He never took chances. Swinging his hand back over his head he belted the end of the gun over his head. The lad fell to the floor like a sack of spuds, he was unconscious.

This was a good crop of weed, around twenty grand's worth and they were ready for chopping down, result. The men knew they had to be quick and get the plants sorted before they died. Harry was getting all the lights down that hung over the plants, they would do for his own grows. The men grabbed the bud and loaded it into the back of a van, it was cleared in minutes. All that was left was dark black soil that trailed on the floor. Harry walked inside the room and saw the young male lay on the floor, he could see he was still breathing. "Right Matty, get that tosser tied up. He could wake up at any time soon and we don't want him ringing anyone until we're well gone. Matty are you listening? I said get the cunt tied up!"

Matty dragged the lifeless body from the floor and slapped the lad around the face a couple of times. Once he started to come round he made sure his own identity was hidden. "One word of this to anyone and I'll be back for you, do you hear me! I'll take your fucking family out, the lot of them, so keep it shut." Matty rammed his finger hard against the youth's mouth and started to tie him up. The lad didn't fight back, he'd pissed his pants too, his pants were soaking wet at the front. The job was done, it was time to leave.

Harry ran outside to the van and started the engine. "Come on Matty, for fucks sake, let's do one. I don't want nosey neighbours getting onto us. That's all we need, a have a go hero on our case." Matty jumped into the van and they sped off with the wheels burning. The other van was in front of them and they were heading to an old lock up Matty had sorted out.

"This is just the start of it Harry," Matty sniggered as he rubbed his hands together. "A few of these a week and we'll be back in the game in no time. I bet we've got over twenty grand's worth." He pointed to the back of the van. He was probably right. There was money to be made from the plants they'd lifted.

Harry was quiet, something wasn't right with him. He wasn't his usual self. Looking at Matty he spoke in a low voice. "I want to ask you something pal, and I want the truth. You're my mate and I expect you to be straight with me."

Matty looked at him and his face was serious. "Yeah mate, you know me I'm as straight as they come, what is it, what's the problem?"

Harry took a deep breath and closed his eyes for a few seconds; he was trying to find the words he needed. The traffic lights were on red and they were stuck in a line of traffic going nowhere. "Has my Gill been shagging about?" Matty nearly died on the spot, he was itching his legs, flicking invisible dust from his sleeve. He couldn't look him in the eyes. "Well?" Harry urged. Matty had heard a few rumours yes, but he'd never seen it with his own eyes. There was no way he was being the one to let the cat out of the bag either. He needed Harry to be focused, and if the truth came out he knew his world would just crumble into two. He lied.

"Nar, is she fuck mate. What makes you think that? Gill's a good woman; everyone knows she loves you to death. You're probably just being a bit paranoid because you've been locked up for years. No way in this world

would Gill fuck about on you, she loves you too much."
Matty turned his head away and couldn't look Harry in
the eye; this wasn't his secret to tell. It was a domestic
affair and he wasn't going to get caught up between man
and wife.

"She's different Matty, something is going on with
her and I'll find out you know, just give me time to find
my feet and I'll get to the bottom of it so I hope for your
sake you're not lying."

It was too late to go back on what he'd said now.
Matty stuck to his guns and carried on with the lie. "Like
I said Harry, Gill loves you. I've not heard one whisper
about her, nothing." The traffic lights changed and saved
Matty's bacon just in time because if Harry would have
carried on probing him he would have bubbled on her
no doubt. He hated lying to him. He changed the subject
quickly. "Ay Harry, Kenzo is working for us now, she's
going to let me know every move her brothers make so
we'll be rolling in cash pretty soon."

Harry smirked and looked at him. "How the fuck
have you ended up banging her anyway? She's a kid, you
have women falling at your feet so why have some young
tart on your arm that's nothing but trouble?"

Matty rubbed his hands together and playfully pushed
at Harry. "She's a dirty bitch. I swear, she's top in bed. She'll
do anything for a bit of sniff, and I mean anything." Harry
pulled the van up at the lockup and jumped out. The men
celebrated their first heist. This was start of things to come
and Harry and his men were on the way up. It was only
a matter of time before the Collins brothers fell flat on
their arses.

Kenzo did the walk of shame home. She was still wearing her clothes from the night before and her make-up was around her eyes smudged all over the place, she looked like a dirty trollop. With no coat on, her silver mini dress was attracting some attention on the main road. Men were honking their horns at her and whistling through their car windows. Kenzo didn't have a care in the world she was a brazen hussy and loved any attention she got from anywhere. Opening the front door she shouted into the kitchen. "Mam, it's only me, bang the kettle on will you while I just get changed."

Mrs Collins ran into the hallway, she could see her daughter walking up the stairs and screwed her face up shouting behind her. "I hope you haven't walked home looking like that? You look like a prostitute who's just finished her night shift. God, have you got no shame. I bet the neighbours are disgusted with you." Kenzo ignored her and carried on walking up the stairs. Susan ran back into the kitchen and stood with her back against the wall, she spoke to John who was sat reading his newspaper. "I know she's my own flesh and blood but she's out of control. She's a slut, I know it. You just mark my words she'll be tubbed soon and she won't have a bleeding clue who the father is. She's like a bleeding sperm bank around the estate I just know it."

John lifted his head up his newspaper and sniggered. His mother was right, but who was he to judge his sister. He had his own secrets to hide and kept well out of it. Peter marched into the kitchen and grabbed a piece of toast from his brother's plate. "Mam, do us a brew will you, and if there's any bacon going, I'll have a butty." Susan blew her breath, she'd just put the frying pan away after making John his breakfast. Peter noticed her sour face. "Just fucking leave it then if it's too much trouble for you. I bet when goldenballs here asks you for a butty you're out of your seat faster than lightening, fucking favouritism again. I'm sick of it."

Susan cracked a smile and realised she'd overreacted. "Oh, be quiet and put your dummy back in you smacked arse. John has been up for ages, that's why he's had his breakfast. If I'd have known you were getting up I would have done you something, so turn it in." The bacon sizzled in the pan, the aroma filled the air. It was mouth-watering. Kenzo stood at the kitchen door and placed her order for food too. Peter stood watching her and ranted. "Oh, where the hell have you been all night," he stood to his feet and ran to where she was stood. He gripped her by the throat and he was choking her to death, she was gagging for breath.

Susan left the pan on the stove and ran at them both screaming at the top of her voice. "Get your bleeding hands off her you bully, what the hell are you doing?"

Peter let his sister drop to the floor and her mother was trying to help her back to her feet. "She knows what's going on mother. Last night she was sat with Harry Jarvis and the rest of the other dick-heads. What the hell is she playing at, where do her loyalties lie?"

Kenzo was struggling to breath and you could see the red hand marks around her neck starting to bruise. Once she could talk she stood behind her mother and screamed at Peter. "I'll sit with who I want and I'll sleep with anyone I want to too. You're not my fucking keeper."

Susan held her daughter tight in her arms, she knew she was a sitting duck. John folded his newspaper neatly on the table and shot a look at his brother. It was always the same in this house, Peter thought he ruled the roost and John had been a victim of his abuse plenty of times in the past. This wasn't his fight though and he wasn't getting involved. As he passed his mother she noticed a love bite on his neck, dark purple blemishes, she had no time to question him on it though, he was gone. Kenzo sat at the table snivelling, Peter grabbed his sandwich and left. On his way out he turned his head slowly and growled at his sister. "Just let me see you with them clowns again. I swear down next time I see you with them I'll make sure I put you in a hospital bed. Nil by mouth and all that."

Kenzo just couldn't keep her big mouth shut; she was chomping at the bit. "Yeah, whatever nob-head. We'll see about that when Harry Jarvis gets his hands on you. We'll see how big you are then won't we you muppet, when you're fighting a real man."

A shoe from the hallway came flying through the air and before Kenzo could duck it hit her right on the nose. Blood splurged all over the kitchen table and Susan was running about like a headless chicken. "Peter you no good bastard, there's no need for that, you're a mental fucker," she shouted after him. Kenzo was in a state; her eyes began to swell almost instantly. She gritted her teeth together tightly and screamed at her brother. "I'll show you now dick-head. Just you wait and see. I'll have the last laugh, just you wait, you prick."

Susan pulled her cardigan around her body tightly. Her family was falling apart and there was nothing she could do about, absolutely nothing - her hands were tied.

Harry Jarvis had definitely upset the apple cart and it was up to her to try and make him stop, she couldn't take anymore.

★

The Collins brothers watched Tony Johnson leave the hotel. He had to be silenced, he was a grass and they didn't trust him. He was the only person who knew they'd had Harry over and without him as a witness, it was Harry's word against theirs. Tony marched along the street, he seemed in a hurry. Peter checked his watch and smiled. "Right on time, he is the wanker. Just let's wait for him to get to the warehouse and we can sort him out there. We need to watch him and make sure he's alone. I don't trust the snitch, there's just something about him that makes me feel uneasy."

Ben nodded, he was the one who was going to end Tony's life. He'd killed men before and it never seemed to bother him. He was ruthless and mentally unstable. Ever since he was a young boy his mother had noticed his behaviour was strange – he was different, sick in the head. Ben used to kill animals, it all started off with spiders first and worms but as he got older he upped his game to hamsters and rabbits. Of course Mrs Collins had him at the doctors and tried to help him, but all they said to her was that he would grow out of it, he never did. Susan knew her son was tapped in the head and always said that one day he would be locked up for his actions. His father was the same – a nutter, a ruthless bastard who only cared only about himself. If his mother only knew what he'd been up to she would have dropped down dead, she didn't have a clue he was a cold-blooded murderer.

Connor was mellow, compared with his brother. He was a watcher, a listener. He was a fighter, a bare knuckle fighter. This was always his way to solve a problem, with his fists, not with guns and blades. People didn't use fists anymore though did they, and he learned the hard way that living on the streets of Manchester meant that guns and blades were just a normal part of everyday life. He was always tooled up, always ready for whatever was thrown at him.

Tony Johnson sneaked into the warehouse, always watching over his shoulder. The warehouse had been empty for years and nobody seemed to be bothered with it, it was derelict. Tony was excited, Peter had told him he was getting another bung of cash today and he was already planning on what he could spend the money on. Tony loved gambling, it was his life. He was always chasing the dream of a big win but it never came. That's how he'd ended up in this mess to start with. He'd owed the Collins brothers money and he was forced to work for them to pay off the debt. Stitching Harry Jarvis up was his job, but when the plan backfired he nearly lost his life and he pledged he would never get involved in this kind of graft anymore. It was dangerous, way too risky.

"Alright Tony my boy, how's life treating you," Ben chuckled. He was always like this before he took someone's life; giddy, cracking jokes. He was a sick bastard and he always wanted to make his victims to suffer right until the end, beg for their life.

Peter walked up to Tony and weighed him up and down, he circled him making him feel uneasy. "I'm great lads; I just need a few quid to get me through this bad time. You know how it is. I wouldn't ask for any more money but I'm on my arse, potless."

Ben couldn't hold his temper any longer he gripped Tony by the throat and threw him to the ground. He was making his skin crawl with all his lies. "Pass me the pliers Connor. I'm going to rip his teeth out one by one for having us over. Did you think you could sponge off us for keeping quiet?" Connor passed the tools over and came to assist his brother.

Peter sat on a small wall facing them and sparked a cigarette up. "You're a grassing cunt Tony. We don't trust you anymore. You have to say goodbye now, you tried to fuck us over and this is what happens." Peter inhaled on his cigarette and blew smoke rings from his mouth as he watched the torture begin. Tony was desperate and he was struggling to move as Connor got him in a head lock. Ben smashed him over the head with the pliers and he stopped wriggling. One by one Ben yanked his front teeth out. Blood was all over the place, bright red claret rolling down Tony's face.

Once Ben had four teeth yanked out he held his head back and started laughing. "We'll post these fuckers to Jarvis to show him that we mean business." Ben crashed the iron tools into Tony's Johnson's skull, crunching, smashing noises that sent shivers down your spine. Connor turned his head away as the final blow was struck. Tony Johnson's body shook for a few seconds then he remained still. He was dead. Ben Collins had taken his life.

Peter stood to his feet when the job was done; he held no remorse for his actions. It was water off a duck's back. "Make sure we leave nothing behind. Connor, double-check nothing is left, check everywhere."

Ben stood up and licked the blood from his fingers,

looking at the four teeth in the palm of his hands he let out a menacing laugh. "I should have been a fucking dentist, me. These bastards just flew out no problem, look at them Peter they're like a fucking horse's teeth. Tony was a right goofy bastard, check them out." Ben held his flat palm out and the teeth were there for him to see. Peter chuckled, the job was done and he could rest again. Tony Johnson was dead and he had no hold over the family any longer. The men left the warehouse without a care in the world. Checking outside, the coast was clear, nobody was about and no witnesses were present.

Matty and his team were parked up in a lay-by watching the Collins brothers from afar. They were watching them twenty four hours a day now and knew they would lead them to the pots of gold they were hiding. They'd put a tracker on Peter's car and they were aware of every move they made. Matty stretched his neck as he watched the Collins brothers drive off. He turned to his wingman and raised his eyebrows. "Where the fuck is Tony? He's not come out has he?"

Jud shook his head and rested his head on the steering wheel. "It doesn't look good for Tony. I bet the fuckers have wasted him and left him in there to rot. I suppose he deserves it though, grassing cunt."

Matty sat thinking. This was serious shit. He needed to know what he was dealing with and what they were capable of. Running from the car he entered the warehouse with caution, ducking and diving. The light was dim and the place had an eerie feeling to it; strange, spine- chilling. Matty covered his mouth as he walked further into the room. He could see a body lay near the window on the far side. Pacing forward slowly he stood looking down at Tony Johnson's beaten body. He could hardly recognise him. Matty could see the dead man had no teeth at the front. He kicked at him to see if there was any life in him. Tony was dead, his eyes were still wide open and they had the fear of God in them. Matty gagged into his hands as he left the room. "Sick, sick bastards," he mumbled under his breath as he sprinted back to the car. Matty was white with shock, and before he got back into the car he spewed his guts up.

The other men were eager to hear what he had to say and Jud opened the car door ready for him to get back inside. "What's happened, where the fuck is Tony?"

Matty wiped his hand across his mouth with a quick movement and got back into the car. "Just fucking drive," he snarled. "They're fucking animals Jud, they pulled Tony's fucking gnashers out before they did him in, fucking sick, twisted bastards they are. I swear, we need to up our game if this is what we're dealing with. We need Jona back on the scene. He's a right sick bastard and he'll soon sort them wankers out. Yeah, Jona will show them what we're all about, he'll wipe the floor with the lot of them with his sick shit he does. Do you know he bummed a guy who owed him money?" The other men looked shocked as he continued. "Yep, on my life, he stuck his cock up his arse and told him that's how it felt to be fucked over. Jona takes no shit from anyone. He's an animal when he's been wronged."

Jud carried on driving, he never spoke a word. This was all getting too much for him. He was a straight head really and just drove the guys around to earn a few extra quid on top of his benefit. He wouldn't be driving for them any longer, no way. Not now he knew a man had been murdered. It was too risky, way too risky.

The men hung all the weed plants up to dry. A couple of days drying out and it would be ready for bagging up. The stench from it was overwhelming and you could taste it in the back of your throat. Matty walked into the room and plonked down next to Harry. He was shaking and seemed traumatised. "Harry they've done Tony Johnson in. They pulled the guy's teeth out before they killed him. What kind of sickos do that? Why didn't they just shoot him?"

Harry sat up straight and his nostrils flared. "They don't scare me. What, so they pulled a few fucking teeth out of some grass's mouth. If I would have got my hands on him, I would have shoved my dick right up his arse, the fucking traitor. Tony got what was coming to him and the Collins brothers done us a favour. Tony would have been at the police station soon anyway, so I'm at ease now knowing that dirty grassing cunt is no longer breathing." Harry's face creased as he looked Matty straight in his eyes. "Are you forgetting he got me banged up for five years or what? Not just a shit and a shave Matty, five fucking years. Five years of my life that I won't ever get back." Matty knew to keep his mouth shut, he was sounding like he'd lost his bottle. He tried to big himself back up again but Harry knew he was shitting himself. Harry gripped his knees and his knuckles turned white. "Watch this space Matty, they want war, I'll give them fucking war."

CHAPTER SEVEN

S usan Collins walked into the ASDA superstore in Harpurhey, it was busy with shoppers all nattering about the latest two for one bargains. The market was on today, kids screaming, mothers looking stressed. This part of Manchester was known as a notorious place to live where crime was rife. Nobody seemed to care who they had over, they lived from hand to mouth, that's just the way it was. If it wasn't locked down it was gone within minutes, everybody knew that. Susan looked at her surroundings as she entered the store. She could see a few drug addicts to the side of her; dirty, sweaty ones out to earn money for their next fix. She clutched her handbag closer to her body. Bag-snatching was well known in this area and if anyone thought they were nicking her bag they had another think coming, there was no way they were getting her bag from her Kung-Fu grip, she gripped it tightly. Susan sighed as she looked at the junkies, they seemed so young yet their faces were aged, grey and sunken. Drugs were a big problem in the area; as they were on most council estates. They wrecked lives and changed people. Susan knew her sons were into all kinds of hooky stuff but she never thought for one minute that they dealt in heroin too. That's where the money was these days, brown and white. There was cash to be earned and plenty of it. Susan sang along to the music playing in the store as she got her trolley from the side of her. It was an old track that reminded her of the years gone by Frank Sinatra. Susan had given up on men nowadays; she'd never had any luck with them anyway and always seemed to go for the same kind; piss-heads and gamblers. Susan was lonely and often thought of finding love, but what about her sons? No, they would never have allowed that, she only had to talk to a man and they put a stop to it straight away. No man would ever be allowed in her life again, well, as long as her children had anything to do with it. Don't get me wrong, she'd had a few knee tremblers in the past but nothing serious, just a jerk and a squirt.

Susan walked up the aisles, it was a big shop day and her trolley was half full of food. Feeding her boys was expensive and she always put a hearty meal on the table for her lads every night, they wouldn't eat shit, they wanted fresh healthy stuff. Susan baked, she loved baking and the smell of the house when she made cakes reminded her of happier times when the kids were small and life was easier.

Stopping dead in her track Susan gripped her trolley tight, her knuckles turning white as her jaw dropped. She clenched her teeth together and made her way down the aisle with speed. "Well, fuck a duck, if it isn't Miss fur coat and no knickers."

Gill was drained of any colour as Susan rammed the trolley into her legs with force. Gill knew who Susan was straight away, and prepared herself for some verbal abuse from her, she was a loud mouth and well known for speaking her mind. Sally was getting some soap powder from another aisle and was unaware of what was going on. Gill moved the trolley from her legs and pointed her finger at Susan. "Susan, just piss off and leave me alone will you. I don't want any trouble. Just give me a break will you?"

Susan held her head back and chuckled loudly, she didn't care who heard what she had to say. "Oh, is that right. I'll tell you what love, if any more trouble comes knocking on my door I'll be looking for you. Who does your husband think he is anyway? Two minutes he's been out of jail and it's been nothing but trouble already," she leaned forward and went nose-to-nose with her. "My lads will break him in two if he continues doing what he's doing. He's underestimating them, trust me."

Gill wasn't standing for this any longer and she stepped forward. Who did this old coffin dodger think she was anyway, the fucking Godmother? Gill retaliated. "Your lads need to pay what's bleeding owed then, Susan. Don't get involved with things that don't concern you. Peter ripped Harry off; he spent five years in jail for crying out loud are you forgetting that? What, did you expect a big fucking party and them all to be friends again."

Susan looked at Gill in more detail and licked her lips slowly; she was going to shut this tart up once and for all. She took a deep breath and kept her voice low. "Perhaps we should have a party for you and Ray Clough shouldn't we? I mean, if we're putting our cards on the table here, Harry should know what a dirty little slut his wife really is. Yeah, perhaps I should fill him in on his so called loyal wife's antics."

Sally was back now and she just caught the back end of the conversation. She knew who Susan was and knew she could strike a blow at any minute; she was a cunning old cow and thought she ruled the roost. Sally stood in front of Gill and went nose-to-nose with Susan. "People who live in glass houses shouldn't throw stones, wrinkled motty. I remember it wasn't that long ago when you were getting banged from Lenny the loan man, yeah, do you remember that you old fossil?" Susan swallowed hard, Sally was right, but that was years ago and Lenny said he wouldn't tell anyone, how the hell did Sally know?

Susan pulled her shoulders back and her chest was firmly out in front of her. "That's a load of shite, whoever has been gossiping needs to get their facts right, me and Lenny are just friends."

Sally knew she'd got her back up and Gill joined in now knowing it was stalemate. "Oh, I bet Lenny's wife would love to know about it too Sally, yeah Susan, let's see you answer to his wife ay."

Susan gripped her trolley and knew the battle was lost. "Do whatever you're doing Gill, but be warned, Harry will find out about you with Ray, it's just a matter of time." Susan stormed off to lick her wounds, she hated being beaten. Anyway, how the hell did Sally know about Lenny? That was top secret and only a handful of people knew about it, Susan was fuming.

Sally blew a laboured breath. "Well, that told the old trout didn't it? See what I mean Gill; everyone has a secret to be told. The truth always comes out in the end, trust me I know."

Gill patted the middle of her friend's arm and sniggered. "How the hell do you know that about that anyway?"

Sally tapped the side of her nose and chuckled. "Ask me no questions, I'll tell you no lies, just let's say I know a lot more about that family than she thinks. So she needs to tread very carefully before I open a can of worms that would break her in two."

Gill studied Sally's face a bit longer than necessary. Sally had always been a dark horse and she always kept her cards close to her chest, she was hiding something. Gill was relieved she was out of the shit and didn't delve deeper. The two women carried on shopping and when they saw Susan again Sally rammed two fingers up in the air at her. "Old cow," Sally shouted over. Mrs Collins kept her head low and carried on shopping.

Callum was twatting Paul who was curled up in a ball on the floor; he was kicking ten tons of shit out of him. "You better start talking you prick before I really start to hurt you. Who the fuck took the grow? Don't give me any bullshit stories, because I know you're chatting shit, come on, fucking get talking before I end your life." Preston was stood over Paul, and he didn't know if he believed him either, he was on the fence. This kid was only the night-watchman and he'd never had any trouble with him before. There was so much back-stabbing in this line of work and he didn't know who could be trusted.

Paul was desperate as he spoke. "Mate, I swear to you, I was stoned and asleep, they just boomed the door in and kicked fuck out of me. I was tied up and left to die," he was pleading with them. "These men were hardcore, they wasn't kids, they were men. Big fuckers." Callum grabbed Paul by the throat and squeezed hard at his windpipe, "you better talk otherwise it's over for you. I swear, I'll do you in." Paul had nothing else to say, he was telling the truth but nobody was listening to him. He was covered in blood and his eyes were swelling every second that went by.

Preston knew Paul had taken enough, if he'd have set them up he would have known, nobody could take a beating like this and not confess. Preston stepped in front of his brother and protected Paul. "He's had enough Callum, just turn it in now. For fucks sake bro, I'm as gutted as you but what could Paul have done against them anyway, he said they were team-handed, just back off."

Callum marched around the room, punching walls, kicking doors. "Fucking twenty grand up the swanee. I owe money left, right and fucking centre, what the hell am I going to do? And, Dan wants a cut no matter what. I'm fucked." Callum ragged his fingers through his hair, he was desperate, and nearly in tears. "Preston we'll have to get on our toes. We owe pure cash out and you know what they're like when we don't pay, they'll cut our balls off." Preston was calmer than his brother and sat on the floor. Making a big spliff he sat staring into space. Callum was watching him with eager eyes; he had something on his mind. He shouted over to his brother. "You don't seem as arsed as me, bro. I mean, why am I the only one who's stressing?"

Preston inhaled hard on the joint and blew large smoke rings from his mouth. "What's the point in stressing when it's gone; you know how it is our kid. Fuck me, how many times have we had someone's grow away?"

Callum snapped and his eyes were dancing with madness. "Unless," he paused. "Unless it's you who set me up. Yeah, it all makes sense now, it's fucking you isn't it?" Callum pounced on his brother and they were half killing each other. Paul struggled to get to his feet and left the room while he had a chance. He knew he would be next and couldn't take another beating, he got on his toes. The brother were smashing holes out of each other, head butts, flying kicks, they were holding nothing back. Preston seemed to be the stronger of the two and he struck a blow to his brother's chin that sank him to the floor.

Preston sat on top of Callum and held his hands down over his head. He could have finished him off but held back. "Listen you daft cunt, you're my brother, I would never rip you off. You're fucking paranoid. Off your head you are, as if I would do that." Preston released his grip from his brother and walked towards the window, he was gagging for breath. His eye was trickling with blood and his lip was swollen. The brothers had fought in the past, horrible fights where they set out to destroy each other, but that was years ago, they'd not had a fight in years. Preston was watching his back, he knew Callum was a snidey bastard and didn't trust him one little bit, he was on his guard. Turning to face him he growled. "Look, we're a team me and you. If we don't trust each other, who the fuck can we trust. We need to think about this, and get back what we're owed. You know what it's like around here, we'll find out soon enough who's had us over. We'll check with the other lads we know too. Surely somebody must know who's responsible for this. I'm gutted too you know, fucking wounded."

Callum knew he'd overreacted, he just couldn't help it. He'd always had an anger problem and once he was in the zone it took him ages to calm down. Deep breaths seemed to calm him, slowly but surely he was seeing his brother's point of view. "Right, okay, I just lost the plot for a second. I'm sorry but my head's done in with it all. We're up shit street. We've not got a pot to piss in bro. Fucking hell," he shook his head and closed his eyes. "Tina thinks she's getting them UGG boots too. I promised her a bung to go shopping too, she'll go sick when she knows we've been had over."

Preston walked over to Callum and helped him up from the floor; he was hurt and holding his leg. "Paul's fucked off. I bet he's shit himself when he saw us fighting. I do think you went overboard with him though Callum; the guy was just a watcher, nothing else. What could he do anyway against a gang of them? It's not his fault."

Callum was thinking straight now. They needed to get out of the house as soon as possible before the dibble arrived. The neighbours must have heard all the commotion for sure and one of them would have reported the noise to the police. They were right nosey fuckers round here, plant pots they were, they didn't miss a trick. Preston helped Callum to the front door; he checked the area carefully before they left. Today was a bad day for the lads and they knew the clock was ticking now before the men they owed money to, started kicking at their door.

Preston was driving today, he had no licence and the car he was driving was plated up. All the grafters found transport this way. It was simple as that; nick a car and find another one the same make and clone it, child's play. Preston placed his screwdriver in the ignition; all the wires were hanging down between his legs. Callum was checking out his face in the mirror, both the lads looked like they'd been through the wars. "Drop me off at Tina's. She's better off knowing now rather than later. Fuck me; she'll go off her head when she knows we've been had over. You know what she's like; she's a right smacked-arse."

"Just tell her straight, bro. You do my head in the way you suck up to her; the girl is a gold- digger."

Callum defended Tina, there was no way she was just after his money, not in his eyes anyway, she loved him to death. "Sort it out Preston, Tina loves the arse off me. You've seen the way she looks at me, I'm her world."

Preston raised his eyebrows and screwed his face up, what fucking planet was his brother on? Did he not see what was right in front of his eyes or what? Tina was after what she could get from him. There was no loving him, no nothing. She was a selfish, self-centred bitch. Preston shook his head; there was no way he was getting into another fight with his brother. He'd had enough for one day. Callum would have to find out the hard way. Tina would kick him to the kerb now for sure. With no money in his pocket, what good was he to her now?

The car pulled up outside Tina's house and you could see her peeping out from the bedroom window. Tina's mother Trisha was at the bottom window looking out too, she was a right nosey cow and didn't miss a trick. Callum turned back to his brother before he got out of the car. "Listen, I'm telling Tina we got done over by some guys and we were fighting with them. I'll say there were ten of them. Yeah, that sounds better that doesn't it?" Preston just nodded his head before banging his head slowly on the steering wheel. His brother was such a prick where girls were concerned, he didn't have a clue how devious they could be. The brothers said goodbye.

Callum was met at the front door by Trisha. This woman was a sight and he cringed when he looked at her in more detail. She was an overweight slob, dressed in black leggings and a t-shirt that was way too small for her. Her camel toe was there for everyone to see and she didn't seem to care that her flaps were as fat as a monkey's arse. "Fuck me, who's give you a good hiding?" she shrieked. "Get inside and get cleaned up. You look like death warmed up. You need stitches in that eye, the gash is massive."

Preston watched his brother enter the house and as he dipped his head he could see Tina waving to him from the window upstairs. He knew she was gagging for it but played it cool. He could never take his brother's woman could he?

Callum sat down at the kitchen table as Trisha ran the cold water. Taking the dirty dish- cloth from the side of the sink she placed it under the tap. "So, go on, who the fuck has done you over then? I can get a team together if you need some back-up. Guns and blades the bleeding lot. But it will cost you, nobody does anything for fuck all do they?" Callum tried to smile. This woman was so full of shit. She loved to play the part of someone in the know, but in reality, she knew fuck all. She'd just watched too many TV programmes and thought she had street cred when in fact she was a geek. Tina came into the kitchen and looked shocked when she saw the state of her boyfriend. She was dressed in her pyjamas and her hair was messy. "Oh my God, who's done this to you Callum?" Trisha was holding the cloth above his eyes now pressing on it firmly, she was listening too.

Callum swallowed hard and it was time to big himself up, time to make himself look as hard as nails. He pushed Trisha away and stuck his chest out in front of him. "It went off big time; fucking loads of them come through the door, tooled up to fuck. I was fighting with four of them and our kid was knocking them out for fun too, but we didn't stand a chance, we were outnumbered."

Tina was horrified and stood with her hands on her hips urging him to continue. "So, go on, did they get the grow?"

Callum sighed and cracked his knuckles loudly. "Yep, the fucking lot. Me and our kid have been tied up for hours. We're not talking kids here either; these guys were on it, no messing about. Like fucking ninjas they were. In and out within a blink of an eye."

Trisha loved the story and her eyes were wide open urging him to continue. "What, so they took the weed?"

Callum nodded his head slowly, he knew he had to make them believe his cock and bull story. "Yeah, lights and everything else, we're fucked now. That money was going to sort us right out. We have fuck all now, not a shekel."

Tina stamped her feet on the floor. "What about the boots and the money you promised me? Fucking hell Callum, I had my heart set on them, they'll be gone now," Tina moaned. Trisha snarled at her daughter, she'd taught her to go for men with money yeah, but she was so rude. They could both see she didn't care about anything else but the money. Trisha was gutted too; she was on a treat too and been promised some bud for her own use. Callum hung his head low and his voice was shaky. "The thing is now; me and our kid have to pay the money back. We borrowed it from Ben Collins; you know just to set us up with the lights and all that. He's a fucking lunatic; he won't listen to anything we have to tell him, he'll just do us in. He wanted money from the grow too, we're fucked."

Trisha rubbed at her arms; the hairs stood up on end. She knew Ben Collins and knew he was not be messed with. Callum was in big trouble. Tina plonked down on the chair with her arms folded tightly in front of her. She was a right smacked- arse and couldn't hide her disappointment. "So, you're skint then?"

Callum looked at her and snarled. "Derrrr... yeah. I've just told you they had the weed away. What, do you think I've got money stashed away or something, because I'm telling the truth, I'm on my arse."

Tina shot a look at her mother and Trisha knew full well that her daughter's relationship would be ended soon. She'd seen it so many times before, once the money was gone Tina didn't stick around for long, she moved on to her next meal ticket. Trisha flicked the switch for the kettle, and stood with her back against the worktop. "You'd better tell Ben what's happened before he comes looking for you. How much do you owe him?"

Callum lifted his eyes to the ceiling and his lips were moving but no sound was coming out. "About ten grand. I'm fucked if I know how I'm going to come up with that amount of money. Our kid owes half too but it's still five grand each isn't it."

Trisha placed the cup of coffee next to Callum, if she'd have had anything stronger she would have given it to him, he was shaking from head to toe and looked like he was going to faint. "Something will come up, can't you do a bit of graft and pay him back. Speak to the Sullivan lads they've always got a few jobs on the go. Do you remember, it was them who done the post office the other month, they got a right few quid from it too, top grafters they are."

Callum shook his head, he'd had dealings with the Sullivan lads before and had left on bad terms. There was no way he could go back to them begging for a money earner. He would have been a laughing stock. Tina checked the clock on the wall, she was edgy. "Right, I've got to go and get ready. Callum, are you getting off or what because we've got to go out soon." Trisha turned her head slowly; she'd not planned to go out today and looked surprised. She was about to speak when Tina put her in the picture. "We have to go into town and pay some council tax at the Town Hall. You know if you don't pay it mam, you'll have them on your case again?"

Tina made a face at her mother to let her know she was lying. Trisha went along with the story. "Yeah, you're right, they said I'll be evicted if they don't get a payment today, bastards they are. Some grassing cunts around here I can tell you. I mean, how else would they know that Terry's been staying here. I'm lucky they didn't take me to court. I wouldn't mind I only done Terry a favour, a few nights he stayed here, four nights tops."

Tina knew her mother was waffling and urged Callum to leave. She pecked him on the cheek and passed him his coat. "I'll ring you later, go home and get cleaned up. Just chill for a bit, you looked traumatised. Try and sleep."

Callum stood and passed the cloth to Tina's mother. He stood at the door and turned his head back to Tina. "I'll get you them boots you know. Just bear with me and I'll be back on my feet in no time." Tina smirked and watched him leave. There was no way in this world she was waiting around for him. She wanted things in life and she wanted them now, Callum was history.

Callum walked down the street, he was limping and his head was low. He looked like he had the cares of the world on his shoulders and in fairness, he did. There was no way out of this, he would have to contact Ben Collins and tell him his money was gone. Reaching into his pocket he pulled his mobile phone out. He looked at his contact list and found the number he wanted. Listening to the ringing tone he closed his eyes.

Preston walked into his home and headed straight upstairs. Gill heard him come in and shouted after him. Stood in the bathroom Preston started to clean himself up, he was covered in blood and his eyelid was swelled hanging over his eye. The bathroom door opened slowly and Harry coughed to get his attention. When he saw his son's face he shouted "What the fuck has happened to you?"

Preston dipped his face in the sink and started to throw cold water over his skin. "It's nothing dad, we just had a bit of a rumble with a couple of lads who were chatting shit to us. You should see the state of them, me and our kid wasted them."

Harry grabbed his son's face and examined it further. He pressed at it and turned his head to the side. "It's going to be a beauty that is. Get some ice on it from downstairs and keep it on it for a bit, it should take the swelling down."

Preston tried to make light of the matter as Harry continued questioning him. "So, which lads have you been fighting with, where were they from?"

Preston clammed up; he wasn't ready for an investigation. He'd never had to answer to anyone in the past and he wasn't going to start now, he snapped. "For fuck's sake dad, just leave it will you. It's been sorted now, so wind your neck in. You're as bad as my mam, she's like the fucking Gestapo once she thinks she knows something."

Harry backed off, his boys had changed, he didn't recognise them anymore, they had no respect for anyone, not even him. Harry went downstairs. Once Preston had cleaned himself up he changed his clothes and headed into the kitchen. He was going to chill today; relax, and think. The clock was ticking and he knew he needed a plan to get himself out of the shit.

"Oh my God, what the hell has happened to you," Gill shrieked. "Harry look at him, he's a bleeding mess. Tell me who's done this and your dad will sort it out. Fucking hell, have you been to the hospital?"

Preston growled at his mother and hated that he had to repeat himself. He plugged the PS3 in and loaded a game. "Mam, chill out it's nothing to worry about, like I've just told my dad, it was just a few nobs who got lippy with me and our kid, it's sorted now so just leave it will you." Gill ran to examine her son's face. As she touched him he pushed her away. "Fuck me, what have I just told you, don't you ever listen woman?"

Harry was about to intervene when Gill stood up for herself, she blew a fuse. "Listen, I'm only showing you I care, but from now on you can take a running jump and fuck right off. I've had it up to here with you and your brother; do whatever you're doing. I don't give a toss anymore." Preston had the control panel in his hand and her last comment went straight over his head. Harry looked at his wife and it was time to see what was really bothering her, he knew she was hiding something and wanted to get to the bottom of it. As she walked into the kitchen he followed her. Gill stood looking out of the window, she was tearful.

"What's up Gill," Harry asked as he sat down at the table. "Don't lie, because I know you, you can talk to me you know, I can help if you let me. We used to be so close, what's happened?" Gill popped a cigarette from her packet, she was nervous and her hands were shaking. Lighting her cigarette up she sat down at the table to join him. She stared at the table as Harry looked at her. "So go on, what's up, open up to me?"

Gill's bottom lip was shaking and at one point she looked like she was going to tell him the truth, she lost her bottle though and started crying. "Harry, you've been gone for a long time, five years. Do you know how it feels to be left that long with no love, no nothing. I struggled Harry, Lord knows I struggled. I had no money, bills were piling up every day and you weren't here to help me, nobody was. I was on my own."

Harry choked up, he hated seeing her upset. He knew this was his fault and tried to comfort her. "I'm sorry love; I know how hard it was for you. I tried my best to help you out, even when I was locked up. The lads brought you money around when they could, so surely that must have helped."

Gill sucked hard on her fag and blew the smoke out in front of her. "Yeah, they did bring money for me, but twenty quid here and twenty quid there, what the fuck is that meant to do for me?" She was sobbing as she continued. "The kids went without too. Why do you think they got caught up in all the shit around here, drugs and all that? It's a vicious circle Harry and someone is going to get hurt. If you loved me you would give it all up and lead a normal life. I can't go on like this. I'm not willing to wait again for you, it's breaking my heart. Can't you see what it's doing to me, to us?"

Harry welled up. He was so hard amongst his friends but in front of his wife it was another story. She was his world and he would do anything to make her happy… but to give up grafting? To go on the straight and narrow? Could he really promise her that and mean it? "Gill, I just need to get us back on our feet. Once we have a bit of money behind us, I'll sit back honest, but for now, you know what I have to do. Don't make me choose, it's not fair. Everything I do, I do it for you, for us."

Gill inhaled deeply and stubbed her cigarette out. Harry reached for her hand and stroked it softly. It was time to ask the dreaded question, the question that was playing on his mind twenty-four hours a day. He inhaled deeply and looked her straight in the eye. "Is there someone else, have you met someone Gill?" There it was, the question she'd been dreading. Her eyes flicked rapidly, she couldn't look him in the eye and Harry knew she was lying even before she spoke, she was so edgy. "Just tell me Gill. I'm not daft; I know you've been lonely. It's my own fault if you've moved on, I've been in jail, shit happens."

Gill looked at him and she knew she had to end his torment, she could see the sadness in his eyes. "What, I tell you what you want to hear, then what? We split up and you hate me forever?" Gill snivelled.

Harry was mellow and he wanted this sorting, no matter what the truth was. "If you still love me we can sort this out. If not I'll pack my stuff and walk away, simple as. I don't want to stand in the way of you being happy. It's my own fault for going to jail. I'll have to deal with it won't I?"

Gill played with her fingers, and tapped her fingernail on the table; it was time to come clean. Silence, such a long silence. "Harry, it just happened. I never meant to hurt you. I was at my wits end and lonely." Harry choked up and swallowed hard, he knew this was coming and prepared himself for the rest. He held his head in his hands and softly played with his hair with his eyes closed. Her words were crucifying him. "I think I love him Harry," Gill whispered.

There was silence, not a word was spoken. Gill's heart was beating ten to a dozen and at one point she looked like she was going to pass out. Slowly she reached her hand over to touch Harry's arm, but he pulled away quickly and looked at her. "Who is it, what's his name?"

Gill hesitated at first, but telling her husband his name would end her torment and she could be happy again without any secrets resting on her lips. "Ray Clough," she said.

Harry stood and walked to the kitchen window. The rain had just started and the noise against the window seemed to be calming him. "I'll never stop loving you Gill. I'm not going to lie. I'm heartbroken here, but if you love him I'm going to leave you to it. It's my own fault. I will just have to deal with it won't I?" Gill ran to his side, she was so mixed up, she thought she loved Ray but at that moment she wasn't sure. What the hell had she done, she should have kept her trap shut but it was too late now. Harry walked from the kitchen and headed upstairs. Gill was crying sat behind the kitchen door, her head in her hands, devastated.

Preston walked into the room and clocked his mother; she raised her eyes to him and screamed at the top of her voice. "There you go, I've told him all about Ray, so you don't have a hold over me no more. Fuck off out of my sight you no good bastard." Preston wanted to comfort his mother, to protect her, but she was making it so hard for him. He filled his glass with water and went back into the front room, he didn't say a word.

Harry stood with his bags hanging over his shoulder; he helped Gill up from the floor and kissed the side of her cheek. His cheeks were wet and she knew he'd been crying. His lips trembled as he spoke. "Take care Gill, I hope he makes you happy, I hope he's worth it." Harry walked away and Gill was screaming his name as he left the house, he didn't turn back once. He walked straight out of the garden and jumped into his car. Pulling off from the cul-de-sac Harry reached for his mobile phone. "Matty, get to the boozer now and bring some of the lads. Ray Clough is a dead man walking. Get there now, pronto. We've got some work to do. This cunt is going down, who the fuck does he think he's messing with shagging my wife? I'm going to cut his balls off the dirty liberty taking twat."

CHAPTER EIGHT

Harry stormed into the pub, he was furious. He kicked the door and flung one of the punters away from the bar by the scruff of his neck. "Bernard, get me a double brandy and fucking hurry up, don't make me wait." Bernard obeyed the order and quickly went to the optic with the glass; he put an extra shot into it too. He could see this man needed it, he was shaking.

Matty walked up to the bar and placed his arm around Harry's shoulder. "Are you okay mate?" Matty scratched at his head. "Are you sure Ray's been sleeping with Gill?"

Harry slowly turned his face and met Matty's eyes, he snarled before he slowly reached his hand over and gripped his cheeks tightly together. "Do you think I would make something like this up? Gill's just told me straight. I swear, Ray Clough is going to suffer. I'm going to break him in two, hurt him bad."

Matty pulled Harry's hand from his face and backed off. There was no way he was getting on the wrong side of him, he was raging. "Well if that's the case let's bring the fucker down. How do you want to do this, are we going through his front door or what?"

Harry knocked back his drink in one gulp and banged the glass on the bar. He clenched his teeth together tightly and growled at the landlord. "Stick another one in there Bernard." The landlord filled the glass again without hesitation. "I want to make the cunt suffer like I am.

Matty, tell me straight, did you know about this, because I know you get to know everything around here so don't fill my head with shit. Fucking tell me."

Matty hesitated; "Harry, pal, I did hear a rumour but I just ignored it you know what the gossip is like around here. I did check it out though, you know ask a few questions and all that, but nobody was saying a single word, so I just left it."

"She's my life Matty, she always has been. I've lost her for good haven't I?" Matty didn't reply he just watched his mate drowning his sorrows at the bar. It was going to be a long night.

Gill pulled up in a taxi at the hotel, she was dressed to the nines, hair and make-up done the lot. She had a suitcase with her and she looked worried as she checked the car park. Walking into the reception she could see Ray waiting for her. They went straight to the room, no talking, they hurried away. Gill closed the door and stood behind it. "He knows Ray; I've told him about us, he knows everything?"

Ray nearly collapsed, he was blowing his breath. "What the fuck have you gone and done that for, you're a daft bitch. For fucks sake, why didn't you tell me this on the phone?" Ray ran to the window and peeped through the curtains. "I bet he's followed you here, fucking hell, check outside the door and make sure no one's there, in fact, lock that fucking door."

Gill stuck her head out and twisted it both ways; she quickly came back inside the room and locked the door with shaking hands. "It's clear, nobody is there Ray."

He was pacing the floor ragging at his hair with both hands. "Are you right in the bastard head or what woman? Harry will be plotting what to do to me now. It's my neck on the line not fucking yours."

Gill was tearful and walked to the bed and sat down. She lifted her head slowly. "You said you loved me. You said we could go somewhere and be happy, what's happened to that?"

Ray inhaled deeply, his chest rising rapidly. He'd never meant any of the words he'd said to her, he just filled her head with shit so he could have sex with her. "I did love you in a way Gill, but come on, me and Regina are married, she's my wife. We were just having a bit of fun. We always knew it would come to an end."

Gill bolted from the bed and thrust her finger into Ray's cheek. "You bastard, so all this time you've been lying to me. Oh my God, why the hell did I ever listen to you? Ray, I hope Harry knocks ten tons of shit out of you now. I can't believe I put everything on the line for you. What a daft cow I've been."

Ray had to take control of the situation; he had to calm her down. "Gill, I do love you, but now he's home do you want to risk him hurting me? How did he take it then? What did he say he was going to do to me? Is he going to tell Regina?"

Gill's blood was boiling; this man was an arsehole, a lying waste of space. Gill spoke in a calm voice. "He took it quite well, he just packed his clothes and left. He hates me now, I've blown it with him."

Ray shook his head and was gasping for breath. "That's not fucking normal, believe you me, that cunt will be planning something, there is no way in this world he will let this go. He'll be coming for me now, what the hell am I going to do?"

Gill realised at that moment that she'd made the biggest mistake of her life. Bending slightly she picked her suitcase from the floor. "So, it's over then. Tell me now we're done and I will walk right out of that door and never look back."

Ray was a mess, he didn't know which way to turn. He walked to her side and knew he had to turn the charm on. His eyes looked sincere as he took her face in his hands. "I love you with all my heart, of course I do. I'm just not ready to face it all yet. We have to plan this, take it easy. You know how it is."

Gill growled at him, she knew he was lying. "No Ray, I'm going home. I should have listened when they all told me about you. Why the hell didn't I listen to them? I give you that Ray…" she paused, "you had me hook line and sinker. I actually thought you cared about me, when in fact, you were just playing me."

Ray was frantic, he knew the moment she walked out of the door he would be a sitting duck for Harry and his men. He tried to buy a bit of time. "Can you not tell Harry you were lying? Just say you wanted to hurt him?" Gill couldn't believe her ears. Her eyes welled up as she went nose to nose with him, she spat right in his face, and walked away. The door closed and Ray was alone, he ran to the window and pulled the curtains back slowly. His arse was twitching and he knew he was a marked man. His head was in bits.

★

Harry was drunk, pissed as a fart, slurring his words. The

juke box was on and a Take That hit called "Back For Good" was playing. Mandy could see Harry as soon as she walked into the pub and made a beeline for him. Mandy was after a free night and looking at Harry knocking the beer back she knew she was in for a good time and a free one at that. Mandy bought a drink from the bar and made her way over. Matty was stood in the doorway and he was on the phone. "Budge your arse over then Harry, let me get here next to you." Harry shuffled over and as soon as she looked at him she realised he was upset. He was humming the words to the tune and seemed a world of his own. Mandy sipped at her drink, there was no way she was gulping at it, she didn't know how long it would be before Harry put his hand in his pocket. She was taking her time. "What's up Harry? Is it something you want to talk about, you know what they say, a problem shared is a problem halved."

Harry raised his head slowly and looked at her. She didn't know what he was going to do next, his mood was unpredictable. "Did you know about Gill and Ray Clough?"

Mandy swallowed hard, she knew it was none of her business but wanted to earn his respect. "Yeah, everyone knew about it. I was going to tell you the other night, but ay, you'd only just got out of the nick. I wanted you to find your feet first."

Harry sighed and shook his head. "How long has it been going on? What are we talking here, months, years, what?"

Mandy went into her bag and pulled two cigarettes from the packet. After lighting them both she passed one to Harry. "Years, love. I've seen them together a few times but just kept my gob shut. I mean, it's none of my business is it and who am I to judge anyone Harry? I've had more nob-ends than weekends, or so they say."

Harry sucked hard on his cigarette and you could see his fist curling into a tight ball at the side of his legs. Mandy tried to console him. "You see Harry, women get lonely. Look at me and Jona. I loved that guy with all my heart and he shit on me from the start. He was shagging anything with a pulse. He broke my heart he did, that's why I carted him. It was hard to let go, so fucking hard, but it was for the best."

Harry was after a shoulder to cry on and after he'd ordered the beers Mandy knew she was there for the long haul. So what, she'd have to listen to his problems, it was a free night and that's all she cared about. Matty come to join them now, he shot a look at Mandy and licked at his bottom lip. He knew she was out for whatever she could get. Usually he would have warned her off but tonight he felt Harry needed a friend, someone to listen to, and she fitted the bill, for now. Anyway, Kenzo was on her way to the pub and she had some exciting news. Matty grabbed his pint from the table and waited near the door.

"So when's that rat out of jail then?" Mandy asked.

Harry smirked and patted her knee. "Next week love, why are you scared? You should be love, he's plotting to do you in?"

Mandy was crapping herself but there was no way she was telling him that. "I'm not arsed Harry, as long as he doesn't come within an inch of me I'll be fine."

Harry fought Jona's corner. "He does love you Mandy. Every night he spoke about you, you've knocked the life out of him you know, he was gutted."

Mandy screwed her face up tightly, and held her head back, laughing. "Oh, is that right? Harry, I wasn't born yesterday, Jona is a dick-head. He only thinks about himself. If he loved me that much he wouldn't have been in bed with all my so called mates would he?"

Harry couldn't fight his friend's corner anymore. This woman was wise and there was no pulling the wool over her eyes. Harry kept his hand on her leg, it was warm, sexy, inviting. Their eyes met and Mandy knew straight away what she wanted. Harry Jarvis was a prize catch and now he wasn't with his wife, he was fair game. She flicked her hair from her shoulder and whispered into his ear. "Do you want to go somewhere else, just me and you? Come on, we'll have a laugh, there's no point in moping around here is there? Let's go and have a good time, what are you saying?"

Harry swigged the rest of his drink and grabbed his coat from the chair. Matty could see he was about to leave and making his way back to the table, he pulled him to one side as Mandy left to go to the toilet. "Where are you going pal? Are you okay or what?"

Harry's eyes were glazed over and his breath stank of stale beer. "I'm sorted Matt, nothing I can't handle. I'll catch up with you tomorrow. This needs sorting out and I'm ready to take some pricks out of the game for good. I have fuck all to lose anymore; prison will be a holiday camp. Like I said, let me sleep on it and I'll fill you in tomorrow."

Matty patted his shoulder. "Kenzo is on her way with some news, so hopefully when I've shagged her brains out she'll tell me about another graft. And, as for Ray Clough," he looked Harry straight in the eyes and his voice was low. "The words out on the street for him, it's just a matter of time before we catch up with him. You just leave him to me for now, the guy's getting tortured when we get a grip of him. Fancy shitting on your own doorstep, what a plonker, he's going to be sorry."

Harry smiled and the look in his eyes was disturbing, he shook Matty's hand and held a tight grip on it. "Cheers mate, see you tomorrow, bright and early and all that. The early bird catches the worm, remember." Mandy came to join them and Harry led her from the pub. Matty watched them both leave and shook his head. This woman was trouble, big trouble.

★

Back in Gill's lounge Sally was trying to console her friend – she was heartbroken and her shoulders were shaking as she sobbed her heart out. "I've fucked it all up Sally, and for what, bleeding nothing. I should have listened to you when you told me about Ray, but I really thought he cared about me."

Sally poured some more wine into the glasses and sat next to her. "The man is a fucking weirdo. Everybody knows him of old; he's been a womaniser for years. He just used you."

Gill banged her hand on the sofa and stamped her feet on the floor. "I know, I bleeding know."

Sally crossed her legs. "It's Regina you need to watch now love. I swear, once she gets wind of this she'll have your guts for garters, trust me, she a crank. I wouldn't like to be in your shoes when she finds out. You need to keep a low profile until all this blows over."

Gill screamed at the top of her voice. "As if I need

to hear that Sally, don't you think I have enough on my plate without you adding to it? Go on; kick me whilst I'm down why don't you."

Sally shrugged her shoulders. "I'm just saying Gill, you know I call it the way I see it and this is not going to go away. That woman will be gunning for you. That's a fact." Sally got a text alert and pulled her phone from her pocket; she gave a cunning grin and quickly replied to the message.

Gill watched her closely, she was up to something for sure. "Who's texting you then?"

Sally went blood red and quickly changed the subject. "Oh, it's just an old friend, no one special."

Gill knew she was lying and delved deeper. "So, what friend. I know all your friends, who is it?"

Sally's back was up and she was on the defensive. "It's just a friend, bloody hell; just leave it at that fucking Juliet Bravo. God, just leave it will you."

The women sat in silence for a few minutes. Gill was watching her friend with inquisitive eyes; she was on edge and acting strange. "Right, I'm going to get off" Sally said at last, "You get in bed and get some shut eye. Things will turn out okay, this will be history soon. You just need to keep strong."

Gill stood up and hugged Sally. "Thanks for being there for me, love. You're always there for me when I need you most."

Sally couldn't get away from Gill fast enough; she pecked her on the cheek and left the house. Gill sat alone, her life was a mess and she knew this was the quiet before the storm; the shit was going to hit the fan big time. Harry was a ticking bomb.

Harry lay on the bed. Mandy was next to him and she was tickling the sprinkling of dark hairs on his chest. They'd gone back to her house and she was dying to get her claws into him, she was like a preying lioness waiting to pounce. "I do fancy you Harry. I know you're Jona's mate but I can't help who I'm attracted to can I?"

Harry's eyes were closing; there was no way any sex was on the cards, his nob was like a shrivelled worm in his boxer shorts, he had brewer's droop. Mandy stared at Harry as his eyes closed. She cuddled up to him closely and inhaled his manly scent as her eyes closed too.

CHAPTER NINE

Preston zipped his coat up tightly and pulled a hat down over his eyes. He hated anyone seeing his face when he was scared, and he was petrified right now. Callum was at the side of him and he was white with fear, quivering in his boots. He wouldn't admit to being frightened but you could see the fear in his eyes. Ben Collins was waiting to see them both, he wanted answers. Callum wanted to bring a gun along but Preston told him he was just adding fuel to the fire, Ben would destroy them if had an inkling that they was even thinking of taking him down. All morning the lads had been on the shitter, crapping themselves. It was the not knowing that was worst, would they still be alive after the meeting? If Ben had told them he was going to do them in they would never have agreed to meet him, but he'd been calm on the phone and told them he wanted to see them as soon as possible. Preston wanted to go last night, but Callum was against it. He was still hurting from their fight and needed a bit of time to recover.

Stood in the front room Preston rasied his eyes to the ceiling and screwed his face up. "She's been crying her eyes out all night you know?"

Callum blew a laboured breath and shook his head. "It's her own fucking fault, fancy admitting she's been getting banged by another man. She's lucky she's still standing because if that was my bird I would have kicked her fanny right in. She's a dirt bag, end of. She deserves everything that's coming to her."

Preston kicked one foot into the floor. "Should we go upstairs and see her before we go. I mean, she's hurting isn't she? No matter what she's done, she's still our mother."

Callum pushed his hand into Preston causing him to wobble. "Nar, fuck it. It's her mess let her sort it out. And, if my dad comes here to give her a good hiding I'm not standing in his way. Yeah, she's my mother but she should have kept her legs closed, innit."

Preston walked slowly out of the room; he had no choice but to leave his mother alone upstairs. He had his own problems to deal with at the moment and a crying woman was the last thing on his mind.

"Come on then, let's do one" said Callum, "If Ben is waiting for us, he'll go sick if we're late. Let's just get this shit over with and see what the prick has to say. I swear bro, if he starts chatting shit he's going down." Preston hurried his brother out of the door, he was so full of shit it was untrue. Callum thought he was a gangster when in fact all he was, was a shit-bag with a big gob who couldn't back it up.

Gill lay in bed staring at the ceiling. All night long she'd been awake, tossing and turning, fighting her emotions. An empty packet of cigarettes was on the side of the bed and the ashtray was overflowing with cigarette dimps. It had been a long night. Reaching for her phone she checked for any updates. No calls, no messages, no nothing. Curling up in a tight ball her knees were pushed deep into her chest. Pulling the duvet over her head she hid away from the world, she wanted to die.

Ben Collins stood tall as he saw the lads walking into the mill. This was an old warehouse where most of his business took place. It was quiet here and nobody ever came unless they were up to no good. Tony Johnson's body had been found there and as yet the police didn't have any suspects. Ben and his brothers were in the clear. Ben Collins knew the security guards who looked after the place and a couple of bungs here and there always kept their mouths shut, the bent bastards. The room was dark, dripping water could be heard in the background. As Preston walked into the room his voice seemed to leave his body, he was choking. Callum took a deep breath and bounced forward. There was no way he was showing this guy any fear, he stood tall and he acted fearless. Ben sat down and pointed to the wall for the lads to do the same.

Ben was with his brother Connor and this kind of work was their own graft, they used young lads to earn them money and didn't care what the consequences were. "So, where the fuck is my grow?" Ben growled.

Callum inhaled deeply and stuck his chest out in front of him. The brothers were covered in cuts and bruises and Ben knew something had gone down. Callum was ready to speak, his hands were held out in front of him and he was constantly moving them about. "Ben, we were had over bro. I swear, they kicked ten tons of shit out of us. Men, big men it was, we didn't stand a chance." Ben was listening but he wasn't buying their story. He'd heard this shit too many times in the past. Everybody was out to earn a few quid no matter who they were having over, he trusted nobody. Callum twisted his head to his brother for some back-up. "Go on, tell him Preston didn't we get leathered, off the bastards."

Preston nodded his head slowly. He knew they were on borrowed time and he was watching his every word. If Ben would have got one whiff of them lying he would have killed them stone dead there and then. "Yeah, we got twisted up Ben. We didn't stand a chance these guys were professionals and they were in and out like fucking ninjas."

Connor stepped forward, his biceps were bulging and the vein in the side of his neck was pumping. "Listen you two pricks, I'm not arsed what happened to the weed, I'm arsed about who's going to pay us the money back." Connor shot his eyes to each of the brothers waiting for an answer.

Callum was flapping, he knew he was going to get a belt anytime soon, he could see it in Connor's eyes, he was raging. "Ben, honest, straight up mate, me and our kid wouldn't try and have you over. We was on an earner too, fucking hell look at the state of us, where do you think these bruises came from ay?"

Connor gripped Callum by the scruff of his neck and bit hard into his cheek, blood dribbled down his face and the lad was screaming out in pain, howling. Preston came to help him out but Connor swung his hand back and punched him in the mouth. Ben remained still, he knew his brother could handle these two scrotes on his own, plus he was wearing a white shirt, there was no way he wanted to get any claret on that, it was too expensive.

Ben shouted out in a loud voice and Connor backed off. He'd done his job and let the lads know he meant business. Ben sat forward and cracked his knuckles; you could hear the bones grinding together. "You owe me ten grand lads; how the fuck do you plan on paying me back?" Callum was trying to stop his cheek from bleeding and he looked like he was going to faint when he saw the amount of blood he was losing. Ben shouted out again, louder this time. "Well, speak to me muppets before my brother sticks his cock up your arses and bums you to death." Connor let out a menacing laugh; he started to unbuckle his belt ready to abuse them both. Preston looked at his brother and panic was in his eyes, he was ready to make a run for it his eyes were all over the place looking for a quick exit.

Ben stood up and walked around the two brothers, weighing them up, poking at them. "You can sell the brown and work your debt off. What are you saying?"

Callum swallowed hard. Selling heroin carried the risk of a big jail sentence. Most of the lads he knew who'd dealt it had all landed up in the nick. No, there was no way he was having anything to do with it, no matter what. "Nar mate, are you having a laugh or what Ben. We're not doing that, we can do other grafts to pay the money back, but selling smack isn't for us." Callum dropped to the floor, and he could see his brother being twisted up by Connor, the lads were taking a beating, a bad beating. There were screams, pounding and crashing noises.

Callum and Preston were lying on the floor begging them to stop. "You'll sell the smack otherwise I'll fucking finish you off," Ben raged, "listen to me you pair of wankers. I gave you a chance to earn some decent cash and look what happened, you took the piss. You owe me and I want my money back, every last penny of it. What? Do you want me to come through your front door and take it out on your family, because I will you know? I'll stick my cock in your mother's mouth while you two watch, is that what you want?" Ben Collins didn't have a clue who their parents were, he never needed to know either. He was just after young kids to do his dirty work for him, he didn't do any background checks on his grafters, he was just out to earn money nothing else.

Callum didn't know his father's business concerning the Collins brothers either. He was just a kid out to get some money. Preston rolled onto his side and covered his face with his hand. He was coughing blood and in a bad way. "Right, we'll do it, just leave us alone, we'll do it." Callum was barely moving, he was on his back just staring into space.

"Now you're talking," Connor sniggered. "I knew you would see the light, you know it makes sense."

Ben walked away from the lads, and lit up a cigarette. "I'll sort you the gear out soon and you can start selling it next week. Monday morning I want you here at nine o'clock sharp. And, if you don't show," he paused. "I'll find you and next time you'll be in a body bag, do you get me?"

Preston nodded as he watched Connor leave his side. Ben flicked his cigarette at Callum and chuckled. "See you Monday lads, bright and early, don't be late." The Collins brothers left, their footsteps could be heard heading towards the door.

Preston crawled over to his brother and nudged him. "Bro, you okay?"

Callum was struggling to breathe. "I think the prick has broken my ribs, fucking hell, I can't breathe proper."

Preston took a few minutes and scrambled to his feet.

He leant against the wall and you could see him spitting blood. "Callum, we need to get off from here, come on, before he changes his mind. The guy is a fucking lunatic." Preston walked to his brother's side and helped him up from the floor. He was in a state, and his legs buckled underneath him almost instantly. "Come on our kid, you need to get you up."

Callum was helped up again, and he leant on his brother as they left the warehouse. Tears were in his eyes as he spoke to his younger brother. "We're fucked aren't we? It's do or die isn't it? If we don't do what he's asking, you know he'll find us, we have no other option." Preston didn't answer him; they walked slowly into the daylight. Covering his eyes with his hand Preston seemed lost, he took a few minutes to realise where he was. The lads headed towards the gate at a slow pace. The security man had seen them leave and turned a blind eye, he knew not to get involved. Preston went inside his pocket and pulled out his mobile. After a quick call the brothers sat on the pavement waiting for a lift. The days ahead looked dark, there future looked set in stone now, they were heroin dealers, the lowest of the low.

*

Gill opened the bottle of tablets on the bed. Her hands were shaking as she popped the white pills to the back of her mouth. She had nothing to live for anymore, all she'd ever loved was gone. She was alone and scared and never wanted to breathe again. Dying was the easy way out; she could never face anyone again. She was ashamed of the woman she'd become, she was a laughing stock. Lying down on the bed she just stared at the walls, her breathing became slower and the grip she had on the tablet bottle loosened. Gill closed her eyes slowly and she seemed to be drifting away. Her mouth was moving but no words were coming out.

Sally opened the front door and shouted her friend. "Gill, where are you? I've got us a bottle of wine to drink; it was two for one in Ads." Sally held her ear towards the stairs. The TV was on and she knew she was in otherwise the front door would have been locked. Sally popped her head into the front room and the kitchen; there was no sign of her. "Gill," she shouted as she started to walk up the stairs. The floorboards creaked as Sally walked along the landing, she was spooked. Seeing Gill's bedroom door opened slightly she popped her head inside with caution. "Oh my God woman, are you still in bed, get your lazy arse up. I've got us a bottle of Jacob's Creek, lovely red wine, come on get up." Sally walked over to the curtains and yanked them open, she was humming a tune. Turning her head slowly Sally held a serious look. "Gill, are you okay?" There was no reply. Sally walked over to the bed and spotted a tablet bottle on the bed lying next to Gill. The colour drained from her face as she yanked the blankets from Gill's body. Sally screamed at the top of her voice. She lifted her up from the bed and slapped her cheeks rapidly trying to bring her round. "Gill, wake up. Gill, can you hear me, wake up." Gill's chest was rising slowly, she was still breathing. Sally pulled her phone from her pocket and rang the emergency services. "Quick, send an ambulance. For fuck's sake hurry up will you." Sally gave the details and ran to the bathroom. She came back with a glass of cold water and flicked bits of it on

Gill's cheeks. Holding the glass with a steady hand she forced the cold liquid down Gill's throat. "Gill, if you can hear me, you better not die on me. Just bleeding wake up will you. Please don't die. Orrr... Gill what the fuck have you done this for? Nothing is ever this bad to try and take your own life. You silly, silly bitch."

CHAPTER TEN

Harry sat in the car alone. He was parked up outside Ray Clough's house, watching, waiting to strike, desperate to seek his revenge. He looked in a deep trance as he tapped his fingers on the steering wheel. Harry was keeping a low profile and it was obvious he didn't want to be spotted. His mobile phone had been ringing constantly all night but he just ignored it, he was in no mood to talk to anyone, his head was in bits. He had more important things on his mind at the moment. He had to right the wrong that Ray Clough had done to him, save his pride. Harry kept closing his eyes and letting out deep breaths. His eyes were sad, empty, something was missing. The radio was on low and you could just about hear it. Harry watched the area eagerly, as soon as he spotted his prey he was having him. He knew that already, no messing about, he was getting it. He'd told Gill he wouldn't go near Ray but, come on, this guy had slept with his missus. This was Harry Jarvis we were talking about, was she that thick to believe he would let this go? No. He wanted payback, he was going to destroy him, make him suffer.

Ray Clough grabbed his coat from the banister. He looked edgy and nervous. It was Saturday and he was heading down to the shops to get a newspaper, he needed time on his own, to clear his head, to think about his next move. His wife Regina had noticed the change in her husband and she could smell a rat. He was being too nice to her, kissing her and doing things he never usually did. "Will you get me a jar of coffee from the shop Ray, I'm gagging for a drink. We must have run out," shouted after him." Ray nodded his head slowly. Regina watched her husband through the blinds and she thought about following him. He never walked anywhere but today he was going to the shops... she sat watching him for a few seconds more. He was up to something, she was sure of it.

Seeing Ray leave the house Harry sat up straight; he was alert and ready to rumble. He clenched his teeth together tightly, grinding them. The time had come to confront his wife's lover. Hands gripped tightly on the door handle he was waiting for the exact moment to strike. If he got this wrong he would have blown his cover and the dirty rat would run free. Harry waited for Ray to walk past him. He dipped his head low and sank down in the driver's seat. He heard footsteps pass the window. In a flash, Harry bolted up from his seat and pulled out a baseball bat from the side of his chair. He knew this would have to be a clean belt to his victim's head, he wanted him dazed. Jumping from the car Harry swung his arm back and you could hear Ray's skull crack as the blow landed right on the top of his head. Ray Clough fell straight to the ground. Harry took the bat and gave him another few belts across his body just to make sure he wouldn't be getting back up any time soon. Ray's lifeless body was flung into the boot of the car. Harry heard rustling behind him and thought someone had seen him. He twisted his head frantically as he closed the boot and jumped back into the car. Flicking the engine over he sped off onto the main road. Harry looked like a mad man, he was shouting now. "Did you really think you would get away with it Clough? Let's see how big you are now wanker! I'll show you. Nobody messes about with my wife, fucking nobody." Harry grabbed his mobile phone from the passenger side. "Matty's it's me. Open up, I'm nearly here. I've got the cunt in the boot of my car. Sort things out for when I get there, this bastard is going to pay." Harry ended the call and sped to the meeting point. He nearly lost control a few times, he clearly wasn't with it at all. Only God could help Ray Clough. His number was up. It was time to pay for his actions.

Matty kicked Kenzo in the legs. "Come on, you need to fuck off home. I've got business to take care of. Get your clothes on quick, I need you gone."

Kenzo yawned and tried to stretch her body out fully but Matty dragged her by the legs out of the bed. "Orrr, you said we could spend the day together remember. Matty, I did tell you about the warehouse full of plants didn't I. I mean, I could have kept that to myself couldn't I?"

Matty snarled at her, she was knocking him sick now. He knew she wanted some more sniff from him and he hated how much she craved the drug. He was just a social user himself, not every day like she was. Rummaging on the side he found some cocaine that was left from the night before. He threw it over to her. "I'm sure this will keep you company until I get back. Just get ready and do one. Harry's on his way and we've got urgent stuff business, it won't wait." Kenzo gripped the sniff with both hands. Her eyes were wide open and she debated having a snort of it before she left. Pulling her pink lacy knickers over her thighs you could see the bones sticking out from her hips, she was so thin, anorexic even. Matty was ready in minutes and he stood anxiously waiting at the window. Kenzo was ready and plonked back down again on the bed sprawling out she yawned. Matty flipped and dragged her back up. "I said you have to go. Come on Kenzo, don't fuck about, I haven't got time for this."

Kenzo was in a strop; she grabbed her handbag and headed to the front door. "I tell you what Matty, you keep treating me like a slut and I'll start acting like one. I mean it; I'm sick of always been last on your list. You said you loved me. If this is love then I'd rather be on my own, it's shit this."

Matty would have slapped her if she'd have been nearer to him, his face was blood red. Who did this tart think she was chatting shit to? He lit a cigarette up and blew the smoke out from his mouth with force. "Yeah, whatever Kenzo. I'm sure your mates will be eager to jump in your place if you're kicking up such a fuss. I'm a prize catch me, are you forgetting that?"

Kenzo flicked her hair over her shoulders and shouted back as she left the house. "Whatever, dickhead, whatever. I might see you in a bit if I'm not busy. That's if a better offer doesn't come along." The door slammed shut and the house shook, she was such a heavy-handed bitch.

Harry pulled the handbrake and turned the engine off. He was watching for Matty at the front door. Within seconds he came running down the garden path and jumped into the passenger side. "Where the fuck is he?"

Harry jerked his head back and let out a menacing laugh. "The cunt's in the boot. Right, where are we heading? I need to get him there before he starts to come round."

Matty pulled some keys out of his jacket pocket; he jingled them in front of Harry. "I've got a little place up in the hills. It's my sister's gaff, she's on a backpacking holiday for a few months so we'll be sorted there. It's nice and quiet, carrot crunching village it is."

Harry nodded his head. "Sorted, that's what we need, somewhere quiet. I don't want any fucking heroes stopping this bastard getting what's coming to him." Matty chewed on his fingernails; he was checking they weren't being followed. Harry lit another cig up, he was smoking like a chimney, no sooner had he put one out he was sparking another one up.

Ray Clough was tied to the bed, he couldn't move. His mouth was covered with thick black tape and all you could see were his eyes flicking rapidly from side to side. Harry came into the bedroom, it was dark and the only light came from the hallway. Harry stood over his victim and growled. Ray could now see Harry for the first time and he pissed himself, big wet patches filled the bed. Sitting on the corner of the bed Harry peeled back the tape from Ray's mouth, he wanted him to answer. Ray's forehead seemed to be hanging over his eyes it was swelled and sore. Harry smirked and bent his head down to Ray. "Well, fuck a duck, I bet you didn't think you would see me again did you?"

Ray didn't reply, his eyes were filled with terror. His mouth moved slowly and you could hear him trying to speak. "I'm sorry," he whispered.

Harry looked at his cigarette burning down in his

hand; he was getting ready to put it out. He lifted Ray's shirt up and dug the cigarette deep into his skin. The smell of burning flesh filled the room. Ray wriggled about and his face creased with pain. Harry gripped his face in his hands. "You've ruined my life, and now I'm going to ruin yours."

Ray was pleading now and knew his life could end at any time. "It was her Harry, I told her no, but she just kept coming back, what was I supposed to do?" Ray was lying through his front teeth; he was doing everything he could to save his own bacon.

"Fucking walk away you daft cunt, that's what you should have done. I've a good mind to cut your dick off you know, perhaps I'll send it to Gill as a token of your love." Harry paused, something was going on with him and Ray knew more torture was on its way. Harry shouted to Matty in the other room. "Matty, bring me the lighter from the stove."

Ray recognised the noise of cupboards opening and closing before Matty's footsteps could be heard heading back into the room. Matty stood at the door and pressing the switch on the ignition. The flame was blue with yellow inside it and when Ray saw it for the first time he started to cry, real tears, terrified tears. Harry stood up and looked at Ray, he was shaking like a scared animal and he had every right to be. "Pull his strides down Matty." Ray wriggled again, but he was going nowhere, he was helpless in the arms of his captors. Matty ripped Ray's pants off. Harry took over now as Matty watched eagerly. This was the Harry he'd remembered. The sick, twisted one who made sure no man ever came back at him. He left them for dead and put the fear of God in them. He was ruthless. Harry pulled down Ray's grey boxer shorts. He could see the man's penis lying lifeless on his pubic mound. Flicking the flame near him he watched Ray twitch. Harry felt sick in his stomach, this was the cock that had been stuck inside his wife. He brought the flame to the side of the penis and started to burn it. Slowly he guided the flame up and down the shaft of it. Ray was screaming in pain as Matty sealed his mouth again with the tape. He wanted to keep this man as quiet as could be all he needed was a nosey neighbour calling the police on him before his reign of terror was over. Ray's penis was on fire and only after a few minutes did Harry decide to end his torment. Ray was howling in pain, the muffled screams filled the walls, chilling cries for help. Matty rubbed at his arms, there were goose pimples all over his skin. The hairs on the back of Harry's neck stood on end. He loved the pain and fear he could see in this man's eyes. This was the man he used to be before jail had worn him down. He was fearless again, king of his domain.

Harry's phone started to ring. He got up from the bed and dug his hand in his pocket. Walking into the hallway you could hear him scream from the pit of his stomach. "I'm on my way Sally, I'm on my way."

Matty was by his side trying to calm him down. "What the fuck has gone on, is it the Collins?"

Harry was white and he ran to the toilet. Stood over the toilet he was gagging. "It's my Gill, she's taken an overdose."

Matty paced the floor behind Harry. "What the fuck has she done that for?"

Harry lifted his head up from the toilet bowl and sprung to his feet. "It's because of that cunt lying in there."

He sprinted back into the bedroom and let rip on Ray, blows were struck to his victim's body – vicious, sickly punches. Blood surged from Ray's mouth, thick claret that looked clotted. Matty closed his eyes; this shit was too much for even him to take. He walked to Harry's side and pulled him away by his arm. "Leave this prick here, Gill needs you. Let's get you back home. Ray can wait here, he's going nowhere, we'll come back soon for him and finish him off."

Harry was in a world of his own, his eyes looked empty. He'd lost the plot. Matty passed him a lit cigarette. "Here mate, get a few blasts of that down you, try and calm down."

Harry gripped the fag and inhaled on it with force, his cheeks sunk in at both sides, he needed to calm down, he was raging. Harry walked back to the bed and bent down to Ray, he was nose to nose with him. "I'll be back for you wanker, don't think this is over. It's just the start of what you've got coming to you." Matty looked at Ray in more detail, he'd be lucky to survive the night, he was in a bad way and barely breathing. Harry left the room followed closely by Matty. The sounds of Ray's moans were chilling, if Harry carried out the torture he had planned for him, death would be a blessing.

★

Sally sat with Gill as she came around. Her stomach had been pumped and the doctors were doing blood tests on her to see what damage she'd done to her liver. Sally reached over and took Gill's hand into hers. It was thin and all the veins on top of it looked sore and bruised from the drips she's had in them. "I'm glad you're still alive, Gill.

Nothing is ever that bad that you have to end your life. You've fucked up yes, but trust me it will get better. Just give it time."

Gill hid her face deep into the pillow, she was sobbing. "I have nothing left Sally, it's all gone. I've hurt Harry for nothing. How do I ever come back from this? I'm a slut, a dirty slapper who can't even wait for her husband to get out of prison."

Sally went around to the other side of the bed so she could see Gill properly. She sat down and looked her straight in the eyes. "You're not the only one to have ever made a mistake. I wasn't going to mention this but Harry cheated on you years ago, so it's all fair and square now isn't it. Why do you think he just upped and left? Don't eat yourself up about him; he's just as bad as you."

Gill turned over and sat up straight away. She ragged her fingers through her hair and was sobbing her heart out. "What and you knew this and never told me? What kind of fucking friend are you?"

Sally took a deep breath and shook her head. "I never told you because I didn't know for sure, but since he's been locked up people talk and I found out that it was all true."

Gill froze, her lips trembling. "Who is it, is it somebody I know?"

Sally dipped her head low and played with the cuff of her sleeve. "I don't know who it is, just that he cheated on you." Sally was lying, it was written all over her face.

Gill threw the blankets from her body and tried to get out of bed, she was hysterical. "For fuck's sake can this get any worse? This is like a TV drama, this can't be happening to me." Sally tried to control her but Gill was fighting back. The doctor came into the room and he shot a look at both the women. Immediately he called for help. Within minutes Gill was sedated and she was slowly drifting off to sleep. Sally sat on a chair at the side of the room, she was rocking to and fro. She should have kept her big trap shut, the shit was going to hit the fan now for sure.

Ray lay staring into space; he was in a bad way, he didn't have long left. He turned his head slightly as the door opened slowly. Footsteps could be heard approaching the bed, his heart was beating ten to a dozen. He could feel someone loosening the rope around his hands. With a look of fear in his eyes he struggled to breathe. "Ssshhh," the voice said. Ray was carried out of the house. He was screaming out in pain. He needed urgent medical help and if he didn't get to the hospital soon his days would be numbered. The engine started and Ray was on the back seat of the car. He didn't look good and every breath he took was a blessing. Staring at the driver he tried to speak but no words came out.

CHAPTER ELEVEN

Harry sprinted into the hospital. He pushed past the nurses sending them flying. "Where is she? Where's my wife?" he ranted. A nurse tried to calm him down, and took some details from him before escorting him to his wife.

Sally bolted up from her chair; she was shocked to see Harry. "I didn't think you'd come," she sobbed. "She's in a bad way; the doctors have just sedated her."

Harry walked slowly to his wife's bedside and fell to his knees. "Fuck off out of here Sally, just give me a minute will you," he snapped. Sally got her cigarettes out of her pocket and headed outside. Harry touched Gill's hand softly, she was out of it and couldn't hear a word he said, although her eyelids flicked rapidly. "Why Gill? Did you love him that much that you'd risk us for him? You've been my world for as long as I can remember, but now look at us, we're like strangers," he made sure they were alone and quickly checked the door. "I've sorted that bastard out anyway. Surely you didn't think he was going to get away with it. He was crying like a baby Gill, if he loved you he would have taken it like a man. You know what," he paused and sank his head into the bed. "He never mentioned you once, he never said he loved you and never said he would die for you. I would die for you Gill, that's love. He just filled you with shit so he could get your knickers off. We'll be back together soon love, but first I need to sort things out. I'm doing what

129

I do best. If we get back together you're going to love me like you used to. There's no way I'm letting you go. I would rather die first."

Harry stayed for a bit longer and stroked his wife's head, his words were chilling and he definitely meant them. Standing to his feet, he checked his watch. "I'll be back soon Gill. We can talk more then. I love you, I always will." Harry left the room and headed outside. Sally was stood shivering near the exit, it was pissing down with rain and she was getting soaked. Harry patted his hand on her shoulder. "Thanks for letting me know Sally, I'll be back soon. If she wakes up tell her I've been."

"I will Harry, she knows about you seeing someone else too. I don't know who told her but she's gunning for you now."

Sally was a lying bitch, why didn't she just tell him that she was the one who'd told his wife? Harry stared at Sally a bit longer than he needed too. He sighed and dragged at his hair. "Fuck me, that's all I need. I'll sort it out when I come back. You just keep her sweet. You know she listens to you Sally." Harry left in a hurry and Sally went back into the hospital.

Harry headed home, well, to the place that used to be his home. He needed to tell the boys what had happened. News travelled fast around here and he didn't want anyone else telling them first. But upon opening the front door he could tell something was wrong. Harry listened carefully, he could hear movement upstairs, creaking floorboards, whispering. Sneaking up slowly he prepared to strike the intruder hard. Harry shouted out, "Hello, who's that?" nobody answered. His fist curled tightly he ran up the last few stairs. Kicking at each door he was trying to find the burglar. The last door stared at him, it was now or never. Harry barged into the room with his shoulder and he was prepared for war. Looking around the room he could see both his sons lying on the beds, relief filled his face. "For fucks sake why didn't you shout to me that you were in. Fuck me, I thought we were being robbed. You're lucky I didn't twist you up."

Preston lifted his head up from the bed covers; he was in a bad way. Harry clocked him straight away and ran to his side. "Who's done this to you son? Tell me the names now. I swear to you they're going down. I'll take them out, kill them, just give me a name."

Callum started to cough behind him and he could see him struggling to get out of bed to reach his drink. Harry's face dropped. Something was going on here and he was going to get to the bottom of it no matter what. Falling to his knees he covered his face as he broke down crying. His lads were in a bad way and somehow he blamed himself for it. None of his sons came to his side, they were unable to move. Harry sat alone, heartbroken. Callum just lay staring into space, his complexion was grey and he didn't look well. Harry sobbed as he broke the news to them about their mother but they couldn't respond. There was just silence.

★

John Collins walked to the back of the club. It was dark and there was very little light in the passageway. He'd always come this way after he'd picked the money up and usually he didn't bother about it being dark but tonight he was unsettled. Rustling, gravel crunching behind him, someone was there. Turning his head slowly, he carried on whistling a tune nervously. John quickened his pace; he was anxious and kept looking over his shoulder. Bushes moved and branches snapped in the distance, he was being watched. John fell to the ground as a sledge hammer was cracked over his head, just one blow, it was a sharp, precise hit. The grip on the bag he was holding was loosened, his fingers were peeled from the handle at speed and then the sound of footsteps could be heard running off into the distance. John lay still, there was no movement in him. The moonlight shone down on him and his body shook for the last time. John Collins was dead.

Susan Collins sat at the kitchen table with her sons. It was the funeral of her son today. They were all dressed in black as she sat sobbing. Kenzo was sat at her side and she looked at her brothers for help but none of them moved. Peter Collins banged his clenched fist on the table causing the bottle of whiskey to fall over, spilling on the table. "Some bastard is going to pay for this. I know it's something to do with Harry Jarvis and his boys. I swear to you now, this isn't over; blood is going to be spilled. My brother is dead because of him, he's getting it, trust me."

Kenzo choked up and dipped her head low. Susan shot a look at her sons and pointed at each and every one of them. "My son is bleeding dead because of you lot. He never wanted any trouble, he kept his nose clean, he hated what you made him do. I'll never forgive you for this, none of you," she broke down as days of emotions poured from her. "I'm dead inside, my heart's broken, I want my son back."

Kenzo's eyes welled up. "Mam, the police will find

out who did it, don't worry. Who ever done this to our John will get what's coming to them. As soon as the lads get one name you know it's over for them don't you?"

Susan screamed as she dragged at her clothing. "It won't bring him back though will it? Nobody can bring my John back, ever."

Ben bit down on his bottom lip. "Mam, I promise you now. As soon as I find out who's done this, I will make them suffer. I'll torture them. They will feel pain, trust me." Kenzo lifted the curtain up from the window, the funeral cars were here. Neighbours were stood on the streets and they were all waiting to show their respect to Susan's son. The Collins family walked from the house. The police were parked up at the end of the street. They knew more than anyone that this was a gangland killing and hoped by attending the funeral they might get a lead on the dead man's killer. Nobody had seen a thing though, there wasn't a shred of evidence to go on.

Susan walked outside and stared at the onlookers. The skies were grey and it looked like it was going to rain. Kenzo was holding her mother's arm and guiding her to the car. The brothers walked behind them with looks to kill on their faces. Susan stopped dead in her tracks. Eyeing the crowds of people she snarled. "One of you bastards know who killed my son. You need to speak up and help us find them. My son is dead for crying out loud. I beg you, please give us a name, please, just end this torment."

Peter Collins took control now and pulled his mother along, she was trying to break free but his firm grip stopped her from going anywhere. He whispered into her ear. "Stop embarrassing us mother, just get in the car. I've told you we'll sort this out ourselves. Since when have we needed help?"

Matty stood watching the funeral from afar. He nodded slowly as he watched the flowers being loaded into the back of the car. The Collins brothers were dropping like flies and he knew Harry would be back on the top rung sooner than he thought. Flicking his cigarette he walked off in a hurry.

John Collins' funeral took place in St Patrick's, Collyhurst. A place Susan had often visited in times of need. She was a Catholic but never really went to church unless she needed help. She'd given up on the Lord many years ago; if the truth was known. She always said if there was God he would have helped her when she had troubles in her life and she'd had her own fair share of troubles. At one point in her life she was at her lowest and often thought the world would have been a much better place without her. There had been horrific domestic violence and violent partners that pushed her over the edge quite a few times, she'd had a bad time. Susan was a seasonal believer so to speak.

The coffin was placed at the front of the church with John's photograph placed on top of it. The aroma from the flowers nearby was strong. They smelt of deceit, lies, and guilt. Kenzo stared at her brother's coffin and couldn't believe he was dead. She was sniffed out of her head and her lower jaw was swinging, she was wired. Her words were slurred but nobody seemed to notice her speech, they were all dealing with their own grief. The priest spoke about John's life to his family. Susan kept shouting things out and everybody was getting fed up with her, she was being a right pain in the arse, constantly chipping in.

Ben spoke about his brother to the people sat there and some of the tales of when they were younger were heart-warming. Stories about go-carts and Grifter bikes, and the adventures they went on with nothing but a brown sauce butty to keep them going all day. He spoke about robbing fifty pence pieces from the meter box at the back of the TV and lots of other childhood memories. Susan was shaking now and she looked like she was going to have a heart attack. As the service finished she walked up to the coffin and rested her head on it. "Son, your death will be avenged; I'll make sure of it." Peter stood tall as he walked to the coffin. He bent down slowly and kissed the top of it, the other brothers followed. Kenzo's legs were buckling as she stood at the side of the coffin, the rest of the family were waiting for her so she didn't have long. Flicking her hair behind her shoulder she kissed her hand and placed it on the coffin.

John's body was laid to rest at Moston cemetery. The mourners stood by the graveside as the coffin was lowered into the ground. The priest said some final prayers and one by one the family took some earth from the side of the grave and dropped it on the coffin. Susan Collins looked at the people and growled. She was ready for snapping again and Ben just got to her in time before she let rip. As the family walked away Susan was screaming at the top of her voice, she was a mess and hysterical. "He was my flesh and blood, he was my boy, I want him back!" The moment was heart wrenching and Kenzo was sobbing. No one comforted her when she was alone. She was a Collins, she was brought up to stand tall. Tears were weak, she wiped her eyes quickly and held a stiff upper lip as she walked back to the car. The family all headed back to the Embassy Club in Harpurhey. The club had once belonged to Bernard Manning the Manchester comedian. When he was alive lots of functions were held there. It had been the place to be. The brothers all headed to the bar as Susan and her daughter sat at the side of the room. Kenzo was on her mobile phone but whoever she was calling didn't answer.

★

Matty, Harry and the boys sat rubbing their hands together. Tonight had been a good night. They'd taken one of the biggest grows they'd ever seen, celebrations were in full swing. Kenzo had done well in telling Matty about this warehouse full of weed, it was a right money earner, they were loaded. Harry looked in a world of his own, and every now and then he shook his head. Matty could see he was struggling and came to his side. "She'll be alright you know, everything will be sorted. I'll go and finish Ray off if you want? That's if the cunts still breathing anyway. I can sort it out; you just do what you have to first."

Harry felt his emotions rising, everything he'd loved was messed up; his boys, his wife, the lot. Matty chuckled loudly. "Well lads, we are officially back on the map, fuck the Collins brothers, we're the main men now. Anyway, they've buried one of the brothers today; hopefully they will drop like flies now. I wonder who done him in? I've not heard a word about it. Twenty grand they got off with too, the lucky jammy bastards. If I'd have known the runt was carrying that amount of money I would a popped a cap in his arse myself." Harry was listening carefully, Matty was right, there were some shady people about that even they didn't know existed. Matty rolled a joint and passed some to Harry. "Here, get a few drags of this, it will chill you out. Help you relax." Harry had never really done drugs, he'd had a bit of cocaine in the past but it wasn't for him, alcohol was his guilty pleasure and even that had a bad effect on him. He steered clear of drugs, he'd seen how much they took over people's lives and destroyed them. After he took a few drags Harry sat staring in to space, he looked to be melting, his shoulders sank low and his eyes were closing. Matty was stoned and got a fit of the giggles. "Ay, Jona's out tomorrow. I can't wait until our full team is back together. I'll tell you what Harry, them Collins brothers don't stand a fucking chance against us anymore. The only way is up mate, all the way to the fucking top."

CHAPTER TWELVE

Ben Collins patted Callum on the arm. "You know it makes sense don't you kid? You'll have this debt paid off in no time if you work your balls off." Preston kept his head low; he hated this man with a passion. He was a bully and preyed on weak people. "Here's the gear, get it bagged and start selling it." Ben smiled and made sure the two lads knew exactly what he wanted from them. Callum was quiet; he'd lost his usual loud mouth. He was actually scared. The Jarvis boys still had bruises on their faces and Callum was walking with a limp.

"I'll be in touch," Connor growled as he left their side. He was a right arrogant bastard and loved that he'd put the fear of God into the two new recruits.

Callum and Preston walked along the road heading toward Tina's house. Trisha had said they could bag the gear up there. She wasn't doing it for nothing, no way, she'd already put her price tag on them using her home for illegal use. Trisha had dabbled in drugs all her life, nothing as bad as heroin though; she was more into popping pills. She knew all about the drugs on the street but she'd yet to try any magic or ketamine, she was a bit wary after seeing on the TV what the drug could do to people.

Tina opened the front door and smiled at Preston. Once she saw Callum though, her face dropped and she headed back inside the house in a strop. Tina was getting ready to end her relationship with Callum anyway. He was pissing her off and now he wasn't getting any decent money she had no further need for him. However Preston had always taken her eye. There was just something about him that made her heart flutter. Callum had asked her in the past if she had a thing for his brother but she'd always denied it. There was no way she was ever admitting that she had a crush on him he would have gone sick at her. Trisha was sat at the table smoking. Once she saw Callum coming into the room she held her hand out. "Come on, cough up the cash, nothing's getting done here until you pay up. I'm no dick-head you know, a deal is a deal." Trisha lifted her leg up and farted, she didn't even flinch, she just carried on as normal. She was a right scruffy slob with no manners whatsoever.

Callum dug his hand in his pocket and passed Trisha some money. There must have been at least fifty pounds there. Shoving it down the front of her bra she chuckled. "Job's a good un lads, do what you have to do."

Tina shot her mother a look and plonked down on the sofa. The house had some nice stuff inside it but you could see it hadn't been looked after, it was shabby and worn. The house stank of cheesy feet. Preston cleared the coffee table and pulled some small scales from his pocket. Trisha was watching him like a hawk. "What's that brown stuff," Tina quizzed.

"It's smack you daft bleeder," Trisha replied. "Don't tell me you don't know that?"

Tina looked puzzled. "What's smack?"

Callum spoke now and he was cheesed off. "It's fucking heroin you geek, you know brown, derrrrr?"

Tina folded her arms tightly across her chest and sat down next to her mother. She delved deeper. "So, once you've paid your debt off you can earn a lot of money selling this stuff can't you?"

Callum nodded his head. "Yeah, and you get a long time in nick for it too. Me and our kid are just paying this debt off and then we're done with it, aren't we our kid?"

Preston had already started bagging up and never replied. Trisha was so on the ball and she held a cunning look in her eyes. "Why don't you put some other shit with it and mix it. You know skank it like every other fucker does. You'll earn more money that way. Do the same with the sniff too."

Callum turned to face her, why the hell hadn't he thought to do this? He never let her know she was right, he made out as if it was his own idea. "Yeah we're on it Trish, we're not daft you know. I've got some lads sorting it out for us. Do you really think we don't know shit about drugs, for fucks sake, we're on it already!"

Preston lifted his head slowly and smirked at his brother, the guy was such a liar. Turning his head, he clocked Tina weighing him up. The slut was gagging for it and he knew she fancied him like mad. Checking his brother wasn't looking he winked at her. Tina looked flustered and her face was beetroot. Trisha was watching them both from the corner of her eye, her daughter was a tart, there was no denying it. Like mother, like daughter I suppose.

The drugs had been bagged up and it was late. Preston had just left, Trish had gone out and Callum was lying on the sofa with Tina. She seemed distant tonight with him and she was bored. "Are you going home or what?" she stressed.

Callum looped his arms above his head and looked at

her straight in the eye. "Nar, I'm staying here tonight with you. It's fuck night isn't it?"

Tina bolted up from the sofa and started to head up the stairs. Standing at the doorway she twisted her head back and spoke. "There's nothing down tonight for you. I'm on my period so stay down here and have a wank. Don't be waking me up either when you come up, I'm knackered."

Tina was gone and he could hear her footsteps going up the stairs. Checking his wristwatch he blew a laboured breath and mumbled. "Fucking hormonal bitch, fuck you anyway I'll sort myself out. Yeah, I will have a wank thank you very much. You've got a baggy fanny anyway, who needs you." Callum flicked the channel over on the TV; he was looking for any sign of porn, there was nothing on, not even a nipple to look at. There was a repeat of Scott and Bailey on TV, but none of the women floated his boat enough to pull one off to. The front door slammed and Callum sat up straight, he'd forgotten Trisha was still out. It was her bingo night and one of the few nights she went out. Callum inhaled, he could smell kebab. Trisha walked into the front room and slung her coat over the side of the chair. She grabbed the white plastic bag and sat facing Callum. "I'm fucking starving, I've had nothing to eat all day."

Callum raised his eyes brows. Who was she trying to kid? Every time you looked at Trisha she was always munching on something or other, she was a right greedy cow. "Are you sharing that kebab or what Trish? I'm starving too, just cut me a bit off."

Trisha was wounded; she hated sharing food and tonight was no different. Opening the food parcel she ripped the end part from the kebab and stuck a few chips into it to make it look fuller, there were two mouthfuls, there tops. They both sat munching their food, you could hear Trisha's chops smacking together. She had no manners whatsoever, she was sickening to watch. Speaking with her mouth full she looked over to Callum. "Where's Tina?"

"Orr she's gone to bed, the miserable fucker. I tell you what Trish, if she carries on like this with me I'll be on my toes; she blows hot and cold all the time. I don't know where I'm up to with her lately. Has she said anything to you?"

Trisha licked her lips slowly, it had been ages since she'd had a leg over and she moved from her place to sit next to Callum. Pulling her top down lower she pushed her breasts out in front of her. "Oh, just ignore her love, you know what she's like, leave her be, she'll come around without water," Trisha started giggling. "Shall we have a bit of sniff, just a bag between us, come on, it will be a buzz, no one would ever know, call it our little secret."

Callum liked this woman, she was fun and up for a laugh. She had no hang-ups like her daughter. Tina was only happy when she was getting gifts or having money spent on her. "Yeah, fuck it, I'm game for that," Callum chuckled. Two lines of cocaine were soon on the table. Trisha went first and snorted her line, she held her head back after it and started laughing. "Fuck me, I've missed the Charlie. I used to always have a few bumps before I went out back in the day. It's just so expensive these days though isn't it?"

Callum snorted his line and he felt the rush surging through his body, his eyes closed and his chest was rising

with speed. "It's fucking mint this. I feel like me again."
It was strange how much the drug changed him, he was
confident again and full of courage. The two of them sat
chatting, they never shut up. Trisha was horny and you
could see she was grooming her victim. Licking her lips
she stood up and closed the living room door. Stood with
her back to it she rolled down her black leggings and
whipped her t-shirt off. "You want some fun or what,"
she giggled.

Callum shit a brick; you could see the fear in his
eyes. Trisha was an older woman, a fatter, rounder older
woman, desperate for any male attention. Throwing
caution to the wind he took a deep breath and smirked.
"What me and you?"

Trisha held her head to the side and clipped her bra
off, she was naked. Callum dipped his head low, he was
ready to burst out laughing. Her vagina looked like a
splattered hedgehog and the lard around her waist was like
a bumper cushion around her stomach. He could see she
wanted an answer, she was twisting her body and licking
her lips, she was gagging for it. Callum walked towards
her. Taking one for the team he called it and after all Tina
was like a nun these days. Sex was a thing of the past so
he was well within his own right to get sex somewhere
else, even though it was his girlfriend's mother, she was
still fair game in his eyes.

Trisha gripped him in her arms and sank her fat lips
onto his; she pulled his head low and rubbed it onto her
breasts. Callum was gasping for air, she was suffocating
him. "Come on then, let's fuck," she groaned. This
woman was like a sex crazed monster, she was pulling
and dragging him all over the place, she sure knew how

to please a man. This was the best sex Callum had ever had in his life. Hot sweaty bodies rolled about the front room, sexual groans. Trisha was boiling hot, sweat dripped from her body and you could see her bright red cheeks. Callum was lying on the sofa now as Trisha grinded hard on top of him, she held her fat stomach up and smiled at him. "Oh, you like that don't you?" Callum was ready to ejaculate, he was off his head and unaware of what was really happening. Trisha covered his mouth as he groaned with pleasure. "Come to mammy, "she chuckled.

After it was over, Trisha found her clothes and slipped them back on. She turned her head back to Callum and whispered. "This is our little secret, keep it that way."

Callum was trying to get his breath, he was done in. Trisha sat down on the sofa and her eyes clocked the bag of white powder. She was wired and ready to party all night long. Making sure Callum couldn't see her she gripped two bags of sniff and shoved them down her bra. Standing to her feet she headed to the doorway. "I'm off to bed, remember, our secret. See you tomorrow." Callum lay on the sofa and reality was hitting home. Had he really just done that? Sex with his girlfriend's mother? He ran to the kitchen and spewed his ring up into the sink. Sat alone in the front room he looked at the drugs on the table. Callum had always experimented with drugs and nothing really scared him. He picked up a bag of heroin and held it up examining it. He flicked the bag a few times and sat thinking. Heading back into the kitchen he came back with some silver tinfoil. Callum was trying smack for the first time. This drug was lethal and he couldn't realise the grip it would take on his life would be so devastating. Lying on the sofa Callum's mouth was

open and spit dribbled from the corner of his mouth, his
eyes were vacant and he was on another planet. Heroin
was in his blood stream and he was already hooked
without him knowing it.

Tina lay in bed and looked at her mobile phone.
She'd been texting Preston all night and she looked like
she was getting somewhere with him. They were flirting
with one another and although they knew they should
have stopped they continued without any fear of the
consequences.

Trisha could see her daughter's light still on in the
bedroom. Creeping slowly she entered her own bedroom.
She had no regrets for her actions either, she was out
for herself and didn't care who she hurt to get what she
wanted.

CHAPTER THIRTEEN

Gill sat on the sofa watching the TV. She looked washed out; her hair was a mess, her skin was blotchy and dark circles had appeared around her eyes. Sleep never came easily to her anymore and her mind was always working overtime, her pulse racing. Ray Clough was missing; nobody had seen sight or sound of him. His wife Regina was on the warpath and pledged when she found him she was going to shoot the bastard herself for putting her through so much grief. Harry had moved back into the family home. Gill needed looking after and he was doing his best to show her he still cared. She'd never mentioned that she knew about his other woman and she was holding those particular cards close to her chest. They had decided to give their relationship another go but both of them had issues with the other and it seemed the best thing they could have done was walk away.

Sally came into the front room; she was eating a bacon butty, brown sauce smudged on the corner of her mouth. "Don't tell me you're not even ready yet, bleeding hell Gill, we said we would go into town today for a new rig out for us both. Remember, it's my birthday tomorrow and we're going out."

Gill covered her mouth with her hand, she'd totally forgotten about it. Her head was all over the place these days and she had the memory span of a goldfish. Harry walked into the room and jumped into the conversation.

"Here, go and treat yourself, Gill, Sally's right you need to get back out there. For weeks now you've been sat in here staring at four walls, it's time to move on."

Gill sighed, she knew he was right but it was more easily said than done. Everything she did was an effort. Stretching her arms above her head she clocked the cash on the arm of the chair. There must have been over two hundred pound there waiting for her. Gill knew Harry was earning now and her financial worries were over; he'd bought a new sofa, new carpet for the house and endless gadgets for the kitchen. Someone was knocking at the front door, rapping the letterbox with speed.

Harry stood still for a minute and shook his head. "Fuck me, who knocks like that?" He stormed into the hallway and he could see Jona through the glass panel on the door. He had his face squashed up against it, licking it, laughing. Harry opened the door. "Fucking hell, you knock like the dibble you do. Just come in for a minute while I shove my trainers on."

Jona bounced into the front room, he was a lively character and so loud. "Morning ladies, how are you all on this fine morning? I'll tell you what ladies, freedom is the best taste anyone can have. It's a top feeling to walk about without anyone breathing down your bleeding neck."

Sally smiled at Jona, "How does it feel to be on the out love, are you coping or what?"

Jona cupped his ball-bag in his hands and walked closer to her and spoke in a low voice. "I'll be alright when I get my knackers emptied. Three days I've been out, and I've not even had a shag yet, nothing." he draped his arm over Sally's shoulders and chuckled. "I don't suppose you want to take one for the team do you Sally? I'll be in and out before you know it, call it a ninja fuck." Sally was doubled over laughing, this man was so funny and he held nothing back. Jona looked over at Gill, he knew all about her affair with Ray and licked his lips slowly. He scratched the top of his head as he neared her. "Are you alright yo-yo knickers? You want your head feeling shagging about on your husband."

Harry was going to shut him up, but he held back to see what she had to say. Gill sat up straight and her face was blood red, she clenched her teeth together tightly. "Since when has my life had anything to do with you, dickhead? No wonder Mandy fucked you off, you waste of space."

Jona held his head back and chuckled. "Mandy wants me back; she just doesn't know it yet. She's been on the blower for three days trying to get me around to her gaff for some sex. But I told her straight. Nar, I don't do sloppy seconds. I've got standards now I have. She's been like a sperm bank since I've been locked up, there's no way I'm going back there. Been there, done that, you know how it is.," he was lying of course, he was just saving face.

Gill walked to the door and growled at Jona. "Just keep your beak out of my business in future will you? Harry, are you going out? Because if you are, take this gob-shite with you. Cheeky bastard he is." Harry smirked at Sally, Gill was back in the game, she was always hot-headed and never let anybody put her down. She was standing on her own feet again.

Jona waved his hands in the air. "Yeah, yeah Gill. Just because I tell it how it is don't be losing your rag. It's a fact. You should be named and shamed just like that tart of mine. I swear when I see Mandy, she's getting a piece of my mind too. I don't know who you women think you are, shagging about on us men when we're locked up, sluts the lot of you."

Harry shot Jona a look. It had gone too far now and he put an end to it there and then. "Oi, keep it shut now motor mouth, we all know what Gill done, it's over now, so button it."

Jona paced around the room he was anxious. Being out of jail had knocked him for six he didn't know if he was coming or going. The world around him seemed to be moving at a fast pace and he was doing his best to keep up. Jona was going with Matty today to finish Ray Clough off. He loved that he was back in the game and he couldn't wait to get blood on his hands once again. Jona was a head the ball, he had mental issues and it was a wonder he'd not been sectioned.

Gill came back downstairs, she was flustered. "Has that prick gone now or what?"

Sally hid her amusement away and nodded her head. "Yeah, they left about five minutes ago. Jona looks well don't you think?"

Gill popped a cigarette into her mouth and reached for the lighter. Taking a long, deep drag on her fag she answered Sally. "He's a prick. I mean, what right does he have to come in here and speak to me like that?"

Sally blew a laboured breath; she was sick to death of Gill and her attitude. "Gill, people will say what they think you know. That's what it's like around here, people say what they see. And," she paused, "you're one of the worst people for it. You always judge people once you get your teeth into a bit of gossip."

Gill was argumentative; she was ready to fight her corner. "Fuck off Sally, so you think it's right that Jona can come in here and verbally abuse me in my own home?"

"Just relax will you, fuck me, are you due on your periods or something, you hormonal bitch."

Gill stubbed her cigarette out in the ashtray. "I'm just saying that's all. I thought you had my back anyway Sally. You've soon changed your tune all of a sudden. What, do you fancy Jona or something?"

Sally was bright red, she was stuttering. There was definitely some truth in what Gill had just said, she was gobsmacked. "Don't be silly Gill. I've known Jona for years. He's Mandy's man. I do have loyalties you know. You don't shit on your own doorstep do you? Plus he's ugly as fuck, but I suppose he's got a great sense of humour. You don't judge a book by its cover do you?" Gill looked at her in more detail, she knew she was lying, the tip of her nose was twitching. She always did this when she wasn't telling the truth. "Are we going into town or what? I'm not standing here and arguing with you all day, come on, it's my birthday tomorrow we should be happy." Gill took a deep breath, she was over the top and she didn't even know herself why she was acting the way she was, she knew she had to snap out of it and get her life back on track.

★

Matty and Jona sat in the car outside the house where they'd left Ray. Jona was itching to get inside, he was ready to end Ray's life. He looked at Matty and his eyes were dancing with madness. "I'll stick my dick up his arse. I'll make sure he suffers too, he'll be squealing like a pig."

Matty chuckled. "It's good to have you back pal. I've missed your crazy face around me I have."

Jona was all skin and bone. His cheeks were sunken in at the sides and the word on the street was that he had been tanning the smack whilst he was in jail. Jona's teeth were brown stumps and his breath stank of arse; dirty sweaty, foul breath. Matty covered his face as Jona spoke to him, his breath was putrid. As his friend he told him straight. "Jona, I swear to you mate, you need to get your gnashers sorted out. Your breath is fucking rancid. Do you need some fillings or something?"

Jona brushed the comment off and looked into the rear-view mirror. "Yeah my teeth are rotten, but I'm scared shitless of the dentist, it's just the sound of the drill that does it, honest mate, I crap my pants as soon as I hear it."

Matty wound the window up. "Come on then fart breath, let's sort this wanker out once and for all. Let's be quick, no fucking about. I'm going to meet Kenzo later and she'll see her arse if I'm late again."

Jona sprang from his seat and stood outside the car. They both headed inside the house. Matty walked down the garden path and his face dropped. He could see a window open and the net curtain was blowing from it. He held a finger up to his lips and darted his eyes at Jona. "Somebody is inside, look, the fucking window's open."

Jona reached inside his jacket and pulled out a silver pistol. He nodded his head slowly at Matty. "Just open the door and leave the rest to me, come on, let's do it."

Matty ran to the door and inserted the key into the lock with shaking hands. He was white and licking his lips constantly. Jona ran straight inside and he had the gun in his hand ready to shoot. They both searched the house from top to bottom but nobody was there, not even Ray. Matty was in a panic. "Where the fuck is he, Jona? I swear he was tied to the bed, the guys not fucking Houdini, so where the hell is he?"

Jona could smell a rat. He went to the open window and looked outside. "It's obvious you were followed here then isn't it? Did you check nobody was on your toes when you were on your way up here?"

Matty was spitting feathers, "Fucking dead right I did. I'm not an amateur. I'm on the ball. Nobody followed us, I'm sure of it." The men looked at each other, it was time to leave. If Ray was missing then someone out there had him and knew what they were up to.

Jona walked to the front door, he looked over his shoulder at Matty. "It's on top here mate, lock up and let's do one. Fuck me, I've only been out of jail two minutes I don't want to end up back there for fuck all. Let's go and see Harry and see what he has to say. This is spooky shit man, very spooky." The two men dived back into the car and screeched off. They hit the motorway at speed and Matty put his foot down. Ray Clough was on the loose and nobody knew where he was.

Gill and Sally were shopping; the two of them looked fed up. Neither of them had bought a thing yet, it was just one of them days when no outfit looked right. Sally was fed up and she was plodding along behind Gill in a mood. "Shall we go for a drink, maybe that will cheer us up. We can go in the pub over the road if you want?"

Gill nodded. If the truth were known she was in no

mood for shopping either. Ray was on her mind and she thinking of going to see him again to see if he'd changed his mind. He must still love her, how could he just turn off his love in a split second. The women walked into the pub, there were quite a few punters in and a few men sat around the table playing cards.

"Do you want a red wine?" Sally asked Gill.

"Yeah why not. I'm just going to the toilet first, watch my handbag."

Gill made her way to the toilet as Sally stood at the bar. The hairs on the back of her neck stood on end as she heard a familiar voice talking behind her. Regina Clough was in the pub, dressed to the nines, she looked tipsy. Sally knew Regina and she was hoping she didn't notice her, she kept her head low. Too late, she'd spotted her. "Hello love, what are you doing in here so early in the day?"

Sally looked pleased to see her and turned to face her. "Oh, we were just in town shopping and thought we needed a livener, you know how it is when you're shopping."

Regina laughed out loud. She clocked Gill straight away and looked alert as she came to join them. Gill looked surprised, she knew of Regina but she'd never met her in the flesh before. Sally introduced them. There was an awkward silence and Sally looked anxious. "So how's everything with you Regina?" Sally asked trying to end the silence.

Regina sipped her drink still looking at Gill and let out a laboured breath. "Not good I'm afraid. Ray's missing again and nobody has seen sight or sound of him. I've been out of my mind with worry. I think he's with another woman you know," she raised her eyebrows high. "This wouldn't be the first time he's just taken off without so much as a goodbye. He's done it lots of time, the cheeky cunt."

Gill swallowed hard, her eyes were wide open, small droplets of sweat started to appear on her forehead. Sally touched the middle of Regina's arm and tried to comfort her, she looked ready to burst out crying. This was so out of character for her, usually she was as hard as nails. "Don't worry love, he's probably caught up in some poker night, you know what these men are like once they get together."

Regina switched and her teeth were grinding together. "Well, when I get my hands on him he's dead meat just like the slut he's with. I swear I'm going to rip her to shreds too."

Sally could see Gill was in a panic and picked their drinks up from the bar. "I hope it all works out for you love. I'm sure he'll turn up, they always do. Anyway, you just take care of yourself." Regina watched them walk away, but she had her eyes glued to Gill. Sally sighed, "Fucking hell, fancy her being in here. I bet you shit a brick when she mentioned Ray had another woman didn't you? I swear to you, I thought she knew about you and Ray, she kept looking at you didn't she?"

Gill swigged at her drink, her heart was pounding and you could see the fear in her eyes. "She looks hard as nails. I'd hate to be on the wrong side of her, she's a mental bitch," Gill whispered.

Sally kept her voice low and moved closer to Gill's ear. "Regina was a right one in her day. I believe she was gorgeous, all the men wanted her. She could have had the pick of the litter, stunning she was."

Gill found this hard to believe, yes, Regina was good looking, but she would never had said she was gorgeous, she was jealous. "I don't know what Ray sees in her. She's podgy now, and look at her hair, she needs a good cut on it."

Sally looked her straight in the eye with a serious look. "I'm telling you straight Gill, on my life, in her day she was hot stuff. She might have let herself go now, but as true as I'm sitting here, she was mint when she was younger."

Gill growled and hunched her shoulders, her face dropped. "Where the hell is he then? She said he's been missing for days. I bet he's with another woman, the lying cunt. Yeah," she paused, "It would all make sense that's why he carted me."

Sally had heard enough, Gill was so vulnerable, did she really not see what was in front her, was she that blind? She couldn't hold her tongue. "Get a grip Gill, Ray never loved you, he was just playing you and you were an easy target, a quick leg-over so to speak. I don't know how you fell for it all?"

Gill folded her arms tightly in front of her. "Oh, says you who can never keep a man. People who live in glass houses shouldn't throw stones. Who was that guy you was seeing, come on, the one you kept all hush, hush. I didn't see him declaring his undying love for you either. I was there for you when that happened Sally and you didn't hear me preaching to you did I? No, I just helped you through the bad times like true friends do for each other."

Sally's jaw dropped, she went white and started fidgeting. Gill was right, she had had her own share of heartache, but that was years ago and she'd learned from her mistakes, unlike Gill. "Oh Gill, why are you bringing the past up? I'm just telling you how it is that's all. Let's not speak about Ray fucking Clough anymore because it's doing my head in now. I hope he never comes back, he's nothing but trouble in my eyes." Sally finished her drink and started to put her coat back on.

Gill was aware she'd upset her and tried to make amends. "I'm sorry, it's just that I loved him. I know I shouldn't have, but what can you do when you fall, nothing."

Sally started to head to the exit. As she reached the door Regina shouted over to her. "You take care love, and, if you see that Ray tell him I'm hot on his trail."

Gill dipped her head low, she didn't want to bring any attention to herself. The women left the pub and headed back to the shopping centre.

★

Jona and Matty ran into the boozer. Quickly scouting around they soon found Harry and the others. Matty looked edgy and he was chewing on his bottom lip. He sat next to Harry and made sure he had his full attention. "He's gone mate, he's fucking gone."

Harry's nostrils flared and he gripped his pint firmly in his hands. "What do you mean, he's gone? How? He was half dead!"

Jona sat down facing Harry and he tickled the end of his chin slowly. "Somebody is on to us Harry."

Matty was getting annoyed. "It's not possible; I checked nobody was onto us. Whoever has Ray, is up to something. The guy is half dead, what use is he to anyone like that. It's doing my head in now, we need to find him and finish the job. If he goes to the rozzers we're up shit street, stitched up we'll be, I tell you now we need to find the prick."

Jona raised his head from the table as Mandy walked into the bar. He smirked at Harry and stood to his feet. Mandy was stood at the bar ordering her drink. Jona grabbed the cheeks of her arse and bit into her neck softly. "Hello there, how's things?"

Mandy pushed him away and gritted her teeth as she looked at him. "Oh, look at what the cat has dragged in. I knew you'd be back around here. Just do one and leave me alone."

Mandy shot a look over at Harry and turned back around. Jona was on the wind-up, his voice was loud. "You wasn't saying that when you was on the phone begging me to come around and shag you was you?"

Mandy chuckled and held her head back. "Give your head a shake, you dickhead, as if that really happened. I wouldn't piss on you if you were on fire you Clampett."

Jona was on a roll, he had everyone laughing in the pub he was a right nutter. A lovable rogue. "Listen, baggy gash, you will never get anyone who's as good as me in bed, so just deal with it and ask me to come back."

Mandy was bright red, this guy was making a mockery out of her and the punters were all laughing. She coughed and cleared her throat, she had to up her game, there was no way this muppet was embarrassing her any more. "Are you right in the head nipper nob, I would rather play with myself than have your dead slug inside me again. Get over me and move on."

Jona wasn't playing anymore and he switched, he'd cried tears over this woman, lots of tears. And, at one point he had been at an all-time low and even thought about ending his life because of her, it was only the smack that kept him going in his hour of need. He was raging. Jona was sweating, wet patches under his arms and droplets of sweat dripping down the side of his face. He'd not scored today and he was doing his best to go cold turkey. Harry would have kicked him to the kerb if he'd have known he was on the brown, he hated the drug with a passion and vowed after his own brother's death from heroin he would never have any dealings with the drug again, not even friends who were on it. Jona smacked his chops together and sucked hard on his gums, he needed to get out of here as soon as possible. He was planning to do his rattle at his mother's house, locked away from the world but looking at him now it was going to be hard. Jona had a habit, he needed to score. He poked Mandy in her cheek, the skin sunk in and he was using force. "Mandy, you better watch your back. I told you what would happen to you when I got out of jail, so all I'm saying is watch your back, sleep tight, slapper. It's only a matter of time until I come for you." Mandy was scared, you could see it in her eyes, this man meant business and she knew from now on she'd have to tread carefully. Jona was a man of his word and it was only a matter of time before he set the record straight.

Tina was sat on the wall facing the park, she was waiting for someone, her eyes looked swelled and she was sneezing constantly, her hay fever was playing up again. Wiping her nose with her tissue, she could see Preston approaching. Tina looked like she'd made the effort to get ready today, her hair was tied up in a neat ponytail and her make-up was on. "So, what's so urgent that you need to speak to me?" Preston said with a smirk on his face.

Tina inhaled deeply and all of a sudden she sneezed, her eyes were watering. "It's nothing urgent. I just thought we could hook up for a bit," Tina shot her eyes about the area. "Where's Callum anyway? He's not rang me for days. I think he's seen his arse with me or something."

Preston sat down on the wall next to Tina. Her perfume was strong and it reminded him of vanilla ice-cream. "I don't know what's up with our kid these days, he's gone proper weird. He sleeps most of the day, and only comes alive at night."

Tina shrugged her shoulders. "He was at my house again last night bagging up. My mam sits with him too. You know what she's like, she loves a bit of company. I just stayed upstairs out of the way, I can't be arsed with him anymore, he does my head in."

Preston moved closer to her, he knew he was playing with fire, but that didn't deter him. He wanted a piece of Tina and by the looks of things she wanted a piece of him too. Tina was in no way shy. She looked him straight in the eye and licked her lips slowly, teasing. "So, what about me and you then? You know you want me. I can tell by the way you look at me." Preston nodded, he couldn't deny it, she was right. Callum wasn't interested in her anyway, he'd told his brother he was banging somebody else, an older woman he'd said, so, she was fair game wasn't she?

Preston pulled her up from the wall. "Do you want to go for something to eat then, we can go to a café in Harpurhey near the market. It's not on top in there and nobody will see us."

Tina placed her hands on her hips, she was annoyed. "Ay, I'm not hiding from anyone so get that thought right out of your head. If we're seeing each other, then we're seeing each other. I'm not ducking and diving for no-one, not even your brother."

Preston blew a laboured breath, he went nose to nose with her. Her hot sweet breath was in his face and he seemed lost in the moment. They shared their first hot, passionate kiss. They were eager for each other's bodies, lusting for it, gagging for it. Tina took his hand in hers. "Come on, let's go to my mate's house. I don't need anything to eat, I just need you."

Preston was buzzing, this was a result for him. He never had to put any ground work in; he was going straight in for the kill. It was a good job she didn't want anything to eat because he only had a ten pound note to his name, the rest of the money he'd earned had gone to the cunts he'd owed money to. He didn't have a pot to piss in anymore, he was always skint. Preston was doing well paying the Collins back what he owed them. He'd told Ben straight that he wanted his five grand paid as soon as possible, he didn't want any connection with what his brother owed. Ben had already warned Callum about paying him late and on a few occasions now he'd been short, fifty or sixty quid each time. Preston had his head screwed on, when this debt was paid, he was getting his own drug circle running. Not smack though, he'd never touch it again after this. Every day he had to watch people scoring from him, kids as young as thirteen craving a hit from the drug, it was so wrong. There was a lad he served up called Pauly and he was only fifteen. He'd been on the gear for over a year. Preston met him through a friend and he was a good punter to have, over eighty quid a day he spent on smack, or more if he could get the money for it. He was a raging bag-head. Of course Pauly had a story behind him and one night Preston had listened to the kid talk about his life in detail. It was such a shame, his story was heart-wrenching. The kid had been abused and battered from his mother's boyfriends. He just got on his toes and left. His accent was different than a Manchester one, kind of a Yorkshire accent, carrot-crunching land. Preston felt sorry for the lad and even though he was still supplying him with drugs he did bring him some leaflets about getting clean and getting help. Pauly just stuck the leaflets in his back pocket. You could tell he would never read the information he'd been given. He was too far gone for that. He was a drug-addict with only one thing on his mind - scoring.

Tina worded her friend up when they got to the house. Her mate just went straight into the living room and Tina led Preston to the bedroom. The house stank of weed and as Preston passed a bedroom on the landing he could see a small grow in one of the rooms. Fucking hell, everyone was growing weed on this estate be it one plant or twenty, everyone was on a little earner. Tina jumped onto the bed and kicked her shoes off. "We're alright to chill here for a bit. My mate's alright, she's going out now anyway so we have this gaff to ourselves."

Preston took his jacket off, you could still see bruises on his body but they were fading now, there were yellow marks under his skin. Preston had always fancied Tina. She was everything he'd ever wanted in a girl; pretty, funny, and a great sense of humour. He looked at her and nodded his head. "I haven't got any money you know.

I'm on my arse, so if you're after any cash you're fighting a losing battle." ·

Tina had a face like a smacked arse. "I'm not bothered about any money, Preston, what makes you think that?" Tina was so hard-faced; she had more front than Blackpool. She looked serious as she continued. I think she even believed she was telling the truth. "I like nice things Preston, but don't we all? Yeah, I've been with lads before who looked after me, but it's not all about the money for me, it's about getting to know a person and respecting them and all that."

Preston was impressed, she knew how to wrap any man around her little finger, she was a conniving bitch. Preston twisted the piece of hair that was dangling on her cheeks. He smiled and leaned over towards her. The betrayal began. He was in too deep now and there was no turning back. Preston unzipped his jeans as the kiss intensified, he was a Judas.

CHAPTER FOURTEEN

Susan Collins looked haggard, she'd lost weight too. Her clothes were hanging off her. Kenzo was sat on the sofa and they were both watching TV. Susan seemed in a world of her own and every now and then she wiped her eyes. Peter walked into the room and plonked down next to his sister, he smelt of alcohol and was ready to pick a fight. "Why aren't you with your boyfriend tonight shag-bag?"

Kenzo rolled her eyes at her mother and ignored him. Susan was watching her son from the corner of her eye and she was ready to pounce on him the moment he laid one finger on her daughter. Peter had always been handy. He'd been the same when his mother had met the love of her life. Trevor Bell was everything she was looking for in a man and Peter put a stop to it from day one. Susan had never really forgiven him for this and she often threw it in his face in any argument they had. Peter Collins had been the man of the house for a long time and even though he was older now, the thought of another man with his mother made his blood boil. He'd seen the way they treated her in the past and heard her crying when they beat her half to death.

Susan growled at her son. "Just go and get in bleeding bed will you, you're pissed." Susan wished she'd kept her mouth shut...

Peter bolted up from his seat and stood raging in front of them both. "Me, sleep, are you having a laugh or what mother? I've not slept properly since our John has been gone. Harry Jarvis is having us over left, right and fucking centre and we're doing fuck all to put it right. Well, mother, things are going to start to change. An eye for an eye and all that. Blood is going to be spilled and it won't be our blood this time, it will be theirs."

Susan snapped, months of emotions were stored up and now it was time to blow. She'd lost a son because of this; her blue-eyed boy, her world. It was all Peter's fault, he was the leader. He was the one who always wanted more, he was so greedy. "They're just words Peter, you're full of shit just like your dad was. Big dreams, that will never come true. If you were going to do anything about Harry Jarvis it would have been done already. So, do yourself a favour and stop talking out of your arse and do something about it or sit back fucking down, you clown."

Kenzo covered her mouth with her hand. Susan was letting rip and holding nothing back. She'd been down for months and very rarely spoke, but now she had the wind back in her sails and she put her son right back in his place.

Peter wobbled about and got his cigarettes from the table. "That little slag there isn't helping matters. I bet she's the fucking mole who's telling them everything," he shot a look at her and gritted his teeth tightly together. "Let me find out it's you Kenzo and I swear I'll burn you alive. Just one word I have to hear and you're gone, do you hear me, fucking gone."

Susan had heard enough of his drunken talk. She placed both her hands on her hips and stood in front of Kenzo. "Listen, bleeding cock of play school, you won't touch one hair on her head. What kind of a man speaks to his sister like that anyway, where's the respect?"

Peter blew smoke in his mother's face. "Respect, for her. Mother she's a dirty sperm bank, do you know what they are saying about her?" His eyes were wide open as he bent down to his sister still sitting on the sofa. "There saying she's a coke whore, a dirty fucking sniff-head."

Kenzo had heard enough, she was scared of Peter yes, but she wasn't standing for this, no way. They all had secrets and she made sure he was aware of his own little guilty pleasures. "I don't touch cocaine at all mam, just ignore him. He's the one who's on the Charlie not me. He sells it, what do you expect?" Kenzo's head jerked with speed to the other side of the sofa. The sound of the slap filled the room. A large hand print was on the side of her face and she was holding it tightly.

Susan rolled her sleeves up and jumped on her son's back. She could fight too; she'd learned that from her five brothers when she was growing up. Susan's fist dug into the side of her son's head and he was doing his best to fight her off. The look in his eyes were menacing and if Ben and Connor hadn't have come inside the room Peter would have set about his own mother, his head was gone. "Fucking hell bro, what the fuck is going down, get your hands off her now. What the fuck do you think you're playing at?"

Ben held his brother back, spit was hanging from the corner of his mouth and he was struggling to break free. "She attacked me, trying to save that bint there, she was. Ben, tell her now to stop seeing Matty. It's her who's telling him where all our shit is, I'm sure of it."

Connor rubbed the top of his sister's head and he was ready to fight with Peter. The family was falling apart and the Collins brothers' reign looked like it was nearly over. Ben settled everyone down and sent his mother to bed. Kenzo followed her, there was no way she was staying downstairs with Peter, he was potty and couldn't be trusted. Ben shot a look over at Connor, they knew if Peter tried to attack any of them they would become a tag team and bring him down. They watched him like a hawk. He was a snidey bastard and could have struck at any time. Ben tickled the end of his chin, he was thinking.

"We need something that Jarvis loves; we need something close to him, we need to find his jugular."

Connor cracked his knuckles, "What about his wife, let's take her."

Peter was slurring his words and kicked his shoes off. "No, I want something else, has he got any kids?"

Connor hunched his shoulders. They all Knew Harry Jarvis well, but his family was unknown to them. Harry always kept them away from any limelight.

Ben licked his lips, "Let me do some research, if he's got kids then they're going on the missing list. If this tosser wants war; I'll give him fucking war."

Peter lay down on the sofa and looped his arms above his head. This was a good plan and at least now they would be back in the game. Connor rubbed his hands together. "Get on this lads, I've heard Ray Clough has been banging Harry's wife. Word on the street is that he's got on his toes and fucked off once Harry found out. I saw Regina, his wife, last night and she was on the hunt for him."

Ben chuckled and high-fived his brother, the sound of them slapping hands in the air filled the room. "That's women for you isn't it mate, they can't be trusted, fucking none of them." Peter closed his eyes, tomorrow was another day and the thought of hitting Harry where it hurt made him relax. Connor and Ben sat counting cash at the table, today had been a good day.

★

Jona walked the streets of Manchester in search of drugs. He'd been out for the last few hours searching. No matter how much he tried to fight his craving he couldn't do it, he needed to score. He was fighting hard with his habit but it had him by the balls and it wasn't letting go. Heroin was his master now and judging by the sweat rolling down his forehead, he was a prisoner to the drug and would do anything to get it, he was rattling. Jona walked to Tavistock square in Harpurhey. If you needed anything illegal this was the place to get it. Jona stood still and clocked some men sat on a wall outside a pub. Pulling his hood up he walked up to them with caution. Callum looked shocked when he saw Jona. This was his dad's mate and he would have bubbled him for sure for selling gear. He dipped his head low and hoped Jona wouldn't notice him. Too late, he patted the top of his head. "Alright lad, how's it going? Fuck me you've grown up, you was just a nipper the last time I saw you."

Callum smiled, he was edgy and hoped he would leave him soon. Jona sat on the wall and bummed a cigarette off him. This wasn't going to be easy, Jona needed drugs and Callum could have answered his question there and then but he had a dilemma, did he admit to the kid that he had a habit, or walk away without any drugs, he was desperate.

Callum was biting his fingernails. There was no way he wanted Jona to know he was licking shot. Callum's mobile phone started to ring; he stood up and walked away slowly. Jona listened carefully, result, his search was over. He had the kid by the short and curlies. They both had secrets and now Jona felt he could reveal his to Callum. He knew how Harry felt about smack and if he knew his son was selling shit he would have ended his life. Jona licked his lips slowly and swallowed hard. "I need some brown, can you sort me out or what?"

Callum was edgy, this was a nightmare. He thought for a few seconds before he answered. "Yeah I can, but this stays between us. If my old man knows I'm serving you up, or anyone else for that fact, my life is over."

Jona rubbed his hands together, "Nar, our secret, I swear my lips are sealed."

Callum was roasting too and he confessed to Jona that he was on the shit as well. Jona didn't seem to give a flying fuck, he smirked and pulled Callum up from the wall. "It's all good then isn't it? Come on I'm rattling. We can share it." They walked off together and headed to Jona's for a toot. They shared a secret now, a dirty, filthy secret that could only end in tears.

Jona got the silver foil ready and prepared the drugs. He wanted to know who this kid was selling for. Who in the right mind would have let one of Harry Jarvis's boys sell smack. He sat down and shot a look to Callum. "Who are you selling for anyway?"

Callum was already stoned and didn't care who he told, he loved bigging himself up and tried to act the hard man. "I sell for the Collins brothers. Do you know them, fucking nutters they are?"

Jona nearly dropped down dead, what a small world this was? Callum had no idea of the war between the two families; he was oblivious to any bad blood. Jona blew a laboured breath, this was bad news. The shit was going to hit the fan for sure. Suddenly Jona had a cunning look in his eye; perhaps this wasn't that bad after all. The two of them smoked the drugs, high as kites they were. Jona lay on the sofa staring into space, he was wrecked. His eyes rolled as the drugs took over his body. Callum now had another drug buddy, a friend who held his secret and could ruin his life at any second he wanted too. The music played in the background. Jona loved The Stone Roses, it made him feel chilled.

CHAPTER FIFTEEN

Sally sat watching the clock tick away; she was waiting for someone and kept blowing her breath as she picked at her fingernails. Sat in her house she walked to the mirror and re-applied her lipstick. The colour was a nice light pink, nothing too much, just enough to give her lips some colour. Someone was knocking at the front door; she gave one last glance at the mirror and headed into the hallway. Peter Collins stood there with one hand resting on the doorframe, he was such a cocky fucker, full of himself he was. "Are you ready or what?"

Sally smiled and fluttered her eyelashes. Her heart was beating ten to the dozen. Peter was her secret lover and had been for over six months. She knew how Gill would act if she got a whiff of her new man so she kept it quiet. It just sort of happened, it was nothing she'd planned. At first she was seeing John, Peter's younger brother, but since he'd been murdered the two of them just fell into each other's arms. Peter looked rough, he was unshaven and his hair needed a good cut. Sally ran into the front room and grabbed her coat. "Where we off to? I hope we're going for something to eat, I'm starving," Sally asked. Peter rubbed the bottom of his stomach, he'd lost a lot of weight lately and the beer was the only thing that was feeding him. They both headed to the car, they were laughing and joking.

Kenzo stood at the bus stop and couldn't believe her eyes. She rubbed her knuckles into the corner of them to check she wasn't seeing things. "Oh, now this is a turn up for the books brother," she hissed. "You sly, cunning bastard!" Kenzo hid away in the bus stop as they drove by in the car, she dipped her head low. This information was going to earn her some brownie points for sure. Sally was a dark horse and when Harry found out she was a spy in the camp the shit was going to hit the fan for sure. Kenzo licked her lips slowly as she waited for the bus. This was great news, she couldn't wait to spill the beans.

Harry sat on the sofa looking at his wife, staring. She seemed to be getting better but he could still see the love for Ray Clough in her eyes, she just couldn't hide it. They'd tried to repair the relationship, but it didn't seem the same as it was. It was broken and looked like it was over for good. Harry moved closer to Gill, he was doing his best to make her love him again. "Shall we go out for something to eat tonight, a country pub, maybe. You used to like going up in the hills when we were younger."

Gill smiled, he was right. Back in the day she loved her husband with all her heart and any time they spent together she was grateful for. He was her world back then and she would have died for him. Gill had changed now though, the years he'd been away had made her turn into a different woman. She had a heart of stone now, and didn't believe a happy ending existed anymore. The kids were grown up and she felt alone, worthless. Ray Clough had made her feel alive again, like a woman; attractive and sexy. Gill still wanted to speak to Harry about his other woman, she was just waiting for the right moment. It had been playing on her mind for weeks and now she was ready to confront him. Stroking a piece of hair at the side of her face, she coughed to clear her throat. Harry was aware she was going to say something and looked her straight in the eyes.

"So, you know about me with Ray Clough, who is your fancy piece then?" Harry was taken back, he didn't expect this, not now anyway, she looked at him and urged him to answer. "I know about her so don't think I don't," she stressed.

This was getting too much for Harry, he was backed into a corner with nowhere to run or hide. "It's a load of shit love, I've never had eyes for any woman while I've been with you. Don't get me wrong, I've had my chances but I've always turned them down."

Gill held her head back and chuckled. "And, you expect me to believe that? I wasn't born yesterday you know. Come on, let's put our cards on the table here and clear the air. You know about me, so tell me about you."

There was no way Harry was ever going to admit who he'd slept with. It was a mistake, a big mistake a long time ago and he'd hated himself for it straight after it. "I'm not having this conversation Gill, are we going out for something to eat or what?"

Gill bolted up from her chair and her temper blew. "And, here was me feeling all guilty about Ray when all along you'd cheated too. I thought you said it was me and you forever Harry? What happened to that load of shit?"

Harry couldn't help himself anymore. He'd kept his mouth shut for long enough. Night after night he'd lay next to his wife and not once did he mention a word about her affair. It was hard, God it was hard for him even when he kissed her red hot lips he could taste the betrayal and forced himself to continue. Not now though, she'd opened a can of worms and he was getting it all out, he had to, before he drove himself crazy. "You were shagging Ray Clough while I was locked up, do you know how that makes me feel as a man," he paused and ran his fingers through his hair, dragging at it. "I have to force myself to kiss you Gill, and even during sex, I can still see him inside you. Do you know how that makes me feel inside? You were mine, all mine, and now you're soiled, dirty, unclean."

Gill was taken back by his words; she ran over to him and gripped him by the arm. "So, what are you saying, that you don't love me anymore?" She was desperate and at that moment she realised what her husband really meant to her.

Harry paced the room and grabbed his car keys from the table. "You love that prick Gill, I can see it in your eyes. What we had has gone. I tried to rebuild it but I can't. It knocks me sick to watch you slip away. I came back here to look after you when you tried to end your life in the hope we could sort things out, but I'm pissing in the wind, I realise that now. We're done Gill, over."

Gill dropped to her knees, she was so mixed up. "Harry I do love you. Don't go, please let's try and work things out. It's been hard for me you know, so fucking hard."

Harry turned to face her; he could see she was upset. He bent down and wiped the tears running down the side of her face. Looking at his wet finger he shot a look to his wife. "Are these tears for me, or for Ray?"

Gill reached her hands up to her husband. "They're for you Harry, I've been a fool, a fucking idiot. I swear to you now, we can work this out. Don't go Harry. I love you."

Harry stood looking at her for a few seconds. He started to walk to the door. Gill was pleading with him before he left. "Harry, I'll change. I'll be like I used to be. Don't give up on us, I'm so sorry."

The front door slammed and Harry was gone. Preston came downstairs and walked into the front room. Once he saw his mother still on the floor he walked over to help her up. "Mam, it's all your own doing this is. My dad's in the right. You should have kept your legs closed."

Gill jumped from the floor, her son was getting an earful now. He didn't have an ounce of respect for his mother, not one drop. "Oh fuck off out you know it all. It's your fault I even told him in the first place. Yeah, it's your fault. You split us up."

Preston was tying his shoes laces and kept his head bent down low. "Mother, you know yourself who's to blame. You're lucky you're still standing; it could have been a lot worse, so you think yourself lucky that you got off lightly. My dad must have mellowed in his old age, because back in the day he would have killed you stone dead."

Gill threw the cushion over her son's head. She knew he was right, and knew it was all her own fault, but come on, he'd cheated too, so wasn't it all fair in love and war now? She made sure she had Preston's attention. "Oh, you don't know about your dad sleeping with other women then do you? That's made you shut up hasn't it?"

Preston stood up and walked to the mirror to check his hair out. "It's different for a man, mother; men are expected to sleep about. So just deal with it. You two need to split up now and move on. I'm sick to death of hearing the arguing every night. The best thing to do is to split up. Look at you anyway, when was the last time you had your hair done? No wonder he's leaving you, you're a walking disgrace." Preston left the room and she watched him leave the house. Gill was going to shout after him, but her words were stuck in her throat, unable to come out. Gill stood with her body against the front door, shaking. Her life was a mess and she knew she'd have to make a choice, did she carry on waiting for Ray in the hope he might come back for her one day? Or did she try and make her husband love her again?

Her head was in her hands and she was sobbing. Standing to her feet she looked in the mirror in the hallway. Her reflection told her all she needed to know. Preston was right, she had let herself go. Looking around the house she sobbed, she used to be so house-proud, but now her eyes could see how much she'd let things slip. The house was dirty and stank of stale tobacco. Gill marched upstairs and looked into her wardrobe, she dug deep to find something to wear. She was going to win her husband back, no matter what. And she was going to get her life back on track. Gill slipped on her shoes and ran back down the stairs. Checking her purse for money she knew she had everything she needed to start making the changes she needed in her life. The first thing she was going to do was to go to ASDA and get some shopping in and some cleaning products. Her home was the first thing she needed to sort out. She'd not cooked a meal in ages and if there was any chance of her winning her man back, she had to show him that she was willing to change. Gill looked for her mobile phone in her handbag. She dialled a number and waited for the call to be answered. "Hiya love, it's Gill Jarvis, can you book me in today for a cut and blow and a spray tan?" She smiled as she headed to the front door with the phone still held to her ear. "Oh, thank you so much. Can I book in for my nails done too?" Gill ended the call and the dark cloud she seemed to have hanging over her head appeared to be disappearing. Everything seemed clear now, Harry was her man, he loved her with all his heart. Ray Clough had used her and if she ever saw the prick again she was going to give him a piece of her mind. Gill wanted to save her marriage and today was the start of putting all the pieces back together.

Sally leant across the table and kissed Peter Collins, slowly passionately. Her eyes were closed and you could see the hairs on the back of her neck standing on end as he gripped her face with his strong hands. Peter had had his fair share of women in the past and he was never short of any female attention. Sally just ticked all the boxes for him and somehow he just felt relaxed when he was with her. "So when are we going to tell everyone about us?" Sally whispered in an excited voice.

Peter pulled away from her and necked a mouthful of his drink. He made sure nobody was listening. "We can't do anything yet, you're part of the Jarvis clan aren't you? I've already gone ballistic at my sister for doing the same thing. I can't just announce you yet can I? I mean, have you told Harry's wife about us yet, what's her name again, Gill?"

Sally licked her lips slowly. "It's got fuck all to do with

Gill who I see. It's my life not hers. Anyway, what could she say anyway? I don't answer to nobody, especially not her."

Peter could sense some friction between the friends and he dug deeper, he wanted to know about Harry's family and what made them click. "Has Harry got kids or what, I've never heard anything about them, do they even live around here or what?"

Sally didn't realise she was letting the cat out of the bag, so she openly told him what she knew. "Harry's got two lads called Callum and Preston. They're a pair of cheeky fuckers they are. Gill's got her hands full with them. Before Harry went into prison they were as good as gold, but not anymore, gobshites they are, the bleeding pair of them, they have no respect for no one, not even their father."

Peter was listening now, the names were registering in his brain and he was asking random questions that would lead him to Harry's family. The two of them sat eating their meal. Sally was a traitor; she'd sold her friend out for her own gain. A total bitch she was, a two-faced sell out.

★

Jona sat outside Mandy's house. He was watching for any sign of life inside but there was nothing. Two hours he'd been sat there waiting to have it out with her. She was angry with him that's all, once he worked his magic on her she would let him come back, she always did. Rolling a spliff he sat on the wall waiting. He could see Mandy's neighbour walking towards him. Sheila was a busybody, she knew everyone's business and wouldn't think twice about dishing the dirt on any of her friends and family.

Jona nodded his head at her as she passed him. At first she didn't recognise him. She wouldn't have, he'd changed a lot since she'd seen him last. "Are you alright Sheila, long time no see ay?"

Sheila stopped walking and twisted her head over her shoulder. Her face dropped. "Well, fuck a duck, when did you get out Jona?"

Jona chuckled and flicked the invisible dust from his pants. "I've been out a few weeks now love, why have you missed me?"

Sheila playfully punched him in the arm. She was a middle-aged woman with the reddest hair you have ever seen in your life. It was like a beacon it was that bright. "Give us a blast of that then," she sniggered as she sat on the wall next to him. Sheila was an ex-brass and if her body hadn't folded on her she would have still being turning tricks. She was riddled with arthritis, her fingers were locked and she could barely move them. "So, why haven't you moved back in with Mandy then?"

Jona shrugged his shoulders and tried to make light of the matter. Sheila knew more than anyone how their relationship was before and knew Jona was hard work. He was a crank and could turn at the drop of a hat. Sheila took a blast of the spliff and closed her eyes, she coughed a little before she spoke. "I think Mandy's seeing Harry Jarvis now you know, he's been here on quite a few nights now, stayed over he did because his car was still here in the morning."

Jona jumped up from the wall, his fists curling at the side of his legs. "What, Harry has been sleeping with Mandy?"

Sheila checked the area and made sure nobody could

hear her grassing Harry up. "Well, yeah. I think so anyway. Keep this to yourself though I don't want my name bringing into this, you know me I like to keep myself to myself. I don't need the hassle I'm just telling you as a friend."

Jona patted her on the shoulder and passed her the last few drags of the spliff. Thinking on his feet he kept his temper. "I bet he's just been checking on her to make sure she's okay, you know while I've been banged up and all that. He's my mate you know, and that's what we do for each other isn't it?"

Sheila was having none of it, she held her head back and chuckled. "Take your head from up your arse lad, he's banging her brains out, don't tell me you don't know that already. Listen," she stretched her neck and came closer to his face. "I heard them shagging all night long through the bedroom walls, trust me, they kept me up all bleeding night."

Jona needed to get away, he was going to be sick, his face turned green and he was heaving over the wall. Sheila looked at him and realised she might have been a bit hard on him but that was her way, she told it as it was, no holding back. Taking a few minutes she jumped down from the wall and patted the dust from her legs. "Jona, if you're looking for another woman, I'm still on the market. I might be a bit overweight and that, but my mouth still works. I can still give a top blow-job if you're interested?"

Jona wanted to pummel his fists into her big fat round face, she was a filthy animal and she knocked him sick. "Nar, Sheila, thanks for the offer but I'm staying single from now on, thanks for the offer though I'll keep you in mind if I ever get desperate."

Sheila sighed and went nose-to-nose with him. "Ay, you cheeky bastard, I'm a class bird I am, just a bit out of practice that's all. Don't think for too long because I'll be gone. Anyway, keep what I've told you on the low. I don't want any comebacks. I've got enough of my own shit to deal with at the moment. Ay, have you got a bit of weed going spare there for me for tonight, just to help with my arthritis and all that? It's bleeding killing me at the moment. I don't sleep a wink you know?"

Jona dug deep in his pocket and passed her a small plastic bag. "Here, it's my last bit, but don't worry about me, I'll get some more sorted, go on take it." Sheila didn't need asking twice, she nearly ripped his hand of for it. Jona watched her leave, he gritted his teeth tightly and the top of his ears were twitching. "Payback time Jarvis, it all makes sense now, what a fucking dick I've been!" he whispered to himself. Jona started to walk off at speed. He was a man on a mission. That bastard was going to pay, nobody took the piss out of him, nobody.

Kenzo chopped out a line of cocaine on the dresser in her bedroom. She was using a twenty pound note to snort it. With her head held back you could see the drug taking effect. Kenzo was a bad sniff head, she was having a bump any chance she got. She was going to meet Matty soon and she wanted to make sure she was at her best. Her mother walked into the bedroom and shot her eyes to the traces of drugs on the drawers. At first she didn't say a word but once she was sure of what she could see she ran at her daughter like a raging bull. "Well, you dirty bastard.

I just knew you were up to something, just you wait until the lads come home you're in for it you are."

Kenzo was shocked, she thought Susan was asleep on the sofa downstairs. "Mam, just relax will you. I'm not a druggie it's just a bit of sniff. I was feeling a bit low that's all. I was thinking about our John and needed something to get me through the day."

Susan looked at her more closely. Just the mention of her son's name tore her heart into a million pieces, she hesitated. "No, don't think you're having me over lady. I know what I saw and I know you've been sniffing that shit more than once. I swear Kenzo, once the lads come home you're getting taken to our Anne's in Cheshire. You need to get away from around here, look at the state of you."

Kenzo was pleading with her mother; she fell to her knees and tried to win her over. "Mam, please, I'll sort my head out, just let me stay here, don't tell the boys please."

Susan ran to the door and held the handle with firm hands. "Not a chance lady, I'm phoning Ben now, the sooner you go the bleeding better."

The door slammed and Kenzo slammed her body on the bed crying. This was a nightmare, she'd been to her aunties before when she was younger and she knew once she got there her life would be over. It was a country village with two shops, no nightclubs, no pubs… nothing. A town filled with fucking idiots. Kenzo hung her head over the bed and looked underneath it. Stretching her body she pulled out a black sports bag. Eyes all over the room, she made sure she was safe and unzipped the bag. There was money, lots of money, inside. Kenzo ran to her wardrobe and started to fill the bag with her clothes.

There was no way he mother was sending her away, she was going to find Matty, he would put her up, he loved her surely. Kenzo threw her bag from the bedroom window and jumped onto the windowsill. She'd done this lots of times before and knew how to keep safe in her escape. Climbing down the drainpipe she held onto it with a firm grip.

A neighbour over the road clocked her and stood watching her curiously. The neighbour was a family friend and started to make her way into the garden. "I'm going to tell your mother Kenzo, does she know you're bleeding doing this or what?"

Kenzo was trying to move with speed, her hair got tangled in the branches nearby and she was struggling. "Fuck off out of the garden, you nosey cow. This is my business, so just piss off."

Nancy York, hammered on the front door; she was rapping the letterbox with speed. "Susan, hurry up. Kenzo is hanging out of the window again," she shouted. She was a right busybody. 'Plant pot' the neighbours nicknamed her. Nancy paced up and down the garden and came to stand at the bottom of the drainpipe. The front door opened just as Kenzo was landing and Susan gripped her by the scruff of the neck. "Get back here you, get back in this bleeding house." Kenzo struggled but with the help of rent a hero Nancy, Susan got her daughter back in the house. The front door was bolted and Susan ran and locked the back door taking the keys out of it. "Ben is on his way for you, do you see what you've made me do now!" Susan ranted at her neighbour who was stood watching it all with eager eyes, she loved a drama. "She's on bleeding drugs Nancy, I just caught her red-handed I did, snorting the shite up her nose."

Nancy was gobsmacked, she loved this gossip and delved deeper. "Do you mean cocaine Susan? I think they call it Charlie don't they?"

Susan snarled and whacked her daughter across the head with a flat palm. "If she was a bit younger I'd put her over my knee and smack her arse until it bleeds, she was always trouble this one Nancy, too much of her own bleeding way if you ask me."

Nancy walked over to Kenzo and started to study her in detail, she was so over the top. "Oh, her eyes do look funny Susan, she looks off her head, should we lock her in a cupboard or something, she might attack us."

Kenzo stood up, this woman was doing her head in, she was making things ten times worse than what they were already. "Listen you beaky bitch, keep your nose out of my business. Nobody likes you around here anyway. Why don't you just fuck off back to where you came from before my foot goes right up your arse?"

Nancy rubbed at her arms and her face dropped. "See what I mean Susan, she's off her bleeding head, I think she's hallucinating."

Susan looked at Kenzo and chewed on her gums, she could deal with her on her own, she was old yeah, but she could still throw a few punches, a craft she'd learned a long time ago when she was with a violent partner. She had to learn to fight the hard way and even until this day she could still pack a punch. Banging on the window, loud banging, someone was shouting outside. Nancy sat down and made herself comfortable, there was no way she wanted to miss this, no way in the world. There was nothing much on the TV today and this was a drama all by itself, she folded her arms across her chest.

"Here's our Ben now," Susan hissed. "We'll see what he has to say about his sister being a bleeding drug addict."

Kenzo snapped and stood up pacing the floor. "Mother for the last time, I'm not a drug addict, it's just a bit of sniff that's all. Everyone does it, it's not just me."

Susan ran to open the door she was shouting over her shoulder. "Oh, so you're a follower now are you, never in my whole life did I expect you to turn out like this. You're going from here, it's for the best."

Nancy piped in with her two pennies-worth from the corner of the room. "I agree Susan, the sooner she moves away from here the better. It's getting terrible around here these days. It's not like it used to be I can tell you."

Kenzo dropped to her knees, hands ragging through her hair in desperation. She could hear talking in the hallway, whispering. Then footsteps headed towards the door and rustling sounds. You could smell Ben's aftershave before you could see him, a strong musky scent. Kenzo could feel his presence before she'd even seen him. He was breathing heavily at her side. Nancy was on the edge of her seat. Her eyes were wide open and she was loving every minute of this.

Ben's feet were near Kenzo as she lifted her head up. Her eyes were red raw and she was hoping he might take some pity on her. Peter would have never have done this, he would have wasted her there and then, but Ben was unpredictable, she couldn't work him out. Holding her hands up towards him she pleaded with him. "Ben, I swear to you it was just a bit of blow. I don't do it all the time, just when I'm feeling down. My mam's going on as if I'm addicted to it. I'm not honest."

Nancy stood up to get a better view, she was hoping that Ben would kick off, but even she wasn't sure of his next move. Susan came to his side now and she was smoking a cigarette, her hands were shaking and you could see she was at the end of her tether. "Just take her to Anne's, Ben. She tried running away you know. Nancy caught her climbing out of the window, if she wouldn't have seen her she could have been on her way to get some more drugs or something."

Nancy stood tall and she felt like the hero of the hour. Ben growled at her, and shot a look to his mother. "I think it's time for Nancy to leave, this is family business and we don't want the world and his wife knowing before the day's over. Thanks Nancy, for helping out, but you can go now."

Nancy was gutted, totally gutted, she wanted to see this girl get what was coming to her and now it was all coming to a head she'd been carted. She moved closer to Susan hoping to get a second chance to stay. "I can bang the kettle on Ben, I mean, look at your mother, she's a nervous wreck, I should make you a nice cup of tea darling to help calm you down?"

Ben's voice moved up a level and Nancy knew her time here was over. "Mother, let her out will you, while I sort this shit out." Susan hurried Nancy into the hallway. She was walking at a snails pace and still trying to look back over her shoulder trying to see what was going on. Ben made sure the door was closed and gripped his sister by the throat, her eyes were bulging out from the sockets and she was turning blue. Ben just stared at her and clenched his teeth together tightly. "You're nothing but a dirty slut, who got you on the Charlie ay, was it Matty?

Come on, just tell me and he's a dead man."

There was no way Kenzo was answering him, she couldn't talk, her feet were off the floor and you could see them wriggling about as he squeezed her windpipe tighter. Susan was back in the room and she covered her mouth with her hand as she witnessed the violence between her two children. "I'll end your fucking life Kenzo. Just tell me now who got you on the shit." This girl was going to die any second now, her head was flopping about to the side and she only had a couple of breaths left in her body. Kenzo nodded her head and that was enough for Ben to let her live. Dark red marks around her neck were visible and they were turning purple with every second that passed.

Susan ran over to her as her body collapsed onto the floor. Ben dragged her away and pushed her onto the sofa. "Leave her mother, just fucking leave her." Susan sat on the sofa and she was rocking to and fro, her legs were shaking. She wanted her son to help her out but not like this, not by trying to end Kenzo's life. Ben kicked his foot into the side of the black sports bag. "What's inside this," he asked. Susan shot her eyes over to Kenzo.

"It's hers, that's what she was taking with her when she tried to run away." Ben sat down and dragged the bag near his feet. Slowly unzipping it he stuck his hand inside it to have a root about. Clothes, lots of tops and jeans, his face changed and he pulled out a wad of cash.

Susan was gobsmacked, she grabbed the money from his hands and ran at her daughter. "Where the hell is this money from lady? Don't give me any cock and bull story either, you better start talking now before I let Ben finish you off."

Ben threw the bag over to his sister and it hit her in the face. "Well," he shouted. "Where the fuck did you get this money from?"

Kenzo was in a panic, she was holding her throat and still gagging for breath, she had no other option than to pretend to faint, she could never answer his question, not now, not ever. Falling to the ground she faked her consciousness, she was a great actress too, she was giving a performance any leading lady would have been proud of, she deserved an Oscar. Ben just sat back thinking whereas Susan was running around like a blue-arsed fly.

"Oh, fucking hell, what do we do, do we phone an ambulance or what? Ben I think you've killed her."

Ben could see she was still breathing, he never flinched. "Just sit down mam, throw a cup of water on her she'll be fine in a few minutes." Ben knew when someone was dead and when they were faking it, it was his line of work and he'd seen men die right in front of his eyes, his sister was going nowhere. He knew she would be awake soon. Susan ran in the kitchen and filled a glass with cold water, as she ran back into the front room it was spilling all over the carpet. Trickles of cold water were placed on Kenzo's forehead. Susan was pouring small amounts of water onto her cupped hand and patting it on Kenzo's head. "Just fucking launch it at her mother, fuck me, give it here." Ben bolted up from his chair and took the glass in his hand. With a quick flick of the wrist he flung the water in his sister's face. She was awake now and knew her nightmare would start again.

Susan was at her side and she was stroking the top of her head, she knew this wasn't going to end well and pleaded with her to tell the truth. "Just tell him where the money is from and it's all over, just tell him for crying out loud. You can just go to Anne's and all this will be in the past, don't make things hard, just tell him."

Kenzo was desperate, her mouth was moving but no words were coming out, she had to make something up. "The money is Matty's. I was keeping hold of it for him. I need to give it him back today. Ben, I'm telling the truth honest, the money is off a graft he did and he wanted me to keep hold of it to keep it safe. We are going on holiday with it. Matty said so himself, just me and him."

Ben bolted up from his seat, this was unbelievable and he couldn't believe his sister was being had over. "Are you right in the head, he's not taking you anywhere, he's just got you holding money for him so it's safe. Matty doesn't give a shit about you, you're just a shag."

Susan dipped her head low, this was filthy talk and she hated that Ben was so blunt with his words. Kenzo pleaded with her brother. "He loves me Ben; he's told me we are going to get a place together soon. That's what the money is for, it's for our future."

Ben had heard enough, he zipped the bag up and banged his clenched fist on the table. "This money is going straight back to the prick, does he think you're some kind of clown," Ben held a cunning look in his eyes. "In fact, he's getting fuck all, this money can go back into the family funds, it was him and his boys who had our grow away so let's call it payback. He's not getting a carrot off us. If he wants his money back, then let him come and get it." He let out a menacing laugh and looked at his mother. "Right, I'll take her to Anne's. No more drugs for you Kenzo, you can stay at her house until things have blown over and that means you sorting yourself out. Do you hear me, let me hear one whisper that you are taking that shit again and I'll make sure you never do it again. I'll chop your fucking nose off, do you get me?" Kenzo knew there was no point in arguing with her brother, he was more than serious and she knew by his past he was more than capable of cutting her nose off. She'd seen men ear's in boxes before now and knew her brother was a sick animal when it came to fighting, he was a lunatic.

Kenzo dipped her head as the car eased out onto the road. Susan stood at the gate watching her leave. It was for her own good, she was a lost cause and staying around here would just make things worse. Susan walked back inside the house and slammed the door. Her life was up in the air and she couldn't cope any longer. With one son already dead and a daughter addicted to drugs, she knew the worst was yet to come. Harry Jarvis and his men had a lot to answer for and if she'd have had a gun she would have shot the bastard right through his heart to save her family from anymore tears.

Kenzo sat in the car crying, she'd secretly texted Matty and told him what had happened. In her heart she was hoping he would come and rescue her but she wasn't holding her breath. Matty would move on without her for sure. Everything she planned had gone to pot and now the money was gone, there was no way she could do the things she wanted. Watching her brother drive she studied him closely, she could just grab him from behind and make him pull over, was she strong enough though? As they hit the motorway she sat forward in her seat, she was waiting like a preying lioness to make her move. It was a do or die moment. Kenzo jumped forward as they came to a junction and gripped Ben from behind, the car swerved and just missed another car. Ben was trying to fight his sister off but before he knew it, she'd bailed from the car. Cars skidded as she tried to make her way to the hard shoulder. Ben was trying to gain control of the car and chasing his sister was the last thing on his mind. Watching her run up a hill through his rear-view mirror he knew she was safe. He chuckled to himself and mumbled under his breath.

"The girls got balls, don't worry Kenzo, I'll catch up with you soon and then you'll see what I'm all about. Say goodbye to your nose you coke whore, big brother is hot on your trail now." Ben drove to the next junction and headed back home. He knew his sister would turn up soon enough, all he had to do was watch Matty and he knew she wouldn't be far behind him. It was all just a waiting game and he had all the time in the world to wait for his sister.

CHAPTER SIXTEEN

Gill looked very different today. She was dolled up. Her skin had changed colour too, she'd had a spray tan. A nice golden touch, that made her look healthy, nothing too harsh, not orange like some false tans, it was just enough to look like the sun had kissed her body. Gill was smiling for a change and she was singing along to the radio. She'd either overdosed on Prozac or she was really happy for once. The door opened and in walked Harry, she'd been waiting for him for hours, clock watching. "I've made you some tea love, steak pie, your favourite."

Harry inhaled and his nostrils flared, he looked like he wanted to tell her to shove it up her arse but he remained quiet. The house smelt clean and fresh, it smelt of lemons. Quickly looking at his wife he could see something had changed in her, he examined her further. Her hair was lighter, a lot blonder and her make-up was fresh, she looked stunning. "I'm not that hungry. I've had something to eat while I was out." Harry could see the disappointment in her eyes and tried to make her feel better. "I'll have it later on though. Anyway, what's with the new you. I mean, you've cleaned the house, made my tea, and," he paused, "you've had a make- over."

Gill smirked, he'd noticed her again. He noticed every little effort she'd made. "Harry, I want us back to how it used to be. Just me and you, no one else. I'll never let you down again. I cross my heart and hope to die if I'm lying to you."

This was a bit too much for Harry to take in, too much too soon. He had to take things step-by-step. He didn't trust her anymore and wondered why all of a sudden she was up his arse, begging his love. "Gill, thanks for trying to change, but things are different now, I've changed. You didn't want to know me when I got out of the nick. For fucks sake, you tried doing yourself in because you wanted him instead of me, do you know how much that hurts?" He nodded his head at her, confident in what he was saying. "Say I've moved on now anyway, let's say somebody else loves me and I have feelings for them."

Gill held her hand around her throat, suffocating. She closed her eyes and took a deep breath. "Harry, don't say things like that, if you didn't want me you would have left a long time ago," she panicked and went towards him. "We can start again, a fresh start. No more lies."

Harry sat down and popped a cigarette in the side of his mouth, he was thinking. "I do love you Gill but let's face it, it will never be the same again, ever. Like I told you before, you're not my Gill anymore, you're his. You belong to Ray Clough."

Gill was spitting feathers. He was just pretending she knew he was. Pulling a black dress from her shopping bag she held it up to him. "I've got a nice dress for tonight if you want to take me out. We can call it a date, let's just go out as friends and see if we still get on together. We used to love each other's company. Harry, like you said before, all we need is each other."

Callum walked into the room and stared at them both. He looked ill, his complexion was grey and he seemed to have lost a lot of weight. His cheekbones were sticking out at the side of his face. Harry watched him anxiously, his son was always so clean and tidy, what the hell had happened to him? As he passed him he could smell his body odour, he stank of stale sweat and cat piss, in fact he smelt like arse. Gill could smell him too and her face changed. "You better get in the bath pongy. Phew... you stink. I've cleaned this house from top to bottom and you stink like a camel's arse. Where the hell have you been to end of smelling like that?" Callum seemed in a world of his own, distant. This wasn't right; he loved an argument and never admitted when he was in the wrong. He sat on the sofa and just played with his hands, his head was dipped low. Harry questioned him too; he was worried about him and tried to get to the bottom of his problems. Perhaps they all needed a bonding session together, some family time.

"Shall we all go out for tea," Harry said. Gill was rubbing her hands together; she was back in the circle of trust. Harry loved her again or so she thought.

Callum shook his head. "Nar, sack that, I'm not hungry, just you two go. You can do your bonding and all that shit, just leave me here to chill."

Gill didn't seem bothered that he didn't want to come out with them, but Harry was. He went to his son's side and tickled him hoping to make him laugh. It was only when he dug his fingers into his waist did he realise how much weight his son had lost. Harry pulled twenty pounds from the wad of cash he had in his pocket. "Here, if you're not coming with us, take Tina out and spoil her for a change, go for a scran or something. What's happened with her anyway she's not been here for ages, have you two fell out?"

Callum tried to put on a smile but his father knew he was lying. "Oh, she's a shag-bag she is, I've carted her. I can't be arsed with all her drama anymore. I'm sick of her blowing hot and cold all the time." Callum's phone started to ring, he flicked his eyes to the screen and stood to answer it. He went into the garden to take the call. Harry held his ear to the window and he was listening. He could hear Callum arguing with someone. "I've got your money, don't worry about it. I know it was one hundred pound short but I'll have it sorted by weekend, just chill out." Harry watched his son return to his seat. He raised his eyes and tackled him. "Who do you owe money to now?" Callum swallowed hard, he knew his father had heard the call. "It's just some geezer who I bought a motorbike off some time ago. It was knackered when I bought it and I told him straight I wasn't paying the asking price anymore. He's getting nothing the muppet anyway. I've told him to stop ringing me too otherwise I'll twist the fucker up."

Harry screwed his face up. Did Callum really think he was that thick not to know what was going on? He'd been in this game too long now and he smelt a rat. Gill grabbed Harry by the arm. "It looks like it's just me and you love, shall I run you a bath??" she moved closer to his ear and whispered. "I can get in with you if you want. I'll wash your back."

Harry smirked, she was trying too hard and she was making him feel sick in the pit of his stomach, she was desperate. He nodded his head; he wanted her gone so he could have few words with Callum. "Yeah, you go and run the bath and I'll be up in a minute." When Gill disappeared Harry turned to face Callum. "Right you, cut the bullshit and tell me what's going on. I wasn't born yesterday and I know you're into something hooky. Fucking start talking." Callum was in a deep trance, he was slavering from his mouth and slurring his words, whatever he'd had was now taking effect. It could have been the pills Jona had given him, chill pills he said they were, but looking at him now they were more than that, he was off his rocker. Harry raised his voice and Callum turned his head slowly trying to focus. He was constantly itching at his skin, really scratching at it. Harry repeated himself, and sat waiting for an answer. It was a lost cause, there was no way in the world Callum could hold a conversation, he was nearly asleep. Harry grabbed his face in his hands, squeezing hard at the skin. "I'll tell you what lad, me and you are going to be falling out if you don't sort yourself out. I mean it son, you need to get your head together and sort your shit out."

Callum smiled, eyes half open. Harry studied his face, brown powder on his teeth, stuck to them at the front. Harry drained of any colour; he'd seen this look before from his own brother. Grabbing his mouth he peeled his lips open. Callum was floppy and he made no effort to stop his old man from doing what he was doing. Harry grabbed him by the hair and went nose to nose with him. "Son, tell me now are you on smack?"

Callum chuckled, a low half- hearted giggle. "Dad, I'm on fuck all. I'm just tired. Fuck me, nothing I do is ever right in this house. I may as well be six foot under."

Harry rubbed at his arms, goose pimples started to appear all over his skin, even the hairs on the back of his neck stood on end as he waited for the answer. "Are you on gear? Just tell me the truth!"

Callum was at rock bottom and he knew his father was a lifeline, he owed money out all over the place and knew sooner or later Ben and Connor would come looking for him. He hesitated before he answered. "Dad, it's my life and I'll sort my shit out myself, just piss off out with my mam and let me get my head down. I'm not on fucking heroin, are you mad. I've just had a weed that's all. Pucka shit it was too, its blew my brains out."

Harry knew he was lying, weed never made anyone act like this. He knew in his heart that his son was on the hard stuff. Callum fell onto the sofa and curled up in a small ball, his mouth was open and his eyes flickered rapidly as he tried to find sleep. Harry just sat staring at him, he was no fool. He knew an addict when he saw one. Why hadn't he noticed this before now? All the signs were there, right in front of his eyes for him to see, he'd been a fool. Harry left the room and you could see a tear forming in the corner of his eye. He'd lost his own brother to the demon drug and in a way he never really got over his death. He dealt in drugs yes, but never the brown, never heroin. He never touched it and made sure he never got involved with selling it. He had standards. When it came to dealing smack he always turned his back on it no matter how much money it would earn him.

Harry headed upstairs and started to take his clothes off. He wrapped a towel around his waist and walked inside the bathroom. Gill was sat in the bath with four candles lit on each side of the bath, it looked calm and inviting. The bubbles from the bath were floating on top of her body and she was stroking her hand over the top of them. "Get in, it's lovely and warm. I'll get near the taps if you want?" Harry's mind was elsewhere and all he wanted to do was have a quick dip. Gill had other things on her mind though, the moment he sat in the bath she was all over him like a rash. Her lips touched his slowly and he closed his eyes as she opened her mouth to kiss him. In his mind all he could see was Ray Clough'. Would he ever get this vision out of his head? He was tormented by it.

Gill straddled him and she was sat on his penis hoping to bring it to life. Stroking her fingers slowly on his chest she noticed a few scratches around the top of his shoulders, red blemishes. "What are these marks, have you hurt yourself?"

Harry turned his face away and reached for the soap. "I must have caught it on the boxes before, will you wash my back?"

Gill didn't mention them again and she moved behind him washing his back slowly looking carefully. Every now and then she kissed his shoulders slowly. "I do love you Harry, and I'm going to make it up to you. From now on I'm going to be the best wife ever. You just watch Harry, you're going to love me like you used to. We're going to get through this, just you wait and see." Their relationship was like the bar of soap in her hand. The more she tried to hold onto it, the more it slipped away.

Later that night Harry and Gill walked into their local. It was packed out and Matty and a few of the other lads were stood at the far side of the room. Jona raised his hand over his head and shouted over to Harry. "Get us a drink pal, a double brandy and coke." Harry placed the order at the bar and gave the money to Gill to pay for it. Gill looked stunning, the black dress showed off her curves and her slender legs. Harry walked over to Matty and passed him a wad of cash. This was from the latest job, another house full of weed they'd found.

Jona held his hand out too and stared at Harry. "Have you got anything for me, you know I'm on my arse at the moment?"

Matty chirped in and nudged Jona in the waist. "You've done fuck all, every time we've told you about a graft you never turn up. What's happening to you, you were always the first in there to earn a few quid?" Matty was right, he'd hit the nail right on the head. In the past Jona was one of the main lads. He could earn money anywhere and always made sure he was on a decent cut of any jobs that were going down in the area. Harry bunged him fifty quid and shoved it in his shirt pocket. "Here, get yourself a few beers, like Matty said, you need to pull your finger out of your arse and get your act together. I can't keep bailing you out you know. I've got a family to feed." Harry chuckled and patted the top of Jona's shoulder.

Matty whispered over to them both. "Here's Mandy now anyway, get over and buy her a drink Jona. Who knows she might even part her tash tonight if you get her pissed enough." Matty was howling laughing and held the lower part of his stomach.

Jona held a stern face and shoved his hands in his pocket. "Nar, I'm not buying that slut a drink. I hear she's got new fella on the go anyway, well, that's the word on the street."

Matty shook his head and looked at Harry. "I've heard fuck all about that, what about you Harry?" Harry shrugged his shoulders as Gill came to his side. Matty was still on the wind-up and prodded Jona in the side of his head. "They'll need to tie a plank to their arse if they're shagging your Mandy. I bet it's like throwing a sausage up an entry shagging her, she must have a right baggy fanny now, pure men she's had."

Jona wasn't laughing. Usually he would have joined in the banter but not tonight, something was bothering him. He moved up to Gill's side and smelt her hair, lifting it up slowly and inhaling deeply. "You look mint tonight Gill, if you're looking for a real man then give me a shout and I'll sort you out," he sniggered.

Harry shot a look at Matty and raised his eyebrows. "Is he dicing with death or what? What's he drinking, is it hard man juice or what?"

Jona turned around and looked over at Mandy, she was dancing with her friends. She looked happy and he knew she was pissed. Her cheeks were bright red and she was as loud as ever, he gave her an evil look and walked away to have a game of pool. Harry blew a laboured breath. "What the fuck is up with Jona tonight? He seems in a right mood, has he said anything to you?"

Matty shook his head. "No, not a word, but I've only just come in. I've had a shit day and Kenzo is pecking my head. They've only tried to have her taken to Cheshire out of the way. The barmy cow tried killing Ben on the motorway and jumped out of the car as he was driving her. She's not right in the head that one I tell you."

Harry found a table and pulled the chair out for Gill to sit down. She smiled at him and tickled the top of his hand. Matty parked his arse next to Harry and poured his heart out. "She wants me to come and pick her up. I can't do that can I? I mean, the Collins know she'll be with me and I can't be arsed with all the shit. I think I'll just tell her to go home. I'm not scared of them pricks you know, but it's just that I can't be arsed with her family problems."

Harry passed Gill a lit cigarette and answered Matty. "She's a young bird, she's got some growing up to do. If she was my daughter I would have locked her up too, she's a fucking nightmare. Come on Matty, think about it, we're at war with the fuckers and she's banging you. I bet they want her in a body bag, because I would if it was my sister. She's bang out of order, where are her loyalties?"

Matty agreed, "Yeah, I know what you mean, she is a good spy though. I mean, look how many grows she's put us onto. We're minted because of her. I feel like I owe her." Harry couldn't be arsed with the drama, he turned his head away and watched the women dancing near him. Mandy was twerking with her friends and every now and then she winked over at him. Gill didn't see her though; she was too busy staring at her husband hoping to win his heart back.

Regina Clough walked into the pub and Gill swallowed hard. She was anxious and stood up to go to the toilet, this was all she needed, someone telling Ray's wife all about how she was the one who had been banging her husband's brains out. She left her bag on the table and rushed across the dance floor. Harry went to the bar and stood with his back to Regina. All of a sudden he jumped and held a look of shock on his face; she'd pinched his arse cheeks. "Oi, what do you think you're doing Regina?"

Mrs Clough moved closer to him and he could smell the whisky on her breath. "I'm just having a feel that's all love, me and you go back a lot of years Harry, are you forgetting about that or what?" Harry couldn't wait to get his drinks; he didn't reply to her and turned away in the opposite direction. Gill was back now, she was eager to leave the bar, she was unsettled and forever looking over her shoulder. Matty was taking a call on his mobile phone, he walked outside and he was shouting at the top of his voice.

Later, Mandy was heading home with some friends. Once they got to the corner of the road they all parted and went different ways. "What a night girls, we sure know how to party don't we?" She shouted behind her. Mandy was swaying about and she was singing to herself as she crossed the road. Her house wasn't far from the pub and if she cut through the small alleyway at the end of the road it would take at least ten minutes off her journey. This was a route she'd taken lots of times; it was just the normal thing for her to do. Walking along with her clutch bag held tightly in her grip you could hear her high-heels clipping along the pavement. She could hear someone behind her, turning her head quickly she scouted the area. "Hello, is someone there?" No one answered. She picked up speed and she was constantly looking behind her, she was being followed. Mandy took her shoes off and began to run. Crossing the muddy grass verge, she could see her housing estate in front of her. Mandy let out a relieved breath, she must have been imagining it, the drink did that to her sometimes, it made her paranoid. Head delving into her bag she pulled out her cigarettes and hung one from the corner of her mouth. Once it was lit she carried on walking into the dark of the night. Tonight the weather was mild, a bit chilly but at least there was no rain. She was wearing a red strapless dress and you could see she was starting to get cold. Sliding the key into the front door she felt a force from behind her. Mandy fell face first into the hallway. The house was in darkness and once the front door was slammed shut, her body was dragged into the living room feet first. Mandy was barely conscious, she was struggling to see who her attacker was. Her hands were bound together tightly and she was flung onto the sofa face down. Heavy breathing and the smell of tobacco filled the air, not normal cigarette smoke, it was rolling tobacco. Mandy knew the smell well as her grandfather used to smoke it, it had a stale aroma. Lifting her head up slightly she couldn't see a thing, it was pitch black, someone was still in the room with her though because she could hear them rummaging about. If this was a robbery, why weren't they ransacking the place? She had a flat screen TV that they could have sold, and a decent music system. Why weren't they taking any of that? Mandy listened carefully; she could hear a buzzing sound in the distance, it was coming nearer to her. Her head was dragged up from behind and she could feel something on the top of her head. Hair falling onto her face, lots of it, mountains of it. This sick bastard was shaving her head! Mandy knew now this was more than just a burglary. This was a mental case, who could kill her at any second. She was wriggling about and every time she tried to scream out a rolled up sock was shoved into her mouth. Her attacker smelt of dog shit – dirty, unclean rancid odours. She could feel his hot breath on her face and for the first time she got a glimpse of him. Her eyes were wide open, and panic filled her body. The man gripped her legs and opened them with force. His knee pressed hard against her vagina and he made sure she couldn't move an inch. He was inside her and she heard sexual moans from behind. Mandy lay face down on the sofa and her hair was stuck all over her cheeks, she was cold, her head was cold, nothing but dark bristles sticking out on top of her head. A tear fell from her eyes as the rape continued. The moonlight shone in through the window and it seemed to be watching the torment she was going through. His hands raked into her flesh, he was biting her now, teeth sinking deep into her skin. This attack was horrific, this man was totally sick in the head. Mandy wasn't moving, she wanted to be dead, her body was being ripped to shreds and there wasn't a thing she could do about it. She felt wetness on her back, on her head, dribbling down her forehead. The dirty cunt was pissing on her. Mandy lay frozen, she was aware her attacker was still in the room with her. Lifting her head up she mumbled, and jerked her body about on the sofa.

A hand now came to her side and pulled the sock from out of her mouth. "Go on Jona, finish me off. You're going back to jail for this you crazy cunt. I'm going to tell them everything," she screamed. Mandy's head jerked with speed to the side. Jona was trying to kill her. The blows she took to her body were fierce and if she ever woke up from this she would be a lucky woman. Jona kicked at her body one last time before he left. Mandy never moved an inch. Looking around the room with evil eyes he run to the TV and unplugged it. This would get him a couple of hundred quid and help him score. Quickly he ran upstairs and searched for anything else of value he could carry. Smashing the house up before he left, he made sure he'd covered his tracks. There was no evidence he was ever there. He smiled as he left the house. There wasn't a soul about and he knew it would be his word against hers. Well, if she ever survived the attack.

Nobody fucked with Jona, nobody.

★

Gill lay next to Harry in bed, she was stroking the sprinkling of dark hairs at the top of his chest. The night had ended sooner than she thought as Matty had to leave the pub suddenly and Harry wasn't in the mood for a piss up. He was quiet tonight, thinking. "We will make this work you know Harry," Gill whispered. "You loved me once and you can love me again."

Harry tickled the top of her shoulder and looked her straight into her eyes. "Perhaps we can, it's just going to take some time. I've got a lot on my mind at the moment Gill, you don't know the half of it. The Collins brothers are giving us a hard time, they think we did their brother in. It's going to off soon, you just watch, people are going to get hurt."

Gill sat up and her eyes were wide open. "Please tell me it was nothing to do with you Harry. I know you're a lot of things but you're not a murderer are you?" Harry looped his hands above his head and he never answered her, she nudged him again. "You're not like that are you Harry?"

"I do what needs to be done Gill. This game isn't what it used to be and you do what you have to do to survive and, if that means stabbing some cunt up, so be it, you do what you have to do. It's a dog eat dog world out there and only the strongest survive."

Gill shook her head, she closed her eyes and took a deep breath. "Make love to me Harry, not just a leg-over. I want you to make love to me."

Harry screwed his face up and sat up from the bed,

she'd rattled his cage. "Is that what he did ay? Did he make love to you?" Gill was stuck for words; she watched him get out of bed and tried to pull him back. He turned his head slowly and growled at her. "Take your hands off me Gill. I'm going downstairs, just fuck off and leave me alone." Gill knew she was treading on thin ice. She backed off and plonked on the bed. The bedroom door slammed behind him and she could hear him going downstairs. "Fuck, fuck, fuck," she sobbed.

Jona hammered on Trisha's door. It was early morning and the birds were tweeting outside. They seemed to know his secret and they were getting louder as they jumped from branch to branch, chirping. Trisha's head appeared at the window. She could see Jona and she shook her head and banged on the window loudly with a flat palm. Ever since Callum had brought him to the house he was a constant fixture here, scrounging all the bastard time. Trisha didn't mind though because if he came to her house he brought drugs and that meant she got a fix for free. Trisha, Callum and Jona were drug addicts now, raging bag-heads they were. They'd do anything for drugs and didn't have any morals anymore. Heroin had numbed everything – they had no feeling of what was right or wrong anymore. Trisha looked thinner; her blubber was hanging out in front of her, loose folds of skin. Opening the door she made sure nobody was watching him come inside. That was all she needed – the dibble knocking at her door. Jona was into everything; burglaries, drugs, and car crimes and she knew he was taking chances by the state of him. He was on top. "Fuck me Jona, do you know what time it is you daft twat. I've only just got to sleep you nob-head it's going to take me ages to get some shut eye now, thanks a bunch."

"Sssh, will you, just let me in. Fuck me, I've been grafting haven't I. Look, money doesn't grow on trees you know." Jona flashed the cash out in front of him and that seemed to quieten her down.

Trisha licked her lips slowly and rubbed her hands together. Money meant more drugs, and she pressed up against him, flirting. "Right, you can get your head down here tonight. Fuck me, what's all that blood on your boat race?"

Jona chuckled and dabbed his finger into his mouth rubbing at his skin. "Oh, I must have cut myself when I smashed the window on the gaff. I got a top flat screen TV and a few other bits, has it gone now, or what?"

Trisha guided his scrawny finger to the blood on his face and it soon disappeared. "What about me bunking up with you tonight. I can keep your back warm if you want?" Trisha was honoured; you could see it in her eyes that she was flattered that someone was willing to have sex with her. Callum was no longer in the picture and sex was a distant memory. She'd tried with him of course but his bits weren't working any more, it was like a dead slug; wet and lifeless. Trisha flicked the light switch and took his hand in hers. She held a single finger up to her mouth and guided him upstairs to the bedroom. Once she was in the room she pushed him down onto the bed. "Are you skinning up first, let's have a joint then you can shake my bones."

Jona seemed up for it, he actually seemed turned on by this overweight slob of a woman. He pulled a small bag of weed from his pockets and a couple of Rizla papers. Trisha stripped off and jumped into bed. What a sight she was - fucking hanging.

Tina opened her eyes and looked at Preston, he was awake too. "Who the fuck has she got in her bed now?" she moaned.

Preston giggled and cuddled up to her. "She's getting some cock, just leave her will you. She needs to get it while she can, just chill and leave her to it." Tina sighed and turned on her side facing the window. Noises came from the other bedroom, it sound like a pig was being slaughtered.

"I'm not having this all fucking night," Tina stressed. She jumped out of bed and banged her clenched fist on the bedroom wall. Preston was doubled over laughing and he stuck the duvet in his mouth as he heard Trisha groaning from the other room. "Fuck me you bony twat, come on, get deeper," she was screaming at the top of her voice. Tina grabbed a t-shirt from the side of the drawers and she was going to her mother's room to end the torment, how embarrassing was this for her?

Preston bolted up from the bed and stood in front of the door, guarding it. "Don't go in Tina. I'm here aren't I? Don't bring it on top for us. Fuck me, if she gets wind that we're together she'll make sure Callum knows about it. You know what she's like, she a right gob-shite."

Tina paused, he was right. She knew more than anyone that her mother couldn't hold her own shit, she paced the room ragging her fingers through her hair. "Well, you need to tell him then don't you. I mean, what can he do anyway? I'm not with him and it's not like I've cheated or anything is it?"

Preston pulled her closer and kept his voice low. "I'm not arsed about Callum and I will tell him when the time is right, not just yet though, let me sort a few things out first then it will be sweet. He's my brother you know and I feel a bit sly on him. Let's face it, he was into you wasn't he?"

Tina plonked back down on the bed and replied. "It wasn't any Romeo and Juliet story you know. I was just bored and he was there, that's all. I never loved him, no way in this world, I was just passing some time."

Preston came to join her; he knew this wasn't going to be easy. Callum was a nutter when his cage was rattled and he knew he had a fight on his hands once he'd confessed the truth to him. "I'll sort it Tina. Just leave it with me. Our Callum seems different these days you know. He seems depressed all the time. I think he's pining for you."

Screaming could be heard coming from the other bedroom, Tina covered her mouth and this time she could see the funny side of things. "She's a right filthy cow isn't she? I swear, she's not right in the head." Preston kissed her shoulder and she shivered as his hot breath tickled her skin. The duvet was pulled over them both and movement from beneath could be seen. It wasn't just Trisha who was having sex tonight; her daughter was getting her fair share too.

CHAPTER SEVENTEEN

The noise of police sirens filled the air. They were swarming the area. Mandy had been found by the postman and the police were all over the estate looking for evidence. A crowd had gathered outside her house and they were all eager to see what had gone on. The postman was in a bad way and he was sitting on a wall shaking like a leaf. "The front door was wide open, officer. I just peeped inside to see if everything was okay. I know Mandy and we usually have a gab together in the mornings. I talk to everyone I do." The officer was writing everything down and trying to calm him down. "She was a mess, just lying there on the floor, lifeless she was. Tied up like a animal. There are some sick bastards out there I can tell you. To do that to another human being is not right. You need to catch this bastard and lock them up for life. Is she going to be alright officer, she was barely breathing?"

The officer turned his head over his shoulder and watched the ambulance leave. PC Birch had been on the force for over ten years and he'd never seen such a horrific attack. He was shaken himself and you could see the whole episode had disturbed him. "Her hair was gone, I barely recognised her at first, she looked so different." The man started to cry now and he was sobbing. "I need to go home now officer. I can't sit here anymore. My head's in bits, can you take me home. I feel sick, I'm not myself."

John Morris had been the local postman for over

twenty years; he knew everyone on the estate and often stopped to chat with the residents. He was fifty-five and enjoyed his job. Everyone was gathered around John and they were shouting out questions at him. There was an attacker on the loose in the area and they all wanted to know the details to make sure they knew what they were dealing with.

Agnes Jones stood with her hands on her hips in front of the officer. She ran a community group for the residents and wanted to make sure the police were doing all they could to make the streets safe, until the attacker was caught. "I live on my own too and if this lunatic comes back what chance do I stand. He broke into her house didn't he? How are we going to sleep at night now, knowing he's still out there?"

The female residents were up in arms and each of them wanted answers. The officer radioed through to his colleges and within minutes a female officer came to join him. "Ladies, ladies, just calm down. I can understand your worries and we'll do our best to make sure you're all safe. At the moment we just need to find out exactly what has gone on, so please just let the officer ask his questions and then we can speak to you all."

The women in the group huddled together. This was a nightmare for everyone living on the estate. Yes, there was a high level of crime here, but nothing like this, never before had such a horrific attack taken place on a woman. A group of youths come marching up to the crowd and they too, were eager to find out what had gone on. The ringleader was known as Frosty and he was a well known troublemaker in the area. "If you need us to sort this out we will. Just give us a name and we'll take the dick-head down."

Agnes blew a laboured breath and folded her arms tightly in front of her. She'd had her troubles with this lad in the past and knew he was asking for trouble. "Frosty, or whatever your bleeding name is. Just leave the police to do their job. They do know what they're doing you know. You're in enough trouble as it is, just keep out of it."

The officer shot a look to the young lad. She recognised his face and knew he was a troublemaker. Frosty marched to his side and bounced about as he spoke. "Ay is it right that Mandy got her head shaved? That's twisted if someone's done that to her. Did they break in too, you know boom her door her?"

The female officer pulled Frosty by the arm towards her. He wriggled and he was aware he was near getting nicked if he carried on. "You lot need to be out looking for this prick instead of gathering evidence. It's simple innit, if she's been burgled just start checking who's bought any of the swag, it's not rocket science is it? Just tell me and the lads what they took and I'll put the word out on the street. I'm not a grass, none of us are, but Mandy was an alright woman and we'll help put the prick behind bars if we can." Frosty stood tall, he was fourteen with bright red hair, he was always in trouble but he was a lovable rogue, he was just misunderstood. The female officer thanked him for his help and moved him and his boys on. She was surprised when he didn't put up a fight, usually this kid was a right head case and he wouldn't take instructions from anyone. He shouted over his shoulder as he left. "Leave it with us, we'll find out who this wanker is, just you watch, we'll have a name before the end of the day." The officer admired his determination and walked back to the witness. If the truth was known nobody had seen a thing and at this moment there wasn't a scrap of evidence to go on.

Mandy was rushed to hospital and the doctors weren't confident that she would make it through the night. The media were all over the story and before long the attack was all over the news. The neighbourhood was up in arms and none of them would sleep tonight knowing that her attacker was still on the loose.

Peter Collins sat with his brothers in the front room. Kenzo was still missing and they knew Matty would know where she was. They were hatching a plan to get her back, and Peter was more than confident that their sister would be back with them before the day was out. Ben sat forward in his chair and he clenched his fist together tightly. "We're going through the bastard's door, taking it off its hinges, no fucking about. The three of us can handle it, we don't need anyone else. Matty will be on his own, he'll shit bricks when he sees us. Trust me the guy's a clown and he's fuck all without his back-up."

Connor agreed, he stood to his feet and paced the living room floor. "Peter, it's time to show these pricks who's boss. We know its Harry Jarvis who's been having the grows away, so let's just destroy them all one by one. He must think we're shit scared. We've done fuck all about it. We've just sat about like a load of women crying over it. He's making us a laughing stock."

Peter inhaled hard on his cigarette, he chuckled. "Don't you worry about Harry Jarvis, that cock is getting it big time. Just let's get Kenzo back first, then we'll sort that wanker out. Ok, we've done nothing about him having our weed away, but it all comes to those who wait. I've got an insider and whatever he's had from us will be coming back tenfold, trust me. We've already got a tracker on his car and a few others of his gang, so give it a few days and we'll know exactly where they stash it all."

Ben was edgy, he kept checking his watch. "Right let's go and get that slut back where she belongs. She's getting a slap off me too when I get my hands on her, the dirty tart. Look at me neck lads, the crazy cow tried to strangle me." Ben revealed his neck, and you could see deep purple bruises all around it, he was right, she had tried to kill him.

Peter stubbed his cigarette out in the ashtray. "Come on then lads, let's Shanghai surprise the daft little bitch. She'll drop down dead when she sees us. Just wait and see, she'll be begging us not to hurt her precious little boyfriend, begging us."

Ben jumped up and grabbed his leather jacket from the table. "He's getting hurt the nob-head, mark my words, he's getting done in. Just you try and stop me. I'll bite his fucking nose off." His words were serious and none of his brothers replied to him. Matty was going down, there was no question about it.

Kenzo opened her eyes. She was right where she wanted to be lay next to her man. They'd been arguing all night and it was only because she broke down crying that he let her stay the night. Sitting up in bed she watched him sleeping, she was so in love. She'd have done anything to keep him but she knew he was slipping away. His eyes flickered open and he jumped up in a panic. "Why are you watching me sleep, you fucking weirdo?"

Kenzo reached over and stroked his leg slowly. "Babes, I've just woken up I wasn't watching you at all. Don't make me out like a nutter when I'm not."

Matty wasn't going back to sleep, no way, he didn't trust her one little bit. Last night was the last straw and he'd told her straight she had to go back home. She was acting strange around him and he knew the drugs were still in her system. "Why can't we just run away together Matty, just me and you? We can be happy. You still love me don't you?"

Matty blew a breath and looked at her. He had to tell her the truth, yes, he'd loved her once, but that was then and this was now. She'd changed and he couldn't be arsed with all of her drama anymore. He tried to keep her calm as he delivered the news to her, he swallowed hard, this wasn't going to be easy. "Kenzo, you're a lovely girl but," he paused and rolled his eyes, "you've changed, you're bad on the Charlie and I can't be with someone like you. I know I have a bit of sniff every now and again, but you're hooked on it love, you need to sort your shit out."

Kenzo just stared at him and then she let rip, she was screaming at the top of her voice, desperate. "You told me you loved me, you said when everything was sorted out we could run away together. What happened to that, ay? You've had me over haven't you? Oh, yeah it all makes sense now you just wanted me to give you all the information on my brothers so you could have them over, what a spineless twat you really are!" Kenzo grabbed her handbag from the side of the cabinet and rushed into the bathroom. Matty looped his hands above his head and just stared into space, this was going to be a lot harder than he first thought. Listening carefully he could hear her moving about inside the bathroom. She was snorting coke, he knew it, he could hear her chopping the powder on the toilet lid. Kenzo couldn't live without the drug anymore and he knew once she'd had a few lines of sniff she might even agree with him.

Suddenly there were banging noises from downstairs. Loud thumping noises and raised voices. Matty was alert and sat up in the bed. There was nothing else he could do. The door flew open and he went white. Ben Collins ran over to the bed and gripped him by the throat, he was helpless. "Where the fuck is she, don't fuck about, tell me, where's Kenzo?" His voice shook the walls, he was in Matty's face and his teeth were clenched together tightly. The large vein at the side of his neck was pumping with rage and Matty knew he was on borrowed time.

"She's in there," he choked. Connor ran to the bathroom door and realised it was locked from the inside. A quick shoulder charge soon opened the door and he was shocked to see the state his sister was in. Head bent over the toilet she was snorting cocaine, there were two lines there and all white powder was visible around her nostrils.

Peter walked into the bathroom and gripped her by the hair. "Get fucking ready slut, you're going home.".

Kenzo's jaw was swinging, she was off her head, she was fighting for her life and screaming in her brother's face. "Just fuck off and leave me will you. Matty loves me and I love him, you'll never stop us loving each other you know, never."

Matty was on the bed and his lip was already bleeding. Ben was stood at the side of him and he was ready to smash his head in, ready to take him out for good. Kenzo could see Matty from the bathroom door and she was doing her best to get to his side. "Connor, just fuck off, let me go. He's my life, please don't hurt him." Peter grabbed her hands behind her back and Connor held her face as they made her watch Matty take another beating. She was howling but nobody listened to her pleas, they just made her watch her boyfriend being beaten half to death.

Peter Collins walked to the bed now and he looked straight into Matty's eyes. "You know who killed my brother don't you? Tell me now and I'll walk away. I know you know, so spit it out, come on prick, tell me who did it."

Matty was spitting blood and his eyes were swelling at speed, he mumbled. "I don't know shit, honest."

Peter jumped onto the bed now and he was like a savage as he bit down into his victim's body. Kenzo dropped to her knees and yelled at the top of her voice. "It was me. I did it, I killed John. Matty doesn't know a thing about it, just leave him alone." The three brothers shot a look to each other, she was lying surely, trying to protect him, there was no way she'd killed John. Kenzo held her head in her hands. "I just wanted the money so me and Matty could run away together. I never meant to kill him, honest."

Connor looked at his brothers, before he dragged her up by her hair. "What did you just say?" he growled.

Kenzo was shaking, her lips quivered. It was time to come clean. Months of covering up her secret had finally come to an end. "I've just told you it was me who killed John, please leave Matty alone, he knows fuck all about it. I've told you now. Ben, the money you took off me, it was the money I took from John on the night he was killed.

I swear to you now, I only hit him a few times. I just wanted to shock him that's all, it's not my fault he died. I didn't mean to do it, honest, it wasn't my fault!"

Peter nutted Matty one last time on the bed and then dragged at his lifeless body. "Connor get this prick in the car, we'll drop him off at Jarvis's house. This will show them that we mean business won't it."

Ben picked Matty up and flung him over his shoulder, Matty was lifeless, blood was dripping down his face. "Connor you just keep hold of that crank while I put this nob in the boot, we can sort her out after we've got rid of this prick." The men left the house. Kenzo was screaming looking about for help, but nobody came to assist her. Curtains were twitching at the windows and people knew to keep well out of things that didn't concern them. This was the Collins brothers they were messing with and nobody wanted to get their back up, nobody.

The car pulled up at Harry Jarvis's house. Ben could see a familiar face coming out from the door. Connor looked at Ben and they both sniggered. "Callum must be Jarvis's lad. What a fucking result! This is a turn up for the books, fancy him being Jarvis's boy, it's a small world isn't it? Now let's see who's laughing, Harry fucking Jarvis." Ben and Connor jumped out of the car. Peter stayed in the back with his sister. He was watching her like a hawk and was aware she could try and make a getaway at any time. Every now and then he slapped her across the head, he was near killing her, you could see it in his eyes.

Matty was flung onto Harry's lawn. His limp body slammed to the ground and he just lay there shaking, naked. Callum clocked the Collins brothers and he was ready to get on his toes. He still owed them money and knew he was in for a beating once they got their hands on him. Callum was roasting his nuts off, sweat streamed down the side of his head as he started to run in the opposite direction. Connor nodded to Ben, "You get in the car and follow me, I'll catch the cheeky cunt, don't you worry." Connor sprinted off and he was fast, very fast. His eyes were all over as he ran down the entry. He could just see the back of Callum turning a corner. Connor motored after him; he was going to catch him, there was no doubt about it. Connor was shouting, and Callum kept looking over his shoulder as he tried to get away. Connor stopped dead in his track and picked a brick up from the wasteland nearby. He was a great shot as he hurled it through the air, it was right on target. The missile hit Callum on the back of his head and he fell to the floor like a ton of bricks. Connor sprinted to where he fell and stood over him gasping for breath, his hands on his knees he spoke. "Not that fast are you dick-head?" Callum never spoke he just sat up waiting to get his beating. Connor dragged him to his feet and scouted the area for his brothers. He spotted the car near the roadside not far from where he was. "Come on you fucking scruff, let's get you sorted out once and for all."

Callum panicked, why wasn't he just giving him a few digs here and now, that's what they usually did? They never usually took him away in a car. It was always dealt with on the spot. "Just do what you have to do Connor. I deserve it, go on, I'm not going to fight back," Callum pleaded. Connor chuckled as he dragged the kid along with him by the scruff of the neck. "Listen up yeah, I'll have the money by dinner time, I swear I'm not lying this time. A guy owes it me and he's promised me today that he'll have it for me, I'm not chatting shit, honest."

Connor wasn't listening. He just opened the boot on the car and flung him inside. Callum could see patches of blood in the boot and he was trying his best to talk his way out of it, it was no good, he was punched in his face and dragged into the boot of the car by his hair, kicking and screaming. Kenzo was sobbing, she was covered in blood too. Peter had busted her nose. "Right, let's get him to the lock- up and we can leave him there until we've dealt with her first," Connor stressed. Kenzo was quiet; she was playing with the cuff of her blouse and kept her head dipped low. She knew any sudden movement and she'd be a dead woman. Peter had his hand around her neck and she knew he wouldn't think twice about ending her life, he was a snapper, a bad mental case.

★

Callum woke up lying on a floor in a room with no windows, except for a tiny one at the back of the room. It was dark and he could barely see. He was bleeding badly and every now and then he would scream out at the top of his voice for help, but nobody heard him, he was alone and craving a fix. He was rattling his balls off. His knees held to his chest he rocked slowly to and fro. "Somebody help me, please," he begged.

Kenzo ran to her mother's side as soon as she got into the house. She was dripping in blood and Susan was hysterical when she saw the state of her. She ran at Peter and started to lash out at him. "I said bring her back, not half bleeding kill her. Look at the state of her now, there's no bleeding need for this. You always go over the top." Ben and Connor stood next to each other and Susan knew they had something to say. Kenzo ran to the corner of the kitchen and dropped to her knees. "Mam, I'm sorry, I'm so sorry. I just loved Matty so much. I wanted us to be together."

Susan went to her side and stroked the top of her head. She was a woman too and knew herself how it felt to be in love with someone who she couldn't have. "He's too old for you love. You need to find someone who's your own age. Look at the state of you, he's had you on drugs, what kind of a man gives drugs to someone they love?"

Ben came to his mother's side and gently helped her up from the floor. "Mam, you better sit down, we need to tell you something."

Susan pushed him away, she didn't need any help, she was pissed off and ready to run at them all for beating her daughter up. "Look at her face Peter, that's going to be swelled in the morning, I hope she's got no scars, God help you if she has." Susan sat down at the table and silence reigned. She lifted her head up slowly and looked at her children. "Well, come on then, spit it out. I've not got all day I've got to go down to the shops and get some shopping, come on tell me."

Peter was the spokesman, he loved every minute of it and you could see he couldn't wait to tell his mother about her perfect daughter. "She killed John," he said pointing at his sister "she was the one who murdered him."

Susan took a few minutes to digest the information and let out a nervous laugh. "Stop fucking about, do you expect me to believe that she would do something like that? She loved John just like we all did. You're pissing in the wind if you think she would kill her own flesh and blood."

Kenzo was sobbing her heart out. Susan turned her head slowly to face her. Ben spoke now. "It's right mam, she's just admitted it to us. She wanted the money John was carrying so she could run away with that prick Matty."

Susan closed her eyes tightly; as she opened them she stood up and walked over to her daughter slowly. "Tell me they're lying, go on, tell me it's not true."

Kenzo reached over and gripped Susan's hand tightly, she was pleading with her. "Mam, it was an accident. I never meant to do it. I swear it was an accident." Susan ran outside into the garden and spewed her ring up. Stood with her back held up against the wall the wind tickled her skin and filtered through her hair. Connor was at her side. "Mam, come back inside, it's cold out here. We need to sort this out."

Susan snivelled and inhaled deeply. She cracked her knuckles as she ran back into the kitchen in a fury. "You dirty lying bastard!" Susan wailed at Kenzo, "You watched us bury your brother and you stood there with us all not saying a word. You're an evil bitch and the lads can do whatever they want with you. I'm washing my hands of you, you're dead as far as I'm concerned, fucking dead." Susan walked around in a circle, she was at her wits end, sobbing her heart out she was. "Phone the police on her Peter, get her locked up. She can rot in hell for all I care. How could she do something like that? How could anyone take another person's life?"

Kenzo stood up and her lips were trembling. "I'll go to prison mam, you're right. I do deserve it. I'm not right in the head. I've lost the plot, I know I have."

Ben turned his head away and bit down hard on his

lips. She was his sister after all and he did care about her. Peter was a heartless bastard and he wanted her to suffer, like they all had when they found out their brother had been murdered.

"You can hand yourself in then can't you?" Peter hissed.

Kenzo nodded, he'd called her bluff and she had no other option left. "I'll go now mam, Peter can take me. I swear I never meant for this to happen. If I could turn the clock back I would. I'm sorry, so sorry."

Susan screamed at the top of her voice. "Get her out of here now; get that dirty horrible bitch out of my house. Burn her for all I care, she's an evil bitch." Peter grabbed Kenzo by the arm and led her to the car. Ben and Connor stayed with their mother and they were doing the best to calm her down. Susan tried running after Kenzo with a knife in her hands and they had to stop her from getting out of the house.

Gill covered her mouth with both hands as Matty fell into the house. "Harry, quick it's Matty!" Gill ran to get a blanket from the bedroom, he was blue and shivering. Harry carried him into the front room. His words were low and he was coughing up big clots of blood. "It's the Collins brothers Harry. They've done this to me, it was them." Matty's eyes closed and Harry knew he had no choice but to ring for an ambulance. This was a nightmare, the police were already on his case and once they saw Matty like this they would know all about the gangland activities in the area.

"Harry, he looks like he's going to die, have you rung

an ambulance?" Gill asked, she was hysterical.

Harry nodded as he sat next to his best friend. "It's on its way. You need to stay with him until it gets here, do you hear me? Keep your mouth shut too, just say he was found like this at the front of the house, do you hear me, say fuck all?" Gill nodded, she was panicking and kept checking Matty was still breathing. His chest was rising slowly and every now and then she shook him to make sure he didn't lose consciousness. Harry grabbed his car keys from the table and rushed out of the front door. Gill shouted after him but he didn't turn back once.

Harry was driving like a maniac; speeding and swerving in and out of the traffic. Picking up his mobile phone he made a call. "Get the fucking lads together as soon as possible, the Collins have done Matty in. We need to get this sorted now once and for all. The lot of them are going down; I swear to you, the lot of them are fucking dead." Harry threw his phone onto the passenger seat. He pulled up outside the pub and ran inside hoping that his enemies were in there. Kicking the door he searched inside for the Collins brothers. The place was dead and just a few punters sat in the corner chatting. Harry's knuckles were turning white as he squeezed them together tightly. This was it, he was ready to wipe the lot of them out.

★

Kenzo sat in the car with Peter. He sat her in the back and he'd already told her if she made an attempt to break free he would shoot her. The silver pistol was between his legs and she knew he wouldn't think twice about ending her life. Peter looked at her through the rear-view mirror, he was studying her. Was she mental, or that in love that she would do anything to keep her man, even go as far as killing her own brother? "You're sick in the head you are Kenzo. I've done a lot of bad things in my time, but to kill one of your own, that's twisted."

Kenzo was staring out of the window, she was still wrecked and it was obvious she was still high on drugs. "Where are you taking me, if you're going to kill me then just get it over with. I'm not scared of dying you know, so just make it quick." Peter rubbed at his arms, goose pimples appeared all over his skin, she was scaring him now and he swallowed hard. Speaking in a deep voice he replied to her. "Don't get smart Kenzo, I'll just slap you if you think you can talk to me like that. You'll see what I'm doing to you in good time but for now, shut the fuck up and zip it before I jump in the back and smash your fucking head in."

Kenzo was humming a song, she held her arms tightly around her body and gently banged her head against the window. Peter turned the radio off and only the sound of the engine running could be heard. Peter pulled over on the roadside and turned to face her. "Tell me everything you know about Harry Jarvis's grows and I'll let you go. I'll give you the money back you took from John and you can fuck off from around here, never to be seen again. Think about it, a new start."

Kenzo stared at him, this was a lifeline, one she thought she would never get from her eldest brother. He was ruthless and never cut anyone any slack. Kenzo had the information he wanted too. She's heard the phone calls Matty had with Harry and the lads, and she'd even been to one of the warehouses where the weed was being grown. She was back in the game and had a bargaining card. "What? You expect me to believe that you will let me go, just like that? No Peter, I don't trust you. You need to give me more than that. Get me the money and I'll think about it."

Peter chewed hard on his lips, the tips of his ears were going blood red and he dropped his head onto the steering wheel, banging it slowly. His voice was raised and as he looked at her she knew she was treading on thin ice. "I'll get you the money once you've told me what I need to know. I'm a man of my word, if I've said you can go, then I mean it."

Kenzo sat upright in her seat; she raised her eyebrows and licked her lips slowly. "What about the others, where will you tell them I've gone to?"

Peter banged his fist on the dashboard and you could see speckles of dust floating up in the air. "For fucks sake. Listen, is it a deal or not? I'm not fucking about with you here; it's either a yes or no. It's not fucking rocket science."

Kenzo nodded, she smirked and sat back in her seat. She was showing no signs of remorse for her brother's death now and was only interested in saving herself. "Right, I'll show you where it is. There is a warehouse full and they have three men watching it every night. Matty said it's ready for cutting down this week, so you're just in time." Kenzo rubbed her hands together and started to give her brother directions.

★

Matty was rushed into an ambulance, he'd lost a lot of blood and it was only since the medics arrived that they'd got it under control. His head was the size of a football.

It was swelling by the minute and his eyes were barely visible. Gill walked to the ambulance at the side of the stretcher. "Matty just hang on in there, you're strong, you're going to make it, trust me." The sirens blared as Matty was rushed to the hospital.

Sally saw the back of the ambulance leaving and ran to Gill's side in a panic. "What the fuck is happening, who's dead, come on tell me. The woman over the road said somebody was flung into the air and landed in your garden, who was it, do I know them? For fucks sake, I thought it was you at first."

Gill started to walk back inside the house. She shot her eyes over to the nosey neighbours and rammed her fingers in the air to them. "There's nothing to see here now you interfering bastards. Keep your bleeding noses out of things that don't concern you, fucking plant pots."

Sally was still eager to find out what was going on, and followed Gill inside. "So who was it then? I tell you what this estate is going right downhill. I can't wait to move away. There's some serious shit going down here. I mean, a woman's not safe anymore. Look at Mandy, Jona's ex, she's on death's door in the hospital. She's in a bad way I hear. And, the police have fuck all to go on, not a drop of evidence. I swear, the sooner I do one the better."

Gill popped a cigarette into her mouth and plonked down at the table. Her blouse was covered in bright red blood and she was shaking from head to toe. "It was Matty. The Collins brothers have done him over. I swear, his lip was hanging off, Sally, they left him for dead. Evil bastards they are, they don't care who they hurt."

Sally had a cunning look on her face as she made her way to the cigarettes on the table. Once she sparked one up she sat down and blew large smoke rings from her mouth. "Well, I suppose what goes around comes around doesn't it. It was only a matter of time before people started to get what was coming to them. It's all about the control you see, the drugs and the money. People are just getting too fucking greedy. There is was more than enough to go around; Harry's just greedy wanting it all for himself."

Gill snapped, she grabbed Sally by her arm and went nose to nose with her. "What do you mean by that? Listen, Harry runs things around here, he always has and always will. It's the Collins brothers who have stepped on his turf, not the other way around, smart arse. Anyway, since when have you given a fuck about who's earning what around here, it's never bothered you before?"

Sally pulled away from Gill, she seemed confident and stood her ground. Usually she would have backed off from Gill in any argument, but not today, she was telling it how it was. "Oh, get a bleeding grip Gill. Things change and Harry is old school. It was only a matter of time before he had to move on anyway. It's a dog eat dog world out there and in time the Collins brothers will be had over too. It's swing and roundabouts in this game. It's a fact, so I don't know why you're getting on your high horse about it."

Gill stubbed her cigarette out in the ashtray and blew the smoke in Sally's face, she hated her attitude. "Yeah, we all know that, but look what they've done to Matty. I can tell you now Harry won't let this lie. There's going to be murders. He's getting a team together as we speak, I swear it will be war around here tonight, nobody is safe."

Sally was interested now and she was getting as much

information out of Gill as she could. "So, let me get this right, Harry's gone looking for Peter Collins and he's got a team ready?".

Gill gave her an evil look and repeated herself. "Oh my God Sally, yeah. I've just told you once. For crying out loud you need to wash your ears out you deaf cow."

Sally was texting someone on her phone while Gill went to make them a brew. She shouted over to Gill. "Mandy's attacker shaved her hair off you know, beat her half to death I've heard. The word on the street is that Jona did it, but I can't see that can you? I know he's a nutter but he's not that low is he?"

Gill placed two cups of coffee on the table and sipped at hers. She was thinking and rubbed at her arms slowly. "Jona is more than capable of it, believe me. Harry's told me a lot of things about him when he was in jail and even then he was planning his revenge on Mandy when he got out of nick. I think it's him too. It's just got his stamp all over it. The man is a psycho, fucking disturbed if you ask me."

Sally crossed her legs and kicked one out in front of her slowly. "It just goes to show you doesn't it, you don't know what goes on in some people's heads. Anyway, is there any news on Ray Clough or what? There's not been a whisper about him and Regina seems as happy as Larry considering her husband has gone missing. I mean, if that was me, I'd have the police out looking for him and all that, but she's not batted an eyelid, she's just acting normal as if nothing has happened."

Gill shrugged her shoulders and blew a laboured breath. "He's probably with another woman, the dirty bastard. I'm so over him now, I can tell you. Harry is the one I love and I realise that now. I just hope Harry forgives me."

Sally let out a sarcastic laugh, and she wasn't aware she was thinking aloud. "He should have kicked your arse to the kerb for what you did, that's what any other man would have done who had any balls."

Sally covered her mouth with her hand, she'd dropped a bollock and she knew it. She tried to backpedal but Gill was on one now. "What's up with you lately Sally, you're doing my head in. I thought you were my friend. If you've got a problem with me then just spit it out."

Sally was on the spot, her blood was boiling; she had so much to say but didn't have the nerve to say it. She swallowed hard as she felt Gill's eyes all over her. "Just calm down will you and put your dummy back in. I have a right to my opinion don't I? I told you from the start that Ray Clough was a nobhead, so it's not something I've hidden away from you is it?" Sally was really pissing Gill off now and for a split second she was going to smack her one.

Gill paced the front room and held her mobile phone to her ear. "Hello Harry, are you alright, don't be doing anything stupid will you? You're still on licence and any spot of trouble they'll bang you back up." Gill was listening eagerly and after a few minutes the call ended.

Sally sat forward in her seat, nibbling at her fingernails. "So, what's going down then is he looking for the Collins brothers or what?"

Gill shook her head and fell to her knees, sobbing. "He's going to wipe the lot of them out, he's fuming Sally. Fuck me, when he's like this he doesn't think straight, he just sees red. What the hell is going on? I just have a gut feeling about this, someone is going to get hurt."

Preston walked into the room and shot his eyes to his mother. He raised his eyebrows to Sally. "What's up with her? Don't tell me they've been arguing again."

Sally knew to keep her gob shut, she dipped her head low. Gill snarled at her son and even though she'd tried to hide her husband's business away from her kids this time she just couldn't hold it in, she was desperate for any kind of help. "No, I've not been arguing with your dad. I need you to go and find him and bring him home. He's going to end up in a lot of trouble if we don't get to him soon."

Preston stood tall; this was a first to him. He stuck his chest out in front of him, at last his mother realised he was no muppet and he could handle himself. He spoke slowly and cracked his knuckles. "Right, you need to fill me in on all this shit, why didn't my dad ask me for help time ago. I could have helped him out, you know me. I'm the man around here. Right, spill then, I want to know what's going on. And, I mean everything mam."

Gill was like a loose cannon, she was telling her son all about Harry's criminal activities and all about the Collins brothers. "Your dad said he was going to the warehouse in Crumpsall, just off Crescent road it is. That's where the weed is, he said he was meeting the boys there."

Preston rubbed his hands together and punched his clenched fist into the air. "So my dad's a main man, fucking hell, so my old man's growing all the weed in Manchester, what a result. Wait until our Callum knows about this he'll be buzzing."

Gill growled at her son and chewed on her lip. "This isn't a joke Preston, you're dad's in serious danger, if the Collins brothers get their hands on him they'll end his life. Is that what you want? Because trust me that's what will happen. Matty's in a bad way, they left him for dead. Do you want your dad to end up the same way?"

Preston was serious now and slammed his hand on the back of the sofa. "Nar, do I fuck. Right leave it with me I'm on it. Nobody fucks with my old man, fucking nobody. Have you seen Callum anywhere, he was supposed to meet me earlier but never showed up, the wank stain, over an hour I sat and waited for him."

Sally grabbed her coat from the back of the chair and headed to the door. She was anxious and couldn't wait to leave. "Gill, I'm getting off. I'll ring you later." Sally waited for a reply but never got one. She rushed into the hallway and left without another word.

Preston was like a blue-arsed fly as he ran up the stairs and sprinted into his bedroom. His eyes were all over and he lay down on the floor with his arm stretched under the bed, he was looking for something. A silver pistol was now in his hands. Standing to his feet he shoved the gun down the front of his pants. Gill was shouting him from downstairs and he stuck his head over the banister. "Mam, just chill I'm sorting it. Trust me everything is going to be alright." He ran down the stairs and pecked his mother on the cheek. He looked her straight in the eyes and spoke. "I'm going to get my dad back home. Who do these cunts think they're messing with? Trust me mother, I'll sort it. These pricks are going down."

Gill gasped, she was sorry she'd even opened her mouth; she was just at her wits end and had nowhere else to turn. "Preston, just bring him home safe, please don't be putting your neck on the line too. It's all I need you ending up in trouble too." Preston stood in the mirror and pulled his bobble hat over his eyes. This was the big time, a time to make his dad proud of him. Making sure the gun was concealed, he left the house.

Gill sat alone smoking; she closed her eyes and wrapped her hands around her body tightly. "Please God, please let them both be alright."

CHAPTER EIGHTEEN

Kenzo sat in the back of the car and rested her hands on the back of the driver's seat. "There it is Peter. Matty said it's the biggest grow they've ever had. There's pure cash in there and it should be ready any time soon."

Peter stretched his neck and tapped his fingers on the steering wheel. It all looked kosher from the outside and if his sister was telling the truth he would be quids in. "You better not be chatting shit Kenzo, if we go in there and it's empty, I swear I'll end you're life." Kenzo was adamant she was telling the truth and when Peter spotted Harry Jarvis pulling up in his car he chuckled loudly. "Watch this space you muppet. I'm taking the lot, let's see who's laughing when your grow has gone, prick."

Kenzo was relieved; she knew he believed her now. "Will you let me go? You know I'm telling the truth and," she paused. "You said I could have the money back too."

Peter screwed his face up, his sister was winding him up, she was a money grabbing bitch. "Just relax, as soon as the weed is out of there I'll stick to my side of the bargain, but for now you will have to keep a low profile. I'll take you somewhere out of the way until it's done."

Kenzo was up in arms and her true colours were there for him to see. "No Peter, you said if I helped you I could go. You said that so come on, stick to your side of the bargain." Peter ignored her and started the engine up, he held an evil look in his eyes and somehow he didn't look like he was going to free her any time soon. Gripped tightly Peter dragged his sister to the lock-up. As he opened the door you could hear someone's voice mumbling in the background. Kenzo was trying her best to break free, punching, kicking and screaming but she was weak and had no fight left in her. Opening another door Kenzo was flung inside head first into the room. The door slammed behind her and she was in darkness, except for a small dim light from a crack in the wall. "Please, Peter, come back. You said I could go. Please, I'm begging you." Kenzo listened carefully but there was no reply. "Bastard, double-crossing bastard," she screamed at the top of her voice. Kenzo heard a noise behind her, somebody else was in the room. Her heart pounded inside her chest and she could barely talk. There were mumbling, rustling noises behind her. "Hello, is anybody there?" Ever since being a small child she'd hated the dark. She was always sneaking into her mother's bed at night and hated being alone when darkness fell. Kenzo turned around slowly and stood with her back against the door, palms held flat on the back of it. "Who's there," she whispered.

Callum answered her from the other side of the room. "It's me Callum, where are you?"

Kenzo was crapping her knickers; she listened carefully to where the voice was coming from and stood on guard. She was planning her attack, and flicked her hair back from her shoulder. "Have you got any gear, anything, I'm ill here. I need to sort myself out?"

Kenzo held her hands out in front of her and made her way to where the voice was coming from. Digging her hand deep in her pocket she pulled out her lighter and flicked it rapidly to get some light. Callum was in a bad way, he was sat with his head in his hands rocking to and fro.

"What the fuck are you doing here?" Kenzo asked sternly. There was no way she wanted this kid to think she was scared, she had to blag it.

Callum coughed and she could see him for the first time, he'd been hurt and dried blood was all over his face, dried and flaking. "Ben brought me here. I owed him some money for the brown, and I couldn't pay him. Ben and his wanker brother did this to me."

Kenzo swallowed hard. She knew what her brothers were all about, but this was a kid, a young man, this was way out of order. Kenzo sat down next to him and pulled a cigarette from her coat pocket, there was a full packet there and she offered Callum one. "It's my brothers you're talking about. I'm Ben's sister."

Callum held his head back against the wall. This wasn't making sense to him, why on earth was she there with him? Was she going to finish him off or what? He backed off and held his hands over his head. "I deserved it, I owed them money. It's my own fault. It's just the smack. I'm hooked on it now and I can't live without it."

Kenzo patted the top of his shoulder; she was battling with her own addiction and knew exactly where he was coming from. Callum was sweating and near his legs she could see a puddle of water, the guy had pissed himself. Kenzo inhaled deeply and checked where she was sat, she could smell shit. Callum watched her and realised what she could smell. His bowels had opened regularly and there was nothing he could do to stop it, the brown liquid just kept pouring from him. "I've shit myself, that's what you can smell. I'm rattling and this is what happens when I don't get a fix."

Kenzo heaved into her cupped hands, the smell was rancid and there was no escaping it. She pulled her coat up over her nose. "That's hanging, fuck me, and here's me thinking I was in a bad way. How the hell have you ended up on heroin, you're still a kid?" Callum choked up and for the very first time he admitted to himself that he was a heroin addict. He told Kenzo all about how he started taking the smack and she cringed when she heard it was her brothers who had introduced him to the drug. Kenzo was curious and started to ask more questions. "So where do you live, do your parents know about you taking drugs?"

Callum shook his head. "Nar, they think I'm just ill. My dad will go sick when he knows he's got a junkie as a son. I've let him down big time."

"Who's your dad then," Kenzo asked.

"Harry Jarvis," he answered.

Kenzo's face dropped, this wasn't right. She asked him again and when he repeated himself she lost all the colour in her face. There was a silence and all you could see was a grey cloud of smoke leaving Kenzo's mouth. She sat playing with her hair and eventually spoke. "My brothers don't know you're Harry's son do they because if they do God help you. Fuck me, this is some mixed up shit. My brothers are at war with your dad, it's been going on for time and it's all going off now, your dad wants his turf back."

Callum didn't answer straight away. "My dad tells me nothing about what he's up to. He thinks I'm some kind of muppet who doesn't understand what all this shit is about. I was up and coming you know, one day it would have been me who was running all the shit around Manchester, I just fucked up."

Kenzo smiled, this guy was full of shit, he was a toy gangster. She'd met plenty of lads like him in the past and knew he was just living in a dream world. Her brothers would eat him up and spit him out. He was a nobody and now he was a druggie, a lowlife with no future ahead of him. Kenzo stood up and stubbed her cigarette out. She looked through the keyhole in the door, it was pitch black. Walking around the room she felt about and tried to find something heavy.

"What are you looking for?" Callum asked.

"Derrrrr, I'm going to try and get out of here. Don't tell me you've just sat here feeling sorry for yourself. Haven't you looked for a way out yet?"

Callum just stared at her. "Nar, I'm in a bad way. I'm weak. I can't even stand up from the floor. Look at me I'm dripping in sweat."

Kenzo looked at him as he pulled his top down. Trickles of sweat were rolling from his body, his eyes looked sunken and he really did look ill. Kenzo found a tool box on the floor; it must have belonged to Ben because she'd seen some of these tools before. This must have been the torture chamber what her brothers used for people who'd wronged them. Her face went white and her heart was beating ten to a dozen. She needed out of here as fast as she could, her life was in serious danger. "Right, get up from the floor and stop feeling sorry for yourself. If they come back here for us any time soon you know it's over don't you?"

Callum held his head against the wall and lifted his eyes up. "What do you mean over for us?"

Kenzo ran over to him and dragged him up to his feet. "Are you a full shilling or what? They will kill us, torture us and end our lives. Are you getting the picture now or what?"

Callum was brain dead, he held on to a ledge to steady himself and you could see he was unsteady on his feet. "You're talking out of your arse. Why would they kill their own sister? And, as for me, I'll probably get another arse kicking, they won't kill me. I still owe them money, surely I'm better off to them more alive than dead?"

Kenzo chuckled, he was so thick she wanted to shake him. "I've just told you who I am and now they know your Harry's son, do you think they will give a flying fuck about cutting you up and posting your body parts to your dad?" Kenzo stood with her hands on her hips waiting for him to answer. "Yeah, now the penny has dropped hasn't it thicko. So, are we getting out of here or what? It's do or die pal, which is it to be?"

Callum bent his legs slowly and placed his hand in the tool box. Picking up a hammer he passed it to Kenzo. "Here, you get a grip of that, you're probably stronger than me and can swing it. I'll just get something light what I can manage."

Kenzo snatched the claw hammer from his hand and held it behind her shoulder, with a almighty swing she attacked the door, hammering at it. Callum stood back and looked scared, this girl was in a wild frenzy and by the looks of things she was taking the door down without any help from him. Callum walked to the side of her, her eyes seemed vacant and her teeth were clenched together tightly. "Here, you have a go beanpole, my arm's knackered, come on, a few more belts and we should be out of here." Callum held the hammer in his hands and he was shaking rapidly as he tried to swing it back over his head. A small banging noise on the door and a small dint appeared where he'd hit it. Kenzo snarled at him. "Fucking hell, give it back here, a fly couldn't get through that gap, you need to swing it like this."

After a lot of loud banging, a hole was appearing in the door and Callum seemed to get a second wind. He cheered her on from the side knowing freedom was only minutes away. "Go on girl, knock ten tons of shit out of it, crack it harder go on, you're nearly there." A large hole was now in front of them. Kenzo slung her coat off and squashed her head through the hole first. Callum was right behind her and as soon as her legs were through he followed her. They both stood quivering in the corridor, eyes looking all around them both for the exit.

Callum crept to Kenzo's side and placed his hand on her shoulder. "Looks like were up shit street, there's no way out." Kenzo jumped out of her skin, he'd scared her. She took a few paces forward and kicked her foot against the wall. "There must be a way out, just have a look around and stop just standing there, fucking do something."

Callum was half asleep, every step he took looked like he was going to collapse. Kenzo patted her hands along the wall feeling for a way out. "Here's another door," Callum shouted, proud that he'd done something right at last.

Kenzo hurried to his side. "Right, get the hammer on it. We'll have to do the same as before. Fucking hell, come on hurry up, they'll be back soon.

Harry Jarvis sat with his men at the warehouse. There were ten of them at least. Harry dipped his head into his hands. "It's now or never. Matty is at death's door, they left him for dead the cheeky twats. They must know it's war now. Who do they think they're fucking with, do they not know what we're about?"

Gerry cracked his knuckles. He'd been part of the team for as long as anyone. He'd served his time in jail too, six years was his last sentence and he always said he never wanted to go back there but having no money always led him back to crime. Old habits die hard and Gerry knew that more than anyone. He promised himself that after this grow he was taking his cut and making it work for him, maybe he'd open a small cafe or something, anything other than crime. Gerry was forty years old, his arms were covered in tattoos and one of them looked quite new. The ink was bright and colourful compared to the others. His round face looked stressed, he knew this was the last straw and he was aware people were going to die during this battle. It was going to be a bloodbath and he just hoped he came through the other side with all his bits intact. "We need to get hold of them Harry, the three brothers need to be wiped out. We can go and boom their mam's door in if you want. If they're not there we'll take the old hag with us. Surely they'll come and meet us then if we've got their old queen on lock down?"

Harry was thinking, he shot his eyes around the warehouse and looked at the cannabis plants. "They're after this fucking lot. I just know it. If they come within an inch of here I'll blow their fucking brains out. This lot is going to sort us all out; we can chill for a bit once this lot is bagged up. We can fuck off on holiday and relax for a bit. I know I need a break."

Gerry stood up and paced the floor, he was agitated and wanted it all sorted straight away. "Harry, you don't know what these Collins brothers are like, you've been away for a long time, they're cheeky cunts, they think they can just have us over. We need to knock them down a peg or two before we lose it all."

A few of the other men agreed, this crop was their bread and butter and none of them wanted to take a chance of losing it. They'd worked too hard for it, just to let it go. Harry was under pressure and knew he needed to sort this out and quick. He patted the top of Gerry's shoulder and sat down with the men. He tapped the spot next to him and shot a look to Gerry. "Right, like you said we'll go through their front door tonight. If they're not there, we'll smash the place up and take their mother with us," Harry paused and chuckled as he gripped the front of his knees. "Yeah, we'll take their fucking mam, at least then they'll know we're serious. I'm sick of being a soft touch. Prison must have messed with my head, what the fuck have I been doing all this time? I should have had this sorted, right lads, game on, we'll boom the door in tonight."

Gerry rubbed his hands together and nudged Harry. "Thank fuck for that soft lad, I thought you'd lost it? You know it makes sense, let's put the fear of God in them, the fucking muppets."

Harry shot his eyes around the warehouse. "Somebody needs to watch this place, there's no way we're leaving this on its own. I've just got a feeling this lot will be gone if we take our eyes off the ball for one second. A few of us will have to stay here with it tonight. I don't want is going AWOL."

Gerry sorted out who was staying the night at the warehouse and left three of the men there. They were tooled up and ready for any intruders. Gerry had told them straight that if anyone came through the door they were to shoot them, no questions asked, just fucking shoot them. Harry and his men fed the plants and left. The team who were on guard all sat together laughing and joking, it was going to be a long night and they knew they had to be vigilant. It was going down big time.

★

Preston lay in the vent in the ceiling. He's sneaked in through the back door when one of the men was outside having a cig. He was meant to be finding his father and bringing him home but all of this action was too much excitement to miss. This was a real gangland war like he'd seen on the TV and he was mesmerized by it all, it was the real McCoy; guns, blades, drugs, the full Monty. Preston watched his father leave and smiled to himself. His dad, his own flesh and blood, a real top man, a fucking gangster. He was proud and couldn't wait to tell his brother all about it. Preston watched the men below skinning up. The three of them were getting stoned and he wished he could have joined them. Lying still he felt his mobile phone vibrating in his pocket. In a panic he looked at the screen, it was Tina. There was no way he could answer the call. He was on a stakeout and she could wait until this was over. He pressed the power button off and slid the phone back in his pocket with a relieved look. Closing his eyes, he listened to the men below talking about his father; he smiled and felt a warmth rise through his body. He was Harry Jarvis's son and at last he was important. This was the life for him and as soon as this was over he was telling his father he wanted to be part of it too. This was all he'd ever dreamt about and now that he knew his own father was the top dog, the life he'd imagined for years didn't seem that far away now.

Kenzo and Callum had one last door to break down and they'd be free. Kenzo was sweating, her face was boiling hot and she'd taken her top layer of clothing off. Callum was neither use nor ornament, he was gagging for breath at the side of her and every now and then he was spewing his ring up. Kenzo told him straight that if he was going to shit himself again he needed to do it away from her, he'd already done it a few minutes ago and she was near hitting him over the head with the hammer never mind hitting the door. Kenzo stopped lunging the hammer at the door for a few minutes; she was exhausted and had bitten off more than she could chew. Time wasn't on their side and she knew if they didn't get out of there within the next hour their number would be up. Peter was due back at anytime now and if he spotted they'd tried to escape he'd go mental.

He was like that Peter; he was a sick mental bastard who liked to see people suffer. All of her brothers were like that and Kenzo held that gene too if she was honest with herself, she got a kick from watching people suffer, begging, and pleading was right up her street. Suddenly she heard noises, people talking in the distance. Kenzo froze and waved her hand above her head trying to get Callum's attention. "It's them they're back, fucking hell, hide." Kenzo was running around in a circle and she knew any second now her number was up, the voices were outside the door. Callum just dropped to the floor, he had no fight left in him and he was ready to face the consequences. Kenzo gripped the claw hammer tightly in her hands and hid away in the corner of the room. "Say fuck all Callum, if they ask where I am, say nothing." The handle on the door was moving and Callum sank to his knees and covered his face with his hands. Kenzo held her breath and you could see her chest rising with speed.

Ben Collins opened the door, shouting behind him. "Flick the switch for the electric, Connor."

Footsteps could be heard and all of a sudden the lights came on. Ben shot his eyes to Callum and he ran to his side as soon as he clocked all the dints in the door, he could see large holes. "Well, you cheeky little rat, were you trying to escape?" Connor and Peter walked into the room now and Peter shouted out in a loud voice. "Where the fuck is she, Connor quick, close the door Kenzo's missing. The both of them were running around the room trying to locate her, she was hid under a table and you could see her feet sticking out from underneath it at the bottom.

Ben yanked Callum up from the floor, he went nose to nose with him and his eyes were dancing with madness. "Tell me now where she is, I swear I'll fucking drop you if you don't tell me where she's gone." Callum struggled to get his breath; he pointed his finger over to where she was. Ben dropped him and ran to her hiding place. Kenzo screamed and shrieked, she was going wild.

She was dragged from beneath the table by her hair. The hammer was still in her hand and she was doing her best to lash out with it.

"You grassing cunt," she shouted over at Callum. "Go on tell them who your dad is, go on shitbag."

Callum was petrified; he was white in the face. Ben flung her to the floor and stood over her. "I know who his dad is. Why do you think he's here?"

A single tear fell onto Callum's cheek and he knew his life was in danger. Peter and Connor came back into the room and as soon as they saw Kenzo, Peter let out a laboured breath. "So, you thought you could escape did you?" Kenzo spat over at her brother, she was ready to attack him but Ben held her back. "I'm not arsed what you do to me dick-head. You promised me if I told you about Harry's grow you would sort me out. I want my money you double- crossing bastard."

Peter ran at her and punched her in the face, blood surged all over as the blow connected. Connor stepped in front of her and Ben pulled Peter away. "Just lock her up out of the way for now. It's this little prick we need to deal with first, remember whose son he is."

Peter wiped some spit from the side of his mouth with a swift movement. His brothers were right, Kenzo would keep for now. Ben and Connor dragged her out of the room and you could hear doors banging as they locked her up in a small cleaning cupboard not far away. Kenzo was pleading with them, begging her brothers to let her go, they never listened.

Peter walked around Callum Jarvis, weighing him up, seeing if he had the balls like his father did. He could see the fear in his eyes, the terror as he walked near him. Peter loved that he was scared; he loved the power he felt over him. Callum was a kid, but that didn't deter him, it just made him even more cocky than he was already. "So, your dad is Harry Jarvis then?

Callum swallowed hard, he was sweating and his vision was poor. "What's my old man go to do with this? I owe the money to you not him. Leave him out of this he's harmless."

Peter was joined by his brothers, they were all stood above Callum and each of them snarled as they looked at him. "I don't think your dad has been telling you the truth mate, your dad is a big grafter just like us. Why do you think he went to jail?"

Callum shook his head, this was a mix- up and he was sure these men were getting his dad mixed up with someone else. "He went to jail because he had a fight, well, that's what my mam told us."

The men laughed out loud, was this guy a comedian or what? Ben held the bottom of his stomach as he replied. "Your dad is Harry Jarvis, you know, the Harry Jarvis who has run most of the crime in this area for years."

Peter paused and raised his eyes and spoke in a sarcastic tone. "That was , until we took over things."

Callum looked puzzled, he seemed to be finding some inner strength. He sat up straight and looked at the three brothers. "Nar, that's not my dad, he against all drugs and that, he goes mad at me for even smoking weed."

Peter couldn't believe his ears, was this kid for real or what, he acted like he was streetwise so why didn't he know the score about his old man? Peter was losing patience and he clenched his fist together tightly. Ben was aware he was going to knock ten tons of shit out of the lad and saved him from a beating at the last minute. "Whoa, just wait up Peter. We want him alive if we are going to use him against Harry, what good is he going to be if he's dead? Think about it; just leave him for now until we've decided what we are going to do with him. He's no good to us dead is he?" Ben was right and Peter knew it, he still wanted to leather him though, you could see it in his eyes.

Callum held the bottom of his stomach and his face creased with pain. A stench now filled the air. Connor covered his nose with his hands as did Ben. They could see wetness appearing around the lad's body. "Fuck me, he's shit himself, what a dirty little bastard," Connor spluttered. Ben walked to the door and stuck his head out, he was gagging. Callum tried to get up from the floor and use the chair at the side of him for help. Taking a deep breath he spoke. "Can you sort me out with some gear lads, just to stop me rattling, I'm dying here. I need a quick toot, you know, to calm me down."

Ben looked at Connor and they knew Peter was onto them now. "What, are you a smack head?"

Callum wasn't afraid anymore and he knew they had to keep him alive. "Yeah, your brothers made me sell the shit to pay the debt off I owed them, it just happened. I only had one go and then I was hooked. I'm a junkie now because of them two."

Peter growled, he was a hard case yes, but to get a kid on heroin, even he wouldn't sink that low. "So you're selling brown then you two, what the fuck is going on? I thought we didn't touch the stuff. I've told you before how I feel about smack."

Ben and Connor had some explaining to do, this was

their own little earner and for months they'd kept this secret from their older brother. "Listen, it's our shit and we'll sort it out. There's money to be had from selling the brown and just because you're against it, it doesn't mean we have to be too."

Peter pulled a face and marched around the room, he knew in this line of work it was bound to happen sooner or later but he felt let down by his brothers, they'd had him over. "Listen, I'm not arsed, do whatever you're doing but don't let me hear about it. Heroin wrecks lives, I know it's good money, but we earn enough from the weed and the sniff, let Jarvis and his lads sell the smack, we're better than that."

Peter zipped his coat up and stood thinking. He hated heroin and remembered a girl he'd grown up with being hooked on it from an early age. As tough as he was, he feared the drug and knew only too well how much it could take over someone's life. Melanie Thomas had been his childhood sweetheart. He loved her with all his heart and always said one day he would marry her. He never did, she died at the age of twenty-six from a drugs overdose. Peter looked sad. He'd never really loved anyone again since Melanie. Sally was his girl now but he was just passing time with her, she'd never fill his heart like Melanie had.

Kenzo was still kicking at the door, her voice was loud and she seemed desperate. "Let me out, please, I'll do anything, I hate the dark. Ben you know I do, please let me out." Nobody replied to her.

Connor gripped Callum by the scruff of his neck and led him out of the door. Ben was in a panic. "That scruffy cunt is not getting in my car like that. Check his pants out, he's covered in shit." Ben was right, Callum's pants were covered in a brown stain, stinking wet, rancid patches. "I'll strip off if you want, just don't leave me here. I'll go in the boot if I have too, just get me out of here."

Peter sniggered to himself. "He can get in the car, if you two deal in smack then this can be a warning to you how much it fucks people's lives up. Come on kid, you can get in the back with Connor."

Ben was looking around the room for something for the kid to wear, there was an old boiler suit slung on a cabinet nearby, he gripped it with both hands. "Here, get stripped off and get this on. I swear, you shit in my car and I'll fucking end your life, do you hear me?" Callum was relieved that he was leaving the building; he twisted his head over his shoulder and listened to the screams from Kenzo. Yanking his clothes off he got changed and left the room.

Kenzo was alone, scared, and abandoned. She sat in the cupboard crying, this was her worst nightmare. She barely had enough room to move, she was trapped, like a caged animal. Drawing her knees up to her chest she rocked about slowly, she hummed a tune trying to comfort herself.

Callum sat in the back of the car, the window was wide open and Connor was sat next to him with his coat pulled up over his nose. Peter was on the phone and Callum was listening carefully to the call. "Yeah Jona, sorted mate. I'll meet you later and we can chat some more. Welcome on board pal, you know it makes sense."

Callum knew Jona and knew he was a friend of his father's, his eyes were wide open and it clicked in his brain that he was a double agent. He couldn't help himself and put his mouth into gear without thinking first. "Jona will be a dead man walking when my dad knows he's working for you lot now, he's a twat, my dad helped him out when he got out of jail. He was always at our house scrounging, the dirty scum bag."

Connor flicked the side of his ears and gave him a warning look. "Keep out of things that don't concern you, keep your trap shut and you'll be okay."

Callum spoke in a low voice, he had to know what was coming next, where were they taking him, were they going to kill him or what? Peter sparked a cigarette up and the car was filled with smoke. Callum was gasping for a blast of nicotine and nudged Connor at the side of him. "Can I bum a fag off you, I'm dying here. It will help me calm down. I mean, you don't want me crapping my pants again do you, I'm shaking like a shitting dog?"

Connor looked at him and dug in his coat pocket for a cigarette. He wanted this kid as calm as could be, if he was stressed he might even shit his pants again, he passed him one. The car pulled up outside the warehouse. Peter was still on the phone and he was gathering all his men together. They were kitted out with guns, knives and other weapons. Peter sat staring from the car window, he wasn't ready to strike yet, it was too early. The roads were still busy and a few pedestrians were walking by. He sat watching the warehouse eagerly – this was the quiet before the storm.

★

Harry and his men went to see Matty at the hospital. He had tubes all over his body and the doctors were constantly running in and out. Only three at a time were allowed in the room to see him. Harry had already been in and he was waiting for the others to come out. Harry paced the corridor outside and suddenly he froze. He checked nobody was watching him and headed up the stairs onto another ward. Opening the door slightly you could see he was debating his next move.

A nurse noticed him and headed his way. "Can I help you sir?" she asked.

Harry was stuck for words at first, he was mumbling under his breath. "Erm, is Mandy on this ward?" The nurse took some more details from him and led him onto the ward. The place stank of misery, old people were coughing and spluttering, and it was obvious to him some of them were living on borrowed time. It was like death's waiting room. Harry could see Mandy lay in her bed, she looked different, her hair was missing. She looked ill. The nurse left Harry's side and he was alone with her.

Sitting on a chair next to the bed he made sure nobody was watching him. "Fuck me Mandy, is this what that crank did to you?"

Mandy turned her head slowly and he could see her full face for the first time. She had stitches in her cheek and her lip was still swollen. "I'm fine now Harry, you should have seen me a few weeks ago, I was a mess. I know it was Jona who done this to me, but the snapper is still on his toes. Nobody has seen sight or sound of him. He's a rat and I'll be glad when the police catch up with him. I hope they lock him up and throw away the key, he can rot in there for all I care. He's a fucking psycho."

"Sorry, I've not been to see you sooner. I've had a lot on my plate, you know how it is don't you?" Mandy smiled at him and reached over to touch his hand softly.

"Harry, I know how things are and I'm just glad

you're here now, it shows you care." Harry bit hard on his lips. Mandy was a good friend of his and the kiss they shared should never have happened. They were good friends and nothing else, she had been a shoulder to cry on when he was at his lowest. Most people seemed to think they'd shared more than a kiss although neither of them had said anything.

"Jona is one crazy fucker, what the hell has he done this to you for. He knew you two were over so why has he done this?"

Mandy took a deep breath and closed her eyes tightly, she was reliving her attack. "I don't have a clue what's going on in his head Harry. What he's done to me I'll never forgive him. Look at the state of my hair, the bastard raped me too, sick in the head he is, he needs sectioning."

Harry sat thinking, he'd been padded up with this guy for months and never once had he showed any signs of carrying out the things he'd spoken about whilst they were in jail, he just thought he was chatting shit, you know, jail talk. Everybody did it in jail and they spoke about cutting people up who had bubbled on them, but it rarely happened. Mandy sipped a glass of cold water at the side of her bed. She looked at Harry in more detail. "So, are you and Gill sorted out now or what?"

Harry sunk his head low and flicked the invisible dust from his jeans. "I don't know where my head is at anymore Mandy, one minute I love Gill and the next I want to twist her up, hurt her bad. She's ruined what we had, and if I'm being honest with you, it will never be the same. I'm just holding on to nothing. Holding on to the past."

Mandy was alert, she licked her dry cracked lips and

tried to sit up in the bed. This was her chance to have him, to make a play for him, to make him her man. Harry Jarvis was a catch and whoever got him next would be a lucky woman. Mandy cleared her throat. "Harry, I know I look a bit dodgy at the moment with no hair and all that, but you know how I feel about you don't you? It might be time to move on from Gill and see if you can be happy somewhere else." Mandy leant over and turned his face towards her. "I can make you happy Harry, just give me a chance."

Harry pulled away slowly; this was too much too soon. He didn't know if he was coming or going. Gill was his life and she had been for such a long time – was she just a habit he had to break or was he still in love with her? Mandy carried on speaking. "I've always liked you Harry, and I think you've felt the same about me. You kissed me for crying out loud, surely that meant something to you."

Harry didn't want to kick Mandy whilst she was down. She was making the kiss sound a lot more than it really was. It was a stupid drunken kiss that meant nothing to him. His heart didn't beat faster and his legs never melted. Harry liked Mandy as a friend and looking at her in more detail he knew he had to put her right before she got her hopes up. "Mandy, you're a lovely woman, and if things would have been different."

Mandy chuckled and held her head back. "Please, don't give me that spiel Harry, fuck me, it's been the story of my life. If I had a penny for every time some geezer had said that to me I would be a rich woman. I understand what you're saying and I'm glad you're being straight with me, but do me a favour, don't start with the wrong time, wrong place, bullshit. I know the score already."

Harry smirked, she was a top woman and she seemed to understand him, she'd listened to him and gave him good advice when he needed it." "Cheers for that Mandy, I will always be straight with you, you're a good woman and I hope you find someone who deserves you one day. It's obvious Jona didn't know what he had with you otherwise he wouldn't have fucked up."

Mandy jumped into the conversation, stopping him dead. "Correct, just the same as you with Gill. She's a dick-head for messing about on you she had everything she ever needed; she doesn't know how lucky she is either."

Harry blew a laboured breath and shrugged his shoulders. "It's not all cut and dried Mandy, I've made mistakes in the past and I suppose its Karma isn't it? What goes around comes around and all that."

Mandy's face creased at the sides, she didn't know what he meant and delved deeper. "You're a good man Harry, you've never cheated on her, so don't beat yourself up about it. It's her in the wrong not you. Unless, that is, you cheated too?"

Harry quickly rolled his sleeve up and checked his wristwatch. He stood up and straightened his clothes. "Right, I've got to get off. I've just been to see Matty. He's in a bad way too, have you heard what's gone down with him?"

Mandy nodded and rubbed at her arms, goose bumps were appearing and the hairs on the back of her neck were standing on end. "Yes, I've heard all about it. The word is the Collins brothers were responsible for it, is that true, you know how people chat shit around here?"

Harry bent over the bed and kissed the top of her

forehead. "It's nothing for you to worry about love, you just get on the mend and I'll come and see you again. You should be out of here soon, so not that long, ay?"

Mandy knew he was keeping schtum about the whole affair. He wasn't one to tell his business to anyone, he'd learned that a long time ago. Women liked to gossip and no matter how much he trusted her, he would never talk about his criminal activities with her, with no one, this was his business and he was keeping it that way. "I'll see you soon, take care Mandy, glad to see you're on the mend."

Harry walked along the corridor to the exit. Mandy was alone in her bed now and lay back down. Her heart was low and she knew any chances of getting her heart's desires had gone forever. Gill Jarvis was a lucky woman and as soon as Mandy was well enough to leave the hospital she was going to tell her straight that she didn't deserve him. Closing her eyes, she pulled the blanket over her shoulders and snuggled down to sleep. Now Harry had been to see her she felt happy again, perhaps there was a chance of her having him, only time would tell.

CHAPTER NINETEEN

Susan Collins watched the end of the film on TV. It was late and usually she would have been in bed by now but she'd got interested in the film and couldn't go to bed until she knew what was happening to the characters in it. She was like that Susan, a bit obsessive sometimes. It was just the way she was. Sat chewing on her fingernails she sat on the edge of her seat, her eyes were wide open and she was scared. Hiding her head behind the pillow, she kept sneaking a look at the screen. "Oh, you bastard, I knew it was you. I just knew it was you." The titles appeared on the screen and Susan flicked the switch for the TV. She was mumbling under her breath as she plodded about the front room. "I should have been a detective I should have. I would have solved that case within minutes, it was so predictable. I'm like Miss Marple I am." The lights were all switched off in the front room. Susan walked into the kitchen and opened the fridge door. She was always hungry at this time of night and started to make herself a ham sandwich. She was a midnight muncher for sure and always had a snack before bedtime. Perhaps that's why she was piling on the pounds. Late- night eating wasn't good for her and she knew it, but carried on anyway. I think food comforted her too, every night she sat alone and her lads were rarely in. John used to stay in with her some nights and they used to watch horror films together. Since he'd been gone she was lonely. Susan started to munch her sandwich as she headed upstairs to bed.

The front door was locked and she had done all her security checks on the house. She was a dizzy swine sometimes and often left windows open, not now though, her lads had warned her to make sure they were closed every night. The crime rate in the area was soaring and everyday you would hear stories about somebody being robbed in the area. If it wasn't locked down it would go missing, that was a fact. Drugs had caused the rise in crime in the area, smack-heads were the worst though, they would do anything to get a fix and robbing people's houses were top of their list, easy graft. They had no morals, they had nothing on their minds other than scoring, so house robbery was an easy way to get money and fast. They preyed on the vulnerable; old folks, single parents, and anyone who was earning a few quid that they thought didn't deserve it. Harpurhey had changed so much over the years, it used to be such a nice area but nowadays money was short and everyone was doing whatever they could to keep their heads above water. Most houses on the estate had a little grow in them, people needed to earn cash, what did the police expect? Drugs bred jealousy though and nobody was safe. The minute anyone found out that someone had a cannabis grow in their houses the door was boomed in and all the plants were taken. It was a dog eat dog environment and only the strong survived.

Susan sat on the edge of her bed and looked at the moonlight from her bedroom window. The silver moon looked peaceful tonight and she smiled softly as she looked at it. The stars were shining brightly too and she studied them further, holding her head to the side. Her father always told her that they were people who had passed away and she often wondered if her son was now a star too. Perhaps he was the nearest one to her, the one that shined the brightest in the night sky. She held her finger out towards it trying to touch it. Susan missed her son so much and the picture of him at the side of her bed was never far from her side at bedtime. Every night she lay the framed photo on the pillow next to her and spoke to it as if it was her son. Tonight was no different. Susan pulled her chunky robe from her body and lay on the top of her bed in a long cotton nightie. She used to like sleeping in the nude when she was younger but since all her body had flopped she hated the way she looked now and always made sure she was covered in bed. "Well John," she whispered. "That film was a load of garbage. You would have hated it. It wasn't one you would have liked, too much blood and swearing in it. I solved the case though; you know how clever I am when I get a bee in my bonnet. I'm like a dog with a bone when I smell a rat." Susan wiped the tears falling onto her cheeks and snivelled. "Why didn't I see it was Kenzo who killed you, son? She had us all right over you know. I've washed my hands off her now, she's no daughter of mine anymore. She's an outcast. I mean it John; she's dead as far as I'm concerned." Susan carried on whispering to the photograph and every now and then her eyes closed, she was tired now and it wouldn't be long before she drifted off to sleep.

Harry and two of his men sat in the alleyway facing the Collins' house. It was late now and not a soul was about. The odd cat walked the streets and you could hear one meowing in the distance. It sounded like a baby crying, high pitched screams as if it was being strangled. Harry was dressed in black and his hat was pulled over his forehead. You could see his eyes just about, but nothing else. Gerry and the other man was dressed the same. "Right, do we all know what we're doing? We're straight in and straight out, once the old cunt's in the car we're off from here, we can't be waiting around, we need to be gone."

Gerry was flapping and he was smoking like a chimney. He was always like this before a job and no matter how many times he'd done things that were shifty he still got nervous. "I'm ready, let's do this. Harry are you taking the door off its hinges or what? Give the door a good fucking belt it should come off in one go. I'll run straight up the stairs and grab her. Hold on, let me check I've got the tape for her mouth, we don't want the old codger screaming do we?" Gerry patted his coat pocket and looked relieved, he'd checked it was there about ten minutes ago but a second check just put him at ease, he wanted everything to run like clockwork.

The car door opened slowly, one side creaked and Harry shot a look at Gerry as they got out of the car. "For fucks sake can't you make any more noise, get that door sorted out, it's so on top." Gerry shrugged his shoulders as they made their way into the garden. There was a strong smell of flowers and Gerry started to sneeze. "It's my bleeding hay fever Harry, don't look at me like that, it's not my fault. It's them fucking flowers over there." Harry carried on walking down the path and now you could see him pulling a sledge hammer out from inside his jacket. Gerry was at his side now and there was no going back, the door was going through.

To the sound of loud crashing noises and with two fierce belts on the door, it came flying from its hinges. Gerry ran inside the house first and he sprinted straight up the stairs. Kicking each door with force he eventually found Susan's bedroom. The old cow was still fast asleep, snoring her head off, she was oblivious to anything that was going on in front of her. Gerry had the tape ready and with a quick movement he slapped it across Susan's mouth. She started to wake up. Gerry pulled her from the bed and pushed her onto the landing. She was like a lump of lead to move and Harry had to help to get her into the car. This woman was putting up a fight now and she was trying to head- butt her attackers, she was a live wire and there was no way she was giving up without a fight. Harry knew he had to quieten her down she was kicking things as they dragged her to the car, the noisy bitch. There was no way he wanted to hurt a pensioner but she was asking for it. Pulling a silver blade from his pocket he held it in front of her and pressed it with force against her neck. Susan gulped and without any further words she ended her fight with her abductors.

The car spun off onto the main road, they were speeding and at one point the driver nearly lost control on the bend. Gerry was going ballistic. "For fucks sake, take it easy will you. We've got a pensioner with us not the fucking crown jewels, we're safe now, just chill your beans." The driver pressed the brake slowly and the speed decreased. Susan sat in the back of the car with Harry and every now and then she tried to make an escape, every time she failed. Harry was sick to death of her already, if this had been a man he would have punched her lights out, but she was old, he wasn't used to kidnapping OAPs.

She was an old woman who deserved a bit of respect at least; she was a victim of circumstances.

Harry pulled up at the warehouse and they quickly scarpered into the building. Susan was still playing up and Harry passed her over to Gerry. He wouldn't take any more of her shit, he would just floor her if she carried on and he let her know that straight away by slapping her across the face quickly. "Carry on old woman, and you'll be meeting God a lot quicker than you think. Move your fat arse now," he growled into her face.

Susan obeyed his orders. She didn't have a clue what was happening and she thought she was being kidnapped to be sold onto some perverted sex ring. She'd watched things like this on the TV and as soon as they removed the black sticky tape from her mouth she told them straight. "Listen, I'm old you won't get any money for me. I've not had sex for ages and I'm not going to start now, so just kill me. Go on; end it now, because I'm not having any foreigner stuck up me, no way."

Gerry turned his head away and sniggered. The old girl had balls, and she was amusing him. He left her for a few minutes and let her carry on thinking she was being sold as a sex slave. They were winding her up. "Men like older women; we should get a few bob for you. You're just what the lads are looking for. They love older women with big tits."

Susan was spitting feathers and she held her hand over her heart, her face was bright red and she was ready to have a heart attack. "Well, take me back home, my next door neighbour is what you're looking for, she's half the size of me and her breasts are massive. I mean, look at me, you're not going to get much for me are you? I'm ready for the knackers yard, my legs won't bend and I've got arthritis."

Harry walked over and ended Gerry's fun. He stood tall and looked Susan straight in the eyes. "Ignore him love, he's just playing with you. You're here because of your lads."

Harry pulled his hat off and the scarf from around his neck. Susan knew him straight away and she ran at him trying to claw his eyes out. "You no good bastard, there was never no trouble until you got out of jail. You're a greedy bastard who wants everything. Why have you taken me anyway, what good is that going to do? Oh, you've dropped a bollock now sunshine?"

Harry bit hard on his lip. She was old yes, but she still needed to know this was serious and her life was in danger. His nostrils flared as he gripped her by the throat. His nose touched hers. "Your sons are the ones who are causing all the shit around here; this is my patch and always has been. They need to know who they are dealing with. We're not dick-heads, you know. We'll destroy anyone who steps in our way and if it means doing you in love, so be it. Nobody fucks with us. Let's see anyway how much your kids love you now. Let's see if the drugs mean more to them than their own bleeding mother. Somehow I think you'll be leaving in a body bag love, l hope I'm wrong."

Preston was still inside the vent, he was trying to hear every word that was spoken, his father was ruthless and this was the first time he'd seen him in action. He was ready to come out of hiding now his father was back; he couldn't wait to tell his old man how much he inspired him. He was sniggering to himself and started to slide out of the vent. Once he was out, he stretched his body out fully, his face looked strained and he seemed to be in severe pain as his body unfolded.

Peter Collins and his brothers were outside the warehouse, raring to go. They were team-handed and ready for action. This was going to be a bloodbath for sure. The men had machetes, blades, baseball bats and guns. It was going to end in tears one way or the other. Peter gathered his men together at the end of the street. Callum was next to him and never far from his side. Footsteps pounding down the pavement made them all turn around. Jona now joined the group. When he met Peter he shook his hand and began to speak. "So, what's the story, is Harry and the firm in there or what?"

Callum tried to barge forward but he was held back by Peter. "You conning cunt, my dad's looked after you. You're a dirty smack-head, go on tell the lads you've been scoring with me. I bet they don't know you're on the gear do they."

Callum twisted his head around and spoke to the men. "Listen lads, he's a fucking heroin addict, a bag-head, just like me. Don't trust him he's probably having you over. I swear Jona, I hope you get what's coming to you. I hope you get done in, you fucking rat."

Peter looked at Jona in more detail, the kid was right he was a smack-head, you could tell that just by looking at him; sunken cheekbones, dark circles around his eyes, underweight, yeah, the lad was telling the truth. Peter nodded his head at Jona. "Well, is he telling the truth or what, are you a junkie?"

Jona knew how to play this part well, he'd done it enough times in the past and lying about his addiction came as second nature to him. He patted the top of Peter's shoulder "Am I fuck guys, ignore this runt, I hardly even know him. I've seen him about twice in all my life. He knows fuck all about me, absolutely nothing. Jack shit."

Callum tried to voice his opinion again but was shut up straight away by Ben. Connor was asking the questions now. "So, why the sudden change of mind, you and Harry have been mates for years, why the change of heart?"

Everyone was waiting on his answer, you could have heard a pin drop, nobody wanted a spy in the camp and they had to make sure he wasn't part of Harry's plan to bring them down. "Harry was shagging my woman. My Mandy. He's no mate of mine anymore. I mean, who does that? That's the lowest of the low if you ask me and I want fuck all to do with him. The guy is a wrong 'un and I won't graft with people like that. I have respect for my mates, but he's crossed the line, he's carted. You don't shit on your own doorstep do you lads?"

There was whispering among the men, they were all looking at him. Peter still wasn't sure but he didn't have time to find out. They were ready to raid the warehouse now and any extra manpower they had was a bonus, especially Jona he was a ticking bomb, scared of nothing. Callum was still shouting at Jona and after a quick slap from Ben he knew he was fighting a losing battle, he remained quiet. Peter and his men knew Harry was inside, they knew he was also team-handed. All the men were prepared to fight to the death for the prize of the plants inside. It was life changing money behind these walls and they all craved the wealth of the cannabis plants.

Ben stubbed his cigarette out and held his head back to look at the night sky. "Let's do this," he sneered. "Let's wipe the fuckers right out." Callum was dragged now by one of the other men, he was being used as a bargaining tool in the raid. If needed the Collins would have shot him dead right in front of his father. This was no game anymore, this was serious, winner takes all.

★

Gill sat clock watching. She'd smoked over twenty cigs and the ashtray was overflowing. Sally yawned; she was tired and ready to go home. She was checking her phone constantly and looked worried. "I better get home, I'm knackered. I bet Harry is in the club, you know what he's like once he gets a few scoops down his neck. I bet he's pissed as a fart, I bet you."

Gill tapped her fingers on the kitchen table, she licked her lips slowly. "You could be right, and here's me sat here worrying for nothing. I'm going down there, are you coming with me or what?"

Sally frowned. "No, I can't be arsed and plus, look at the state of me. Gill it's nearly three in the morning, you'll have to bang on the door at the back so they'll let you in, it's after closing time." The club was well known for doing after time and it was only usually the main heads who got invited to stay. In the past Harry had fallen out of there at six in the morning unable to walk. It was common knowledge that the club did a lock- in.

"I'll bang the bleeding door down if I have to Sally. You go on as if I'm a nobody. I'm Harry's wife are you forgetting that. The lads down the club respect me."

Sally sniggered and grabbed her coat from the side of

the chair. She knew what she was going to say and held nothing back. She was sick to death of pretending it was all rosy in the garden. "They used to respect you Gill. Well, they did until you got your knickers off for Ray Clough. Everyone was talking about it you know. You lost a lot of friends around here because of it. Come on Gill, let's face it, you are a slapper."

Gill was bright red, she knew Sally had had a few drinks but she wasn't that drunk, she must have been speaking her mind. "Oh, so is that how you feel too? Come on, get it off your chest, say what you think."

Sally put her coat on and stood with her hands on her hips. "Harry is a good man and like I've told you before you're lucky he's stood by you. Any normal man would have fucked you off sometime ago. I think you've changed since you were with Ray. He was a bad influence on you."

This was turning into a full blown argument and neither of them were backing down. Gill could fight, but Sally could hold her own too. "Get the fuck out of my house if that's how you feel. What is it ay? Is it because you've not had a leg-over for ages; are you jealous because I'm getting plenty?"

Sally held her head back and let out a sarcastic laugh. "You don't know shit about me anymore Gill and for your information I'm getting plenty too. Oh, you're quiet now aren't you? Yes, you heard me right, I've got a man."

Gill's face dropped. Sally was her best friend and if she'd not told her about finding love something was definitely wrong. "Sally, if you would have met somebody I would have been the first to know. You can't hold your own piss, so don't come that with me."

Sally paced the floor slowly, she was going to deliver the blow and she chose her moment wisely. "I've been seeing Peter Collins for months. There you go, stick that in your pipe and smoke it. Yes, Peter Collins, go on, what do you have to say about that?"

Gill stood frozen to the spot, Sally knew the trouble her husband was having with him and yet her best friend had gone behind her back and was having a relationship with him. Gill curled her fist into tiny balls at the side of her legs, her knuckles were white and she ran at her, swinging punches. "You lying slut, you know how much shit that man has caused. How could you Sally? How could you?"

Sally held her own and threw a few punches back, none of them were winning and after a few minutes they let go of each other's hair. Gill dragged her fingers through her hair and chunks of it landed on the carpet. "Get the hell out of my house. I swear, don't you ever come near here again, you snidey bitch. Oh my God, I bet you've been telling those fuckers all about what Harry's been up too. You're finished with me; don't ever darken my doorstep again."

Sally sucked on her gums, she didn't care anymore. "Listen fucking yo-yo knickers I'm not arsed about our friendship, you've not given a shit about me for years, it's been all about you, you, you for years. Go on, when was the last time you asked me how I was?" Gill started to push her into the hallway, she was hysterical. "I've always been here for you Sally, what about when Donkey Don finished with you, who was there for you then? Go on tell me," she stared at Sally. "Yeah it was me. Fuck off, we're done, go and have your life with Peter Collins. Let's see how long that lasts ay?"

Sally was outside the front door now and she was screaming at the top of her voice for everyone to hear. Curtains were twitching in the distance and lights were going on across the road. "You're so up your own arse. Harry's not as white as you think, ask him about the night of your birthday ten years ago, ask him where he was when he stayed out all night. I think there's only you that doesn't know the truth, you clown. Not so perfect is he now, Gill is he?"

Gill slammed the front door behind her and stood with her back against the door, she was shaking. Sliding to her knees she ragged her fingers through her hair. What had Sally meant about the night of her birthday, had Harry wronged her in some way, was she that daft that she didn't pick up on it? Sally said everyone knew about it. Why the hell didn't she know? Gill jumped up from the floor and grabbed her phone. She tried Harry's number one last time before she launched it at the living room wall. Using the landline she rang a taxi to take her to the club. There was no way he was getting away with this, she wanted answers.

Gill paid the taxi driver the fare, she didn't even wait around for her change, she was like shit off a shovel leaving the car. Running to the back of the club she hammered her clenched fist onto the steel door, kicking at it, screaming at it. The door opened rapidly and one of the bouncers dragged her inside. "Fuck me, why you knocking like that, you'll have the dibble here if you carry on like that." Gill broke free from his grip and tried to walk inside the club. The bouncer gripped her by the arm and this time he wasn't taking any shit. "Where the fuck do you think you're going, get your bony arse back here."

Gill was in a wild frenzy, she was pushed against the wall and the man held her by the throat, he was pissed and she didn't know what he was going to next. "Is he here? My husband Harry Jarvis." The bouncer let go of her and stood back, he was apologising. "Sorry about that love, you should have said Harry was your hubby, fucking hell, don't mention this to him will you?"

Gill straightened her clothes and looked confident now she was being treated the way she should have been in the first place. "I won't say anything, it was an easy mistake, is he here or what?"

The bouncer shook his head. "Nar, he's not been in all night, none of the lads have." Gill's face creased. She'd been here before when the lad's wives had phoned or come to the club looking for them and the code of practice had always been to say they'd not seen them.

She poked her finger in his chest. "Go and get him please, it's important."

"Honest love, come in and check for yourself, I'm not lying, honest." Gill barged passed him and stuck her head into the club, there were groups of people sitting at tables and a few women dancing about, but she couldn't see Harry.

A voice came from behind her and she turned her head quickly to see who it was. "Who you looking for love, did you say you're Harry's wife?"

Gill was happy to hear a friendly voice and let out a laboured breath. "Yes, have you seen him?"

The woman now came from out of the shadows and Gill swallowed hard as she saw it was Regina Clough stood right in front of her, she was ready to leave when

Regina grabbed her back. "Oh, I've heard quite a lot about you love. I think we need to talk don't you?"

Gill's legs nearly buckled from underneath her, she placed her hand on the wall to steady herself. "Listen, I've got to go. I'll chat with you soon, but not now, I need to find Harry."

Gill was gripped by her hair and dragged into a small office at the side of the corridor. The bouncer watched the commotion but turned a blind eye. Regina was a nutter and there was no way he wanted her on his case, she was a handful, fucking mental. Regina slammed the door shut behind her and paced the room looking at her prey with menacing eyes. She could have twisted her up there and then and there was nothing Gill could have done about it, she knew her number was up. "So we meet at last, don't you think for one minute that I don't know who you are. I've always known it was you. So, do you want to start explaining what the fuck you have being doing with my husband or what?" Regina sat on a chair facing Gill and crossed her legs; she popped a cigarette into her mouth and flicked the lighter slowly. "So, come on, let's hear the bullshit he fed you before I decide what I'm doing with you?"

Gill sat up straight and hunched her shoulders, she was trying to play this cool but guilt was written all over her face. "I don't know what you've heard but it's just gossip. You know what people are like around here. Chinese whispers and all that."

Regina was losing her rag and she had to remind this woman who she was and what she was capable of. In the past she'd put women in hospital and she was well known for being a fighter. Being brought up with a big family had taught her from an early age, how to fight and it was said she packed a punch like a man. Regina flicked her cigarette at Gill and watched as she tried to remove it from her body. The smell of burning filled the air and Gill was stood up trying to find out where the cigarette had landed. "Listen, I don't know what you're going on about, just move out of my way and let me go." Gill fell to the floor with a crash, she landed on the table and instantly she was in pain.

Regina growled at her and stood over her ready to strike again. Gill was howling and she was in bits. "So, I'll ask you again, tell me about the affair you were having with my husband, and cut the bullshit."

Gill was backed into a corner, she had nowhere to run. She had to come clean if she valued her life. This woman could have ended her life at any moment and she wasn't taking any chances. "Okay, just sit down and be calm. I'll tell you what you need to know."

Regina flung Gill by the hair onto the sofa at the back of the room and she poked her finger into the side of her head with force. "Did you think I didn't know you daft cunt. I knew from the moment he first slept with you. Things are not what they always seem at first, my dear." Regina was playing with her for sure; she was like a cat playing with a mouse. "I hope you're ready for this Gill, don't you ever think you can have me over. I'm too clever for that, you have to get up early in the morning if you think you can outsmart me." Gill's jaw dropped, she wasn't sure what to say next, she remained silent and waited for Regina to talk, she was playing it by ear. "Ray wanted his revenge when he found out I slept about, he was a man and wanted his pride back. You know what men are like, fucking smacked-arses. It's all about what people are saying about them behind their backs, bullshit if you ask me. They should just deal with it like us women do. I'm not in the habit of sleeping about; don't think that for one minute. But, this one guy took my eye and I couldn't help myself. He got under my skin." Gill was listening now and she wanted to know the full story, she inhaled deeply and tried to control her breathing as she continued. "I told Ray to sleep with you and then we would have been fair and square. An eye for an eye and all that."

Gill chirped in and sat forward in her seat, she was confused. "Why me, if you cheated on Ray, why would you want him to sleep with me. I don't get it, it doesn't make sense?"

Regina chuckled and turned her head away for a second. "You're just not getting it are you. I slept with Harry and Ray found out. I told him if he slept with you then we would be equal."

Gill was white with shock, this wasn't real. Was this some kind of sick, twisted joke? Regina was making things up, surely. "Stop lying Regina. Okay yes, here's the truth. I did sleep with Ray but it was a mistake and I'm sorry about it. Every day I regret what I did and I can only say I'm sorry, but, stop lying about sleeping with Harry. I know you're only trying to hurt me."

Regina dropped her head low and played with her fingers, stroking them softly. "It's the truth darling. Sorry, but that's the way it is. It just happened. Lust is a funny thing, it just takes over you."

Gill studied her face and looked for any sign of deceit; there was none. Nothing, no twitching eyebrows, no nothing. Gill wanted to know more, she wasn't taking this lying down, no way. "So, go on then, when was it, because me and Harry are joined at the hip and he's never far from my side. Come on then smart arse, when was it. Yeah, I thought you would be quiet now, you lying cow?"

"Remember the night of your birthday, sugar; you must remember it because he never came home."

Gill bolted up from her seat and she was treading on thin ice as she went into Regina's face. "How long ago are we talking here, fucking hell, Harry has been in jail for years."

Regina stood up and made sure Gill knew who was calling the shots. "It was before he got slammed, Harry has always had a soft spot for me if he's being honest with himself, he would never admit it to you but he has. We just clicked and couldn't keep our hands off each other. He wanted me just as much as I wanted him. I don't regret it for one minute either. It was the best night of my life, if I'm being completely honest with you. Harry sure knows how to treat a woman, especially in the bedroom."

Gill held the lower part of her stomach and remembered what Sally had said to her earlier. She fell to her knees and held her head in her hands. "So, the one and only night he stayed out he was with you?"

Regina nodded her head slowly. "Well fuck a duck. At last, the penny has dropped, yes, he was with me. We spent the night together."

You could see the pain in Gill's eyes, tears forcing their way into her tear ducts ready to roll down her cheeks. "You bitch, Harry is a married man you should have kept your filthy hands off him."

Regina retaliated and made sure Gill was looking at

her. "And so should you. Remember Ray was married too, are you forgetting that. You're no better than me. Like I said, I gave him a pass to cheat, just once though, not the amount of time he was banging you, he was taking the piss. He thought he was smart and got carried away, that's why he's ended up half dead."

Gill was alert, Regina must know something about Ray's whereabouts, she'd told everyone he'd ran off with a woman, she must have been lying. "So you know where Ray is then?"

Regina sat staring at the floor she seemed in a deep trance and Gill was afraid of what she would do next. "Of course I know where the wanker is. I bleeding saved him. I should have left the bastard to rot for the way he's treated me, but I just couldn't do it. I knew Harry had him and watched where they took him. He deserved his beating too, if he would have just kept to the rules it would have been fine, but no, he thought he could have me over. So that's his mistake isn't it?"

Gill wasn't thinking straight, her head was in a whirl, she was going to pass out. She loosened her top, yanking it down from her neck blowing her breath down it. A red rash was appearing on her skin, she always got this when she was angry. "What did Harry do to Ray? I swear to you, I didn't know a thing about it. Harry never breathed a word to me, honest."

Regina licked her lips slowly and twiddled her hair, her words were slurred now and she was slavering. "Harry and Matty took Ray from the street. I was following him thinking he was going to meet you again. I'd had enough, come on, don't you blame me? I was going to put a stop to it once and for all, he was taking the piss. Honest, he had me down as a right nob-head." Gill walked to her side and shot her eyes to the door, she could have made a run for it but she stood frozen. "He's in a bad way, it's sick what they did to him. His dick is burnt to a cinder. I just couldn't leave him there, I had to save him."

Gill ran to the side of the room and retched into the bin. She was gagging for breath and she didn't look well. "He loved you Gill. That's what hurts the most. I could see it in his eyes that he'd fallen for you. I suppose it's my own fault. I should never have told him to sleep with you. I should have known it would end up like this." Gill felt warmth rising through her body. Regina had just said Ray loved her, she knew he felt something for her, she just knew it.

"Where is Ray, can I see him?" Gill asked in a low voice.

Regina was calm and licked her lips slowly. "He's hid away; he can never show his face around here again. He's a dead man walking if the lads ever get their hands on him again."

"I just need to see him Regina, just to make sure he's okay."

Regina choked up, she snivelled. "You still love him don't you?"

Gill didn't know what she was feeling. She thought she knew in her head what she wanted but that was before she knew Ray still loved her. She was so mixed up, she didn't know if she was coming or going. "Can you take me to see him?"

Regina stood up and walked to the desk facing her. Picking up a pen she started writing an address down on a white piece of paper. Digging deep in her bra she pulled out a gold key. "There you go, you'll find him there. I know when I've been beaten. He will never love me again while you're still around. You're welcome to him. Go on, fuck off before I change my mind. I'm going back into the club to get a drink. I think I deserve one don't you?" Regina left the room and Gill was stood there looking bewildered holding the key in her hand. Harry seemed to be a million miles away from her thoughts; at that moment all she wanted to do was see Ray, to make sure he was alright, to see if he still loved her. Walking out of the room she headed into the night.

CHAPTER TWENTY

Tina lay in her bed looking at her phone. Preston's phone had been turned off all night and she was unsettled. Using the app on her I- phone she used the find my phone app to see if she could locate her boyfriends whereabouts.

Trisha was restless tonight; she was rattling and needed drugs. Jona told her he would sort her out earlier that night but there was no sign of him, the prick had left her roasting her tits off. Sweat was dripping down her forehead and she was gripping the lower part of her stomach as the hunger for drugs took over her body. She looked in pain, her face was green.

Tina slipped her shoes on and tied her hair back in a ponytail. She'd located Preston's whereabouts and decided to go and see what he was up to. No one would ever have her over… Tina opened her bedroom door slowly, it was so late in the night and she never expected her mother to be awake.

Usually at this time Trisha would have munched everything in sight and been well away in bed but she was up and about and didn't look well. "Where the fuck are you going at this time of the night? Why aren't you in bed Tina? I shit myself then, I thought you were a robber."

Trisha came out of her bedroom now and followed her daughter downstairs. Watching her put her coat on she stood at the doorway. "You're not going out at this bleeding time, go and get back in bed. What's up, I can tell something is going on so you better tell me."

Tina slid her shoes on and lifted her head up slowly. "I think Preston is up to something, his phone is off and he's not been in touch all night. I swear, if he's shagging someone else he's going to be so sorry."

Trisha blew her breath and raised her eyes. "You wouldn't be told would you? You thought you knew it all. Didn't I tell you he was a sly bastard. I mean, banging his brother's woman, what does that tell you about him. If I was you, I'd cut my losses and have done with him. He's not got a pot to piss in anyway, why are you wasting your time on him? Get with someone who can show you a good time."

Tina stood up from the sofa and walked to the doorway. "He's earning money now, he's just getting back on his feet. And, for your information he's not one bit sly, he was the one who wanted to tell you about us because he thought you should know before anyone else told you."

Trisha chuckled. "Did he fuck want to come clean, wake up and smell the coffee. He wanted to make sure I would keep my gob shut. Why do you think he was always bunging me the weed all the time, yeah, that was a sweetener if ever I've seen one."

Tina reached over to the chair and grabbed her coat. "Listen, I'm going to see where he is. If he's with someone else then he's history isn't he, you know me mam, I won't stand for any shit, especially from any man."

Trisha quickly slipped her shoes on too. "Hold up, I may as well come with you. I can't sleep anyway, and plus there is no way I'm letting you walk the street on your own at this time of night, you could be attacked." Tina and Trisha left the house together. Trisha was really going out to see if she could see Jona or any other smack-heads who were out and about. This was the time they were out grafting and she was hoping she might bump into one and bum some smack from them to sort herself out.

The night was cold and the wind was picking up. Even though it was late there were still cars out and about on the main road. A few of the neighbours were still up partying and you could hear music being played as they left the estate. Trisha stood frozen; there was a crack house not far from where she stood. There was a light on inside the gaff and she had a gut feeling Jona might be in there. "Just wait here two minutes while I just check something out. I'll be right back." Trisha waddled off down the garden path and she knocked on the window. Tina was rubbing at her arms and she was cold as she waited for her mother to return. The door opened slowly and a young girl opened the door, she must have been only about eleven years old. She looked tired and as she spoke she seemed distressed.

Trisha bent down a little and held the top of the kids shoulder trying to make her feel at ease. "Is Jona inside love, can you get him for me, tell him it's Trisha."

The young girl shrugged her shoulders. "You can come in and have a look for yourself. My mam is asleep so she won't mind that I've let you in."

Trisha looked over her shoulder and placed one finger in the air to her daughter. Tina snarled and kicked her foot on the floor, she was in a rush and Trisha was just adding extra time to her journey. Trisha covered her nose as she walked into the house. It smelt of arse, dirty, sweaty arse. The carpet in the hallway was filthy and parts of it were ripped up from the floor. Trisha heard people talking from the room in front of her and she prepared herself to go inside. The young girl smiled at her before she headed up the stairs. "Can you tell them to be quiet? I've got school in the morning and I'll never get any sleep if they carry on like this. My teacher has told me sleep is important for my brain but none of them seem to care in there they just keep at it all night long."

Trisha licked her lips slowly, her heart went out to the kid and she walked back to her. "Don't worry I'll sort them out. You need your sleep, go and get back in bed and close your door. I'll have a word with your mam."

The young girl started to walk up the stairs. Each step she took seemed a big effort, the girl looked as thin as a rake and it was obvious she was being neglected by her mother. Trisha opened the living room door and all she could smell was weed, it went straight to the back of her throat. A man looked at her and nodded his head slowly. He looked shocking, thin, sweaty, and undernourished. "Is Jona here?" Trisha asked.

A man shook his head and carried on sucking on a bong in front of him. Once he'd finished he fell back onto the chair and giggled. "Jona's not been here for time. I saw him last night, but I've not seen him since then. What's he been up to anyway, has he had you over?"

Trisha smirked at the man. "Does this face look like anyone could have me over? No, I'm just waiting for him to come back. I'm roasting my tits off here and need to score." The man looked vacant as he carried on smoking. He never answered her and just carried toking. Trisha scanned the room just to make sure he wasn't having her over and after a few seconds she knew he was telling the truth.

"Here, get a few blast of this," the man said, "it should help until he comes back. It's pucka shit too, it blew my brains out." Trisha sat down next to him and sucked hard on the bong. Once the cannabis entered her body she melted into the chair. You could see she'd already forgotten about her daughter waiting outside. Trisha was like that, she only ever cared about herself and if drugs were involved they always came first, before anything and anyone. Tina had never had any support from her mother. Even when she was growing up she had to make do with whatever she could steal or get free. Trisha never gave a flying fuck about anyone but herself, some things never changed.

Tina walked up and down on the street. Standing under the lamp- post she lifted her head up and stared at the orange light. Scraping her finger against the cold pole, she shot her eyes to the house. After a few seconds she headed off on her own. She knew her mother was never coming out anytime soon and decided she was better off where she was. Trisha would have only caused a scene anyway and made things ten times worse than what they already were. She'd cause trouble in an empty house.

★

Gill pulled up in the taxi at the address Regina had given her. Once she'd paid the fare she watched the taxi driver move off. She looked anxious and she kept walking forward and stopping. What would she do when she saw him again? Would her heart melt and would she fall into his arms again or had too much time passed? Gill slid the key into the door and turned it slowly. There was silence in the street and everything seemed so eerie. Her heart pounded in her chest as she opened the door. As she entered she faced a set of steep, narrow stairs. There was a light on upstairs and she heard someone coughing. As she stepped onto the first stair it creaked loudly. Gripping the banister she made her way up to the top. Four doors now faced her, from one she could see a dim light inside. Tiptoeing to it she tapped gently on the door. Her mouth was dry and she was constantly licking her lips. "Ray, it's me. Are you awake?" Gill walked inside the room. She could see a figure lay in the bed and stood frozen. "Ray, it's Gill." The body moved slowly in the bed and you could hear Ray's voice for the first time, it was low and seemed hoarse.

"Gill, go away. I don't want you to see me like this, just go will you." Gill walked closer to the bed. She could see lots of medication at the side of the bed and bandages and dressings. There was some old fruit in the bowl next to the bed which had never been touched. The curtains in the room were closed fully and very little light came into the room. Gill touched the end of the bed with her fingers. She could feel his feet. "I need to make sure you're alright Ray then I will leave. Regina has told me what happened and I want you to know this was nothing to do with me. I didn't know a thing, I swear to you."

A head now appeared from under the blankets. Gill covered her mouth with her hands and cringed. Ray was a mess, his hair was missing in places and his nose was swelled beyond belief. Looking at him made her stomach churn. Is this what her husband was really capable of? Ray was a mess. Without thinking she moved towards him and cradled him in her arms. He screamed out in pain and she released him straight away. "Oh, I'm so sorry, it's just that I needed to hold you again." A tear ran slowly down his cheek and she watched as he wiped it with his fingertip. "

"Gill, it's best you just walk away. If Harry finds out you're here we will both be dead." Suddenly he sat up in the bed and his jaw dropped. "How the fuck did you know I was here? Is this some kind of sick joke, is Harry with you? Are you going to finish me off?"

Gill tried to calm him down, he was terrified and he was trying to get out of the bed. "Ray no, just relax. Regina told me where you were and Harry doesn't even know I'm here."

Ray was still watching the door with eager eyes, he trusted nobody, not even Gill. "Why has Regina told you where I am? She's up to something, this isn't right. Gill, she's a sick, twisted bitch; you don't know her like I do. I bet she's set us up. Yeah, that's it; she's probably been on the blower to Harry saying we're together. We need to get away from here as soon as possible. We don't have long, please help me."

Ray yanked the covers from his body and Gill could see for the first time his injuries. His body was mutilated and his wounds were there for her to see. Gill dropped to her knees. His manhood was nothing like she'd ever seen before. It was disfigured and full of scabs. All over his body were yellow and purple bruises and as he stood up his legs give way on him. Ray lay on the floor and curled up in a tiny ball. He was shaking rapidly and looked like he was having a fit or something.

Gill dragged the duvet from the bed and covered him up, he was shivering. "Ray please believe me, nobody will come here. I will protect you. Look, I've got a gun." Gill dug inside her jacket pocket and pulled out a small silver pistol. It was one that Harry always kept at their home, he said he needed it for the lifestyle he led; there was always firearms in the house. Holding it in her hand she gritted her teeth tightly together. "I said I'll use it if anyone comes here," her eyes looked deep into his as she continued, "and, that means Harry. I swear I'll use it on him."

Ray reached his hand up and his fingers stroked her face slowly. "Would you do that for me Gill, would you really do that?" Gill nodded her head as she helped him back onto the bed. "Regina has told me all about her affair with Harry and how she gave you permission to sleep with me."

Ray lay flat on the bed and ragged his hands through his hair in a desperate state. "She's right, that's what happened. When I found out about her with Harry I was all set for leaving her, she was begging me to stay you know, but I told her it was over. But once she said I could seek revenge with you it all seemed so much better. You are gorgeous Gill and I knew Regina would be hurt if I slept with you. I was heartbroken when I found about her you know. I was a player myself, but she never knew about it. I suppose it was karma wasn't it?"

Gill banged her clenched fist on the bedside cabinet at the side of her and turned her head to face him. "So, it was just all a joke to you then? I ruined my marriage so you and Regina could fix yours. What kind of sick bastards are you two? How can you just play with people's feelings like that?"

Ray grabbed her arm and looked her straight in

the eye. "It started off as a game Gill, but I fell for you. Once I got to know you I couldn't let go. I told Regina it was over, but she knew deep down in her heart that my feelings for you had grown. Night after night she sat crying down my ear begging me to stop seeing you. I denied it, I told her it was over and I know now I should have just packed my stuff up and walked away but Regina is evil, she would have never let me go, she would have made my life a misery, so the easiest thing to do was lie to her."

Gill looked at him in detail, he was telling the truth. The front he'd put on in the past was just a cover-up, he really did love her. Ray kept his voice low and reached for the glass of water at the side of him. "But, you won't want me now will you. My dick is fucked and you've seen what my body is like. Harry did a good job on me and I suppose I deserve it, but he should never have slept with my wife."

Gill sighed and twisted the piece of hair dangling near her cheekbone. "So, what happens now?"

Ray closed his eyes and sucked on his bottom lip. "I love you Gill, more than life itself. If you still love me I want us to leave here together, me and you, a new life away from all this shit. The ball's in your court, what do you think?" Gill knew it would never be as easy as that. She would never be able to leave and have a life with Ray. As long as Harry was still breathing she knew he would search high and low to find her and make sure she paid the price for her deceit. Ray asked her again. "I love you Gill with all my heart, no woman has ever made me feel like you do. We can have a good life together. I've got a bit of money to get us started, that's all we need isn't it?"

Gill was in a deep trance, he was speaking to her but nothing he was saying was going in, she was in a world of her own, in deep thought. "Ray, I have to go but I'll be back. I just have to sort my life out before I leave." Ray smiled and clutched at her fingers. "So, we're going to be together then. Do you still love me?" Gill walked to the bedroom door and slowly turned around to face him. Ray was sat up on the bed searching for an answer, desperate. "Where are you going Gill, please speak to me. I need to know if you're going to come back or not, tell me you still love me, tell me something that will keep me going. I may as well be dead without you Gill, honest, you're my world. Please talk to me." Gill closed the bedroom door slowly and headed down the stairs. The sound of the door slamming shook the walls and all Ray could do was lie back down in the bed. He didn't know if Gill was ever coming back, all he had was his faith in love. In his heart he knew Gill couldn't just walk away. He'd seen love in her eyes and hoped and prayed it was enough to bring her back to him so they could run away together and start a new life. Covering his eyes with his hands he sobbed his heart out. "Please Gill, please come back."

Tina walked along the street with her mobile phone held in her hand. If the details were right on her phone Preston was just around the corner. She was puzzled as she kept checking the buildings around her. This was an industrial estate, not a housing estate, what the hell was Preston doing here? Tina zipped her coat up and dug her hands deep inside her coat pockets. Walking around the corner she could see a few men stood at their cars talking.

Sneaking into the shadows she hid away trying to see what was going on. Tina noticed Jona straight away and she nearly shouted him but stopped at the last minute when she saw Peter Collins come to his side, he was dragging Callum with him. Tina covered her mouth with her hands and her eyes were wide open. Whatever was going down here was heavy shit and she knew people were going to get hurt. Hid away she kept out of view, there was no way she wanted any part of this, no way in this world.

CHAPTER TWENTY ONE

Harry made sure Susan was locked up in a room nearby. She was screaming at the top of her voice and Gerry was ready to knock her out until Harry stopped him. "Just leave her alone pal, she'll quieten down soon enough, she's old, just leave her."

Gerry spat on the floor at the side of him and wiped his mouth with a swift movement. "Right, let's get this lot cut up then. It's going to take hours, it's like a fucking jungle in here, but ay, we will be loaded when it's all done. Fucking result." Harry got his men together and they all started to cut the cannabis plants down. Some of them were stoned and had a fit of the giggles. Suddenly there was a loud crashing noise at the back end of the warehouse and the men stopped dead in their tracks. "Gerry, go and check that out, it doesn't sound good." Gerry pulled an iron bar from the front of his pants and sprinted to the other end of the warehouse. A few of the others ran with him too.

Preston hid behind a wall. He'd tripped into some large boxes and knocked them over, he knew it was on top and found cover straight away. He could hear voices coming towards him, they were getting nearer. Bending his knees he dipped down low and pulled his hood up over his head trying to blend into the background. His breathing was heavy and his heart was pumping. "Check behind that wall there," Gerry shouted over to one of his men. Preston felt a hand grip him by the scruff of the neck and within minutes the man had informed the others he'd been found. Gerry was at his side in minutes and he was ready for knocking Preston out. He yanked his hood down and squeezed he's cheeks together so his lips touched at either side. "You'd better start talking dick-head before I end your life. Trust me you're a goner if you don't start talking. Come on, what the fuck are you doing here, who sent you?"

Preston wriggled to break free and stood with his back up against the wall. "Get the fuck off me you clown. I'm Harry's son."

Gerry examined the lad and he wasn't sure, he'd been to Harry's house in the past and he knew he had kids but he wasn't sure, he was taking no chances. Gerry and the other man dragged Preston out from the shadows. They frog-marched him back to his dad. Harry's jaw dropped when he saw his son for the first time. "What the fuck are you doing here?" he yelled at the top of his voice.

Preston stepped forward and turned his head back to Gerry. "See ya muppet, I told you he was my dad." Harry was livid and dragged Preston to the side of the room and told the men to carry on with what they were doing. "Dad, why didn't you tell me you was into all this shit. I'm your man for anything like this. I swear this is top, we'll be rolling in cash once I'm involved."

Preston went to shake his father's hand but Harry backed off. "Are you right in the bastard head or what? What have you come here for? How did you know I was even here?"

Preston was wounded and hated he didn't get the welcome he thought he deserved. "My mam was worried about you and told me to come and find you. Dad, you were mint before. I swear you're one mad mother-fucker. I honestly thought you were as straight as a die. You've had me over, that's for sure. Wait until our kid knows he'll be buzzing."

Harry gritted his teeth together tightly; there was no way in this world any son of his was getting involved in this world. It was dangerous and he'd always said his sons would never turn out like he had. He was a youngster when he started his life of crime, but he had to, he had no other choices. Harry's mother and father were potless and it was very rare they had any money. Harry's dad was a man's man and he was never scared of using his fists on his family, especially his son. Harry had left home at sixteen and most of the time he was getting his head down at his friend's houses. He craved a family unit in his life and when he met Gill he knew his prayers were answered, she was everything he'd ever wanted. Crime paid, everybody knew that in the area and they were all fighting to be the top dog but Harry was hard as nails; he'd had to be, to deal with his old man. When the time come for him to step up he showed everyone what he was capable of and half-killed the former top dog. From that day on, Harry gained the respect of his men and always made sure he kept on top. It was a dangerous world he lived in and he knew he was lucky to still be breathing. Many had come to take his crown in the past and many had failed, well, until the Collins brothers that is. They struck their blow when Harry was sent down. Five years was a long time for them to plan their takeover. They would have done it too if Harry would have still have been in nick, but he got out just in time to end their reign of terror.

"You can get back home now. I'll get one of the lads to

drive you. Tell your mother I'll be home when I'm ready. Is she fucking on this planet or what, fancy involving you? You're a kid, king of the see-saw that's about it, fuck me can this get any worse? This is another level son and nothing like you've been involved with before. Men get killed, people go missing, is that something you want to be involved in, son? Sleepless nights, always watching your back, and knowing any day soon someone bigger and better is going to come along and knock the smile right off your face."

Preston kicked his foot into the floor and kept his head low. "Dad, just let me stay here with you. I'll just sit over there and watch, honest, I won't say a word to anyone. I'm not a kid anymore, so stop treating me like one."

Harry was ready for snapping, he ragged his fingers through his hair. "Fuck, fuck," he whispered under his breath. Walking up and down he shook his head and let out a laboured breath. "Right, just sit there and don't fucking move. It's going to be a long night you know?"

Preston tried to play it cool. "Dad, you won't even know I'm here. If you want I can chop some of them plants down, me and our kid have done it loads of time, I know what I'm doing honest." Harry walked away from his son and headed towards Gerry. Preston could see them talking and moved closer to one of the plants. With quick movements he pulled some buds off and shoved them in his coat pocket. No one would miss it anyway, the gaff was packed with the stuff.

Susan was banging on the door with her clenched fist and Preston could hear her shouting. Making sure nobody was looking he sneaked into the corridor at the side of him. Listening to the noises from inside he held his ear to the door. "Shut the fuck up with your whining woman, if my dad's put you in there, then that's where you're going to stay. Now shut up before I deal with you. I'm his son, the new kid on the block, Preston Jarvis, remember the name, bitch." Preston went for a mooch around, checking things out. Walking into the toilets he sat down in a cubicle and turned his phone back on. The message alert started beeping at speed. Twenty two he had and all from Tina. He smiled to himself and started to read them. Placing the gun on the floor he sat back and started to have a dump without any further hesitation.

Peter Collins was ready to strike. The van they had just pinched from a street nearby was ready for action. Ben was driving it and Connor was at his side. The engine turned over and Peter gave the nod. The van started to move at speed and it was heading straight for the steel shutters. It collided with a loud crashing noise and black smoke was coming from the exhaust of the vehicle telling you the engine was ready to burst into flames. Ben and Connor jumped out of the van and after a few seconds they jumped from either side of the vehicle. It was all going off now, gun shots were fired and Harry's men were running around like headless chickens. Ben ran straight to Gerry and blasted him in the face with an iron bar, he never stood a chance and just dropped to the floor in a daze. Harry lay behind a box and he could see his men dropping like flies. A few of them were fighting back but they were outnumbered and the odds were against them. Harry made a run for it and ran to the room where Susan was. Hands shaking he unbolted the door and gripped Susan by the throat. There was no fighting back from her this time, she knew it was serious and remained quiet. Harry grabbed the gun from his jacket and pointed it at Susan's head. Walking into the main warehouse he walked behind her with his body hid securely behind hers. Not a sound was heard and Harry stood tall scanning the room for any sign of the Collins brothers. "Come on then pricks. I swear, I'll kill her stone dead. Come out now before she gets it."

Ben stood up from his hideout and held the gun out in front of him. "Let her go Harry, she's fuck all to do with this. If one hair on her head gets hurt I will cut you up into tiny pieces I swear to you."

Connor was by his side now and the rest of the men revealed themselves. Harry counted the men slowly. Over twenty of them there were, he was fighting a losing battle and knew without Susan he would be leaving here in a body bag. Harry's men came to join him. There was a silence and you could hear a door opening at the back end of the building. Ben shot a look over his shoulder and watched as Peter made his grand entrance. Harry nearly died on the spot as he watched Callum being dragged in by his hair. "Now we're equal Harry. Stalemate isn't it."

Callum was shouting at the top of his voice over to his father. "Dad, just shoot the old cunt. I'm not arsed what they do to me, just shoot her."

Peter held the gun over his head and sent it crashing over Callum's head leaving him dazed. He fell to his knees but still he refused to be quiet. "Jona is with them dad, he's a fucking spy, he's had you right over."

Harry scanned the room looking for Jona and shouted

his name at the top of his voice. "Is that right Jona, are you with these cunts?"

Jona stood up and came out of hiding. "Yeah fucking dead right I am. Did you think you could fuck my Mandy and get away with it? You know I loved her and this is how you treated me."

Harry licked his lips slowly and growled before he answered him. Susan was wriggling and he gripped her hair tighter and ragged it about. "Jona, you've got it wrong. I never touched Mandy, she's a good friend but that's it. Whoever has told you this bullshit was lying."

Jona bounced about waving his hands above his head. "Nar, don't think you can have me over. I've been told Harry, you're a snidey cunt, a proper shady twat."

Peter stepped forward and dragged Callum with him. "Look at the state of your son Harry. Do you know he's been tanning the gear, yeah he's a fucking raging bag-head."

Harry's eyes were wide open. There was no way this could have been true. Callum sobbed from the other side of the room. "It was these bastards who got me and our kid to sell it. When our grow got robbed they made us pay for it by selling heroin. I only tried it a few times dad honest but it just got a grip of me and took over my life. I'm sorry dad, I've fucked up."

Peter Collins held a menacing look in his eyes as he pointed the gun at Callum's head. "I should just end his misery shouldn't I? You know what the gear does to you Harry, he'll be selling his arse next and robbing from his own, you know the story don't you Harry?"

Susan stuck her neck out and screamed at the top of her voice. She was terrified and hoped she could talk a bit of sense into everyone. "Peter, just walk away. You can earn your own money you don't need to earn it like this. Harry is a nobody and we all know his time is up. Just walk away and do things the right way." Peter was having none of it. His mother was right he could have set up more grows and got the money back that way, but this was more than just about the money, it was about being the lord of the manor, the top dog.

Callum could see the gun in Peter's hand just above his head. He was weak and didn't know if he had the strength to jump up to his feet and grab the gun. It was a do or die moment for Callum and using his inner strength he jumped to his knees and tried to grab the gun. A single gunshot was fired and Callum lay lifeless on the floor, his body shook for a few seconds and then there was nothing. Harry's face creased and he pressed the gun deep into Susan's head at the side. "Fuck you," he snapped as his finger pressed the trigger on the gun.

Ben and Connor were running at Harry now and they both were tooled up. Harry was ready to fight them both and yanked his coat off. "Come on, let's have it," he yelled. Ben dropped to the floor as a bullet hit him in the chest. Another shot was fired and Connor fell to his knees. He screamed a few times but after that he spoke no more, he fell to the ground with his eyes just staring into space. Preston stood behind his father with the gun in his hand. "Let's get the fuck out of here dad, it's on top." Harry was frozen as his eyes shot to his son on the other side of the room. The gangs were fighting now and shouting and screaming could be heard. Harry watched Peter Collins flee from the building and within seconds he was hot on his trail. Preston ran to his brother's side and lifted his head up into his arms. "Don't die our kid, come on, just hang on in there." Preston was sobbing as he kissed the top of his brother's forehead. Callum was gone, his body was cold and no matter how much he tried Preston couldn't wake him up.

Peter Collins jumped into his car and tried reversing from the street. Harry jumped onto the bonnet of the car and brought his knees up to his chest. With almighty force he sent them crashing through the windscreen. Peter let go of the steering wheel and the car skidded into a wall. The two men went blow for blow once Peter scrambled out of the car. Blood surged from Peter's mouth as Harry connected a punch. Grabbing him by his neck he flung him on the floor and sat on top of him. Harry never stopped punching Peter until he was dead. His fist covered in blood he smashed his head against the concrete slab next to him. Harry held his head up to the sky and let out a roar from the pit of his stomach. "Fuck you all," he screamed. Staggering to his feet he stood looking about the area. This was a bloodbath for sure and he could see some of his men falling out from the warehouse with serious injuries to their heads and bodies. Peter's men were the same; none of them were fit to fight anymore. Harry was gagging for breath at the roadside, his body was in shock and he was retching into his hands. Trying to get to his feet to go back inside he received a blow to his head from behind, his attacker smashed the concrete slab onto his head until he moved no more.

Tina edged out from her hiding place and moved. She'd phoned the police after hearing the gun shots and just hoped Preston was still alive. Opening the door slowly she covered her mouth with two hands. Bodies were just lying on the floor and some of them weren't moving. Her legs were like jelly as she made her way further inside. She spotted Preston straight away and ran to his side. "Come on the dibble are on their way, we need to get out of here as quick as we can." Preston lifted his head up and Tina could see Callum for the first time in his hands. Taking a deep breath she shuddered. "Is he dead?"

Preston wiped the tears from his eyes and nodded. "The bastard just shot him in cold blood. Tina, he's dead, what the hell am I going to do. It's all fucked up. What am I am going to do now?"

Tina rubbed the top of his head and tried to console him. "We need to go Preston, you can't be found here otherwise you'll be slammed for it. You could go to jail for years."

Preston snapped, "Do you think I'm arsed about going to jail Tina. Look at my brother, he's fucking dead."

Tina was the stronger of the two and knew time wasn't on their side. "Preston, he's gone, we need to go."

Preston kissed the top of his brother's head slowly. His voice was low and tears were streaming down the side of his cheeks. "Sorry bro, sorry I never got to you in time. I'll make sure your death is avenged; trust me, until my dying breath I'll make sure somebody pays for this." Tina tugged at his arms slowly and urged him to hurry up. With one last look over his shoulder Preston and Tina fled into the night.

The birds were tweeting now and each of them seemed to be telling the other what they had just witnessed, it was a bloodbath. Tina and Preston ran from the scene of the crime at speed. Police sirens could be heard in the distance and they were only minutes away. Harry's body lay on the roadside not far from Peter Collins. This was a murder scene for sure. The police would take weeks to work out what had happened here. Bodies lay all over the place and guns and blades scattered around the building. This was a gangland massacre, one of the worst Manchester had seen for a long time.

CHAPTER TWENTY TWO

The streets of Manchester were quiet as the funeral for Harry Jarvis and his son took place. The Collins' funeral had already taken place at another church the day before. Gill sat waiting for the cars to come with Tina and Preston. Tina was stepping up to the mark for a change and she was the one doing all the running about. Gill sat staring into space, she seemed in a world of her own. The police had been with her throughout the ordeal and as of yet they didn't know who killed her husband. Jona was in custody and he'd already told the police everything he knew about the fight. He was a right grassing cunt but he was roasting his nuts off for drugs and sold his soul to get some medication rather than do his rattle. Jona was looking at a long time behind bars and he knew it. Not only did they want to interview him about what went on at the warehouse they also wanted him regarding Mandy's attack. They had a witness now who had come forward and told them all about the TV they'd bought off Jona, he was bang to rights and there was no way out for him this time.

The streets were crowded with people paying respect to Harry and Callum. Even some of the old time gangsters had come out of hiding to come to the funeral. They knew more than anyone that death was inevitable in this line of work and they were the lucky ones who'd got out before their time came too.

Flowers were placed into the back of the hearse.

Mandy handed her wreath over to the funeral director and dipped her head low; she was sobbing her heart out. Her hair had started to grow back now and she looked like she was turning a corner regarding her injuries. Gill walked from her front door and there was a strange silence that filled the air. There was whispering from the onlookers, discussing the murders. They all had a version of events at the warehouse, who knew what was fiction and what was fact? Then again no one wanted to be seen to get involved with the police, it just wasn't done. A grass was the lowest of the low and none of them wanted to be known as a police informer.

Preston walked at his mother's side and held his hand on the top of her shoulder. She was quiet and every now and then she let out a flood of tears. Once they were inside the car they headed to lay her husband and son to rest in Moston Cemetery. The service was held at St Malachy's church in Collyhurst. Harry had attended this school as a child and always loved the inside of the church there. He could never have been called a devoted catholic despite his parents drumming it into him from an early age, but he had still believed in God. Few knew that whenever he was at a low ebb he would visit the church and ask if the big man could help him out.

The service began and Gill turned her head to look behind her. The church was packed and a lot of the faces were unfamiliar to her. From the corner of her eye she clocked Regina Clough stood at the back of the church trying to keep a low profile. Gill looked around and wondered how many more women Harry had slept with, she would never know now, his secret had died with him. He was a dark horse and even to this day she could never fully work him out. The funeral went to the cemetery. The sun was shining down brightly behind several big black clouds. It was threatening to rain though; the clouds looked ready to burst. Preston held a stiff upper lip as he spoke about the loss of his brother and father at the graveside. Tina held his hand tightly and she was sobbing her heart out too. Trisha was at the funeral too but she was stood at the back out of sight. She was probably looking for an unattended handbag; she was a right low-life and never missed a chance to earn some extra money.

Preston cleared his throat and tried to stop his voice from shaking, it was hard for him but now he was man of the house he had to put on a front. "My dad was a good man and he loved his family. He did everything he could to give us all a better life. Callum was the same he was just misunderstood. I know they're together now and I hope they are both at peace." There was mumbling in the crowd and Gill turned her head to see who was talking. She snarled as she caught the eyes of the two women who were speaking. She knew they were slagging her husband off and hated that they held no respect for the service taking place. The coffins were lowered. Gill just stood watching and didn't move an inch. After she picked some soil up from the side of the grave she sprinkled it softly into her son's and husband's coffins. As she stood over Harry's resting place she paused and her lips were moving but nothing was coming out. She lifted her head to the sky and walked away slowly. Preston followed behind her with Tina at his side. As they all headed back to the cars to go back to the pub, Tina turned around as she heard her mother shouting her name.

Trisha hurried to her side and held her hands on her

knees gasping for breath. "Have you got a couple of quid before you go love? I want to come back to the wake but I've not got a carrot, I'm bleeding on my arse."

Tina growled at her mother, she had no shame. "Mam, will you just piss off and leave me alone. Look at you, you're a bleeding disgrace."

Trisha had her back up and as per usual, she was the victim again. She placed her hands on her hips and spoke in a loud voice so everyone could hear. "Oh, so it's a no then. Selfish you are, all I want is to have a drink to show my respect to Harry and Callum. Are you begrudging me that?"

Preston came to Tina's side now and rested his hand on her shoulder. "I'll get you a beer Trisha, don't worry about it you'll be sorted."

Trisha was red in the face. Preston was onto her game and smiled at her. "No, I'm no charity case love. I don't want you to buy my drinks for me I do have some pride left you know."

Tina was spitting feathers; she went nose to nose with her mother and gripped her cheeks. "You just want money for heroin don't you? Go on admit it, you have no intentions of coming back to the pub you're just scrounging again. You can fuck off if you think you're getting another penny from me. I'm done with you now mother. I'm moving in with Preston. I've had enough of you and your skanky life."

Trisha scooped her hair from her face and scratched the side of her arm, she was full of blotchy marks on her skin and several scabs were visible on her forehead. "Oh, so you're leaving me are you? Go on, go and live your life. Selfish self-centred bitch just as you've always been."

Tina was just about to get into a full blown argument but Preston dragged her away. "Come on leave her to it, you know what she's like, she'll come around without water, let's do one. My mam's waiting for us." Trisha was left on her own and she rested her hand onto the wall debating her next move.

The pub was packed out as Gill arrived at the pub. She was greeted by a few of Harry's old friends. Gill blew a breath and she knew for the next few hours she would have to listen to tales of what a great guy her ex-husband had been. No one wanted to talk about her son, her flesh and blood, it was knocking her sick. Sipping her double brandy she held her tongue, holding back years of frustration. Years of the truth about the perfect man all her friends and family thought Harry was. Gill looked at her mobile phone and looked around the room making sure nobody was watching her. She sent a quick text message and stretched her neck looking for Preston she needed to speak to him as soon as possible before she lost her nerve.

Gill made her way through the crowds of people and finally found her son sat among the old-timers. She could hear them talking about the days they were grafters and how much money they'd earned over the years. Looking at her son's face her stomach churned. He was excited by it all and she knew he was going to follow in his father's footsteps. Waving her hand above her head she tried to get his attention. "Preston, Preston," she shouted. Her son never replied and he was telling the men how he'd seen his own father take the Collins brothers out. Her spirits were low as she left the pub.

A little later, Gill sat on the bed and looked at her suitcase. This had been her home for as long as she could remember. Sally had just been around to try and make amends but their friendship was broken, no matter how much they both tried to make it work. Checking her wristwatch she sat nibbling on her fingernails. This was it; she was leaving Manchester for good with Ray. A new life. A new beginning without the shadow of her husband hanging over her head every minute of the day. She had to kill him, she had no other choice he would never have let her be happy with Ray, his blood was on her hands.

The front door opened and Preston walked in shouting his mouth off. "Mam, are you in?" Gill popped her head over the banister and panicked. She thought her son would have been in the pub for the night, now she would have to tell him she was leaving for good. Slowly, she made her way down the stairs with her suitcase. Preston had his head stuck inside the fridge, he was a right starver and his stomach was never full, he was always hungry. Gill had her coat on and stood at the doorway. "Mam, have we got any ham or what, them butties in the boozer were shite. I'm Hank Marvin now. I swear to you." Slowly Preston looked at his mother and shot his eyes to the suitcase near her feet. "Where you off to?"

Gill swallowed hard and dug deep to find the strength to tell him she was leaving. Holding onto the doorframe with one hand she tried to steady herself, she was a nervous wreck. "I'm leaving Preston. There's nothing around here for me anymore. I just need to get away. Do you think the Collins family will just leave it like this, because they won't you know. Your father killed Susan, do you not think she has brothers and sisters who want revenge. We're not safe around here anymore, none of us."

Preston stuck his chest out in front of him and sat down at the table munching on some old meat he'd found in the fridge. "As if that's going to happen mother. I'm sorting things out now and nobody will come near us. I swear to you mam, I'm never going to let anyone hurt us again, so go and put your suitcase back upstairs and stop being silly."

Gill snapped at him. "Are you right in the head or what? Do you think for one minute the Collins family are not conspiring to finish us off? Give your head a shake Preston, it doesn't work like that. You're a kid and you don't know the half of it."

Preston banged his clenched fist onto the table and the colour drained from his face, he was white. "Stop saying I'm a fucking kid. I'm a man now and I'm going to show everyone what I'm capable of. My dad ruled the area and there is no reason why I can't too. I've got respect mam, the lads in the pub all told me they would back me up if I needed help, so what's the problem?"

Gill bent her knees slightly and picked her suitcase up. "You're not getting it are you? If you stay around here you'll just end up dead in a gutter somewhere. If you're willing to take that chance then it's up to you. I'm not. I'm leaving while I'm still breathing."

Preston looked at his mother and realised she was serious. He panicked. "What, so you're getting on your toes and leaving me. Don't you care what happens to me? I've only got you left mam, don't you desert me too." Preston shook his head as a single bulky tear travelled down the side of his face. He was waiting for her to reply but she never did. The front door slammed shut and Preston was alone with his thoughts. Raising his eyes to the ceiling he spoke. "Dad, our kid. I swear to you now, no one will ever fuck with us again. I'm going to make sure the Jarvis name is something that everybody knows and remembers forever."

Gill sat at the train station on the bench. The large clock in Piccadilly train station just stared at her. Ray should have been here over twenty minutes ago. Looking nervously around her she looked towards the entrance, there was still no sign of him. A message alert from Ray appeared on her phone. Gill read the message and sighed. "For fuck's sake Ray, What's going on?" Gill stood to her feet and headed out of the exit dragging her suitcase behind her. Head twisting left then right she searched the area for him, he was nowhere in sight. Another text alert appeared telling her to go down the back alley opposite her. Ray was paranoid of being seen by anyone, but this, this was way over the top. For crying out loud all he had to do was cross the road and board the train. It was night-time now and nobody would have noticed him anyway, nobody.

Gill stuck her head into the alleyway, it was pitch black and there was no lighting. "Ray, are you there," she whispered. There was no reply so she shouted louder this time. "Ray, come on we're going to miss the train if we don't get a move on." A noise at the other end of the alleyway made her stop dead in her tracks. She took a deep breath and slowly moved forward with caution. There were crunching gravel noises then an eerie silence, a small breeze passed over her shoulder causing her to shudder. Gill zipped her coat up tightly and rubbed at her arms, she was scared now and her eyes were wide open. "Ray, I swear if this is some kind of a joke then you're not funny. Just bleeding hurry up before I change my mind and go back home." There were more rustling noises, someone was definitely there. Gill gripped the hand gun in her pocket; she was carrying it with her all the time now. She knew more than anyone how shady the Collins family could be and didn't trust them one single bit. The pistol was cold on her fingertips and she placed her finger inside the trigger just in case she had to use it. Gill walked forward a few more steps and she could see a shadow. She halted and blew a laboured breath. "Thank fuck for that. I thought you weren't coming. Come on; let's hurry up the train's due in fifteen minutes, if we miss it we'll have to wait another hour." The figure stepped out from the shadows and Gill nearly dropped down dead. "Regina, what are you doing here?"

The woman walked forward and you could smell the alcohol on her breath. "Did you think for one minute I would let you take my husband? Are you that tapped in the head to think he would want you over me?"

Gill put her back against the wall before her legs buckled from underneath her, she was wobbling about and her heels weren't helping much. "Where's Ray, what have you done with him? He told me he loved me and wanted us to run away together."

Regina chuckled and her laughter echoed throughout the alleyway. "He thought he loved you Gill, he thought he could actually leave me until it came to the crunch. I look after him. I feed him, are you willing to do all that for him?"

Gill walked forward and she could see the whites of Regina's eyes. "I would have done whatever it took. So, it's you who was texting me and not Ray?"

Regina stood cracking her fingers and smirked, showing her tobacco stained teeth. "Yep, all the texts have been from me. Ray can't use his fingers properly and once I saw your pathetic messages it was me who was replying to you not Ray."

"I don't believe you, you're lying. Get Ray on the phone and let him tell me himself that it's over, go on you lying cow get him on the phone."

Regina dug her hand in her pocket and looked at the screen on her phone, she dialled a number and you could hear a ringing tone. "Come on then if you want to speak to him." Gill marched forward and gripped the phone in her hand. Suddenly her stomach felt warm and then her back, boiling hot pain surged through her body. Regina had stabbed her. Gill fell to the ground with the phone still held in her hand; she crashed to the ground like a lump of lead. Regina pulled the silver blade from her back and continued stabbing her until she moved no more. Looking at the knife in her hand now she slid her finger along the sharp edge and smiled. "Nobody messes with me and gets away with it. Did you think I would just let you leave with my man Gill? No, you got what was coming to you." Regina shoved the knife inside her jacket and fled from the scene of the crime. Gill was dead and all that was by her side when she took her final breath was a black cat. It sniffed her face a few times then walked over her body as she lay in a pool of thick red blood

Preston walked out from his front door. His heart was low and he was going back to the pub to meet Tina. His head was spinning and the brandy he'd drunk earlier was now taking effect. As he walked along the roadside he noticed a car in the distance following him. He couldn't see the driver but he was aware something wasn't right, he had a gut feeling. His heart was beating ten to the dozen and when he turned the next corner her sprinted off away from the roadside. Lighting a cigarette he hid away watching the road with eager eyes, within seconds a car turned into the cul-de-sac and he was doing his best to see the identity of the driver. He couldn't see properly the light was poor. Watching the car pull off he came out of hiding and scratched the top of his head. Was he imagining it, or was this real? Walking off slowly he headed back on his route to the pub, he was on his guard and constantly looking over his shoulder.

Kenzo sat behind the steering wheel and tapped her fingers rapidly. She was off her head on drugs, she was as high as a kite. It was lucky for her that some kids from the estate who were playing at the warehouse freed her from the cupboard otherwise she would have died in there, alone and scared.

All the Collins' money was now hers. Once she was freed she had gone straight back to the family home and realised nobody was there. She ransacked each of her brothers' safes and removed anything of value – she was a rich woman. Kenzo stared into the night sky as she watched the pub eagerly. She'd had to watch her family's funeral from a distance and nobody even knew she was there. Her mother and her three brothers were buried that day and watching it broke her heart into a million pieces. Kenzo pledged to herself that the bloodline of Harry Jarvis would never go on. There was one last family member left now and once he was out of the picture she had her own plans to rule the crime scene in Manchester. Money talks and she had loads of it, more than she knew what to do with. Surely with cash behind her she could do anything she wanted, but first Preston Jarvis had to go, he needed showing that the Collins family had had the last laugh. One way or the other she was going to make sure Harry's family name died with him. This was war and she was ready to fight to the death to avenge her family name. If it took a week, a year, a decade, she would never give up. She wanted Preston's blood no matter what; it was only a matter of time before he met his fate.

Kenzo had booked herself in rehab. There was no way she could fight this battle with drugs still ruling her life. She needed to be level-headed, she needed to be aware, she needed to be strong for the days ahead. Blood was going to be spilled and there was no way she would rest until Preston Jarvis was six feet under. The Collins' family name would mean something again; they would rule the streets of Manchester.

THE END

Other Books by Karen Woods

Broken Youth
Black Tears
Northern Girls Love Gravy
Bagheads
Teabags & Tears
The Visitors
Sleepless in Manchester
Covering Up
Riding Solo

To order any of these titles visit:
www.empire-uk.com